ROSE THORN

SOFT PETALS, SHARP EDGES

GAURAV ANAND

Made with ❤ on the Notion Press Platform
www.notionpress.com

To the one who taught me the most valuable lesson—

That words are easy, but actions carry the weight of truth.

You showed me that not every promise deserves belief,
and not every smile hides sincerity.

In trusting you, I learned to trust myself.
In losing you, I found a clearer lens to see the world.

This book is a tribute to that awakening—
To the wisdom that sometimes, the people who break us
also build our vision.

Thank you, for being the mirror I didn't know I needed.

Contents

Contents

Prologue

There are some stories that don't begin with a spark. They start in silence—beneath flickering streetlights, in the corners of old book pages, or in the eyes of a boy who never quite belonged.

Shaunak's story isn't loud. It doesn't shout for attention.He grew up believing in a love he hadn't met yet. A love that would make everything make sense. A love that would know him without words and stay through the storm.

Shaunak once read something that stayed with him for years:
"When you like a flower, you pluck it. When you love a flower, you water it daily."

It sounded beautiful, even noble. So he believed in it—with all his heart.
He believed that love meant care.
That staying meant trying.
And that giving more was always the answer.

But life, as it often does, taught him differently.

He learned that watering too much can drown the roots. That even a flower, no matter how delicate or lovely, doesn't bloom through obsession—it wilts.
And some plants, like the cactus, don't need water. They grow through silence, space, and solitude. Some things are meant to survive, not to be nurtured into something they're not.

Shaunak had always lived in stories—the kind where soulmates existed, where love was enough, and where the right heart could fix a broken one. He thought life was just a waiting room, and one day, she would arrive—the one he was made for. The one who would see him, understand him, love him.

And when someone did arrive, he convinced himself she was the one.

Even when her silences hurt.

Even when her presence felt like absence.

Even when every sign screamed otherwise—he stayed.

Because belief is a powerful thing.

It can blind, it can bind.

And when it is rooted in longing, it can make you stay in places you were never meant to remain.

Rose Thorn is not a love story in the way we're taught to understand love.

It is about loving too deeply, too innocently, too stubbornly.

It is about the cost of holding on, not because it's right, but because letting go feels unbearable.

It is about confusing effort with destiny.

And learning, the hard way, that sometimes love isn't about watering the wrong flower—it's about walking away before you lose yourself.

This is Shaunak's journey.

From fairytales to reality.

From blind belief to bitter truths.

From bleeding hands holding roses to finally seeing the thorns.

CHAPTER I

The Invisible Boy and his dream

Shaunak sat at his wooden desk, waiting for the exam results to be announced. His fingers drummed against the surface, his heart steady but expectant. He wasn't hoping to be the best—he had never been the best. But second place, or at least third, seemed within reach.

Deep down, though, he knew the truth. No one could surpass Sharat. Even if Shaunak copied his entire answer sheet or had the textbook right in front of him, he wouldn't beat him. Sharat wasn't just smart; he was different—someone born to top the class.

Shaunak, on the other hand, had spent most of the year lost in a different world, one that fit inside a small, scratched-up geometry box. The cover of the box displayed a mesmerizing image of planets scattered across the universe. During long, dragging lectures, when the teacher's voice faded into background noise, he would stare at it, his mind drifting into space.

He loved Saturn, with its golden rings circling it like a royal crown. Sometimes, Jupiter fascinated him—the largest of them all, demanding attention without trying. But the one he felt the most connected to was Pluto. A tiny, distant world, demoted from the ranks of planets, left alone at the edge of the solar system.

Shaunak understood Pluto.

Like the forgotten celestial body, he, too, was invisible. He wasn't popular, nor was he disliked. He wasn't among the best students, nor was he considered the worst. Even his teachers barely noticed him, never calling his name for praise or punishment. He simply existed—a drifting planet in a classroom of stars. And yet, Pluto still belonged to the solar system, even if it stood at its edge. Shaunak wondered if, someday, he too would find his place.

Shaunak had grown up surrounded by stories—tales of gods and their mighty battles, of how planets shaped destinies, and of distant lands where magic was real. His mother often spoke of celestial alignments, explaining how Saturn's slow march or Jupiter's mighty presence could alter a person's fate. He never understood whether it was truth or myth, but he listened, always listening.

He had also heard fairy tales—stories of kings and queens, of cursed lands and enchanted forests. They were not just bedtime tales to him; they were lessons. Whenever people around him spoke of a story—be it a legend, a folk tale, or even a simple anecdote—Shaunak absorbed every word as if it were going to be tested in an exam.

While others laughed, dismissed, or forgot, he remembered. Every word, every detail. It wasn't just interest; it was instinct. Stories, after all, were the only things that never ignored him.

Shaunak was a small boy with a brown skin tone, always swallowed by the oversized clothes his parents bought for him. His sweater hung loose, the sleeves covering his hands, and his long pants bunched up at the ankles. His parents believed in buying bigger clothes so they wouldn't have to replace them every year. While the other students in his class wore well-fitted, neat uniforms, Shaunak's attire made him feel out of place, like he was wearing someone else's skin.

He often wished for better clothes, but whenever he convinced his parents to buy him something new, another necessity would fall apart. If he got a new shirt, his shoes would wear out. If he finally got shoes, his school bag would tear at the seams. It felt like an endless cycle—by the time he got something, another thing was already ruined.

One day, while reading his textbook, he learned about India's first Prime Minister, Jawaharlal Nehru, and how he wore fresh clothes every day. The thought fascinated him. To have a new outfit daily—what a life that must be! He dreamed of the day he would earn his own money and wear the finest clothes, ones that fit him perfectly.

Inspired by Nehru's habit of wearing a rose on his coat, Shaunak decided to do the same. But he had no coat, and no garden of his own. So, he found his own ways. Sometimes, he plucked a flower from a roadside bush, sometimes from the neighbourhood gardens, and sometimes, when he passed a flower shop, he would take a fallen petal from the ground, pretending it was just as grand.

With a wilted rose tucked in his pocket, Shaunak walked into class—still in his oversized clothes but carrying a small piece of his dream with him.

Shaunak had so many dreams—big, endless, and full of colour. But every time he wished for something, a question followed: **"Why didn't God give us more money?"** Wasn't life supposed to be fair? If others had everything without asking, why did his family have to struggle? Did he really have to wait for things to change, or was there some secret way to get what he wanted?

Whenever he voiced his frustrations, his mother would smile softly, her hands busy kneading dough or folding clothes. She never scolded him for his questions. Instead, she would say, **"With time, everything clears up. One day, when you look back, you won't even feel like these were problems at all."**

Then she would remind him of the people they saw every day—families living under bridges, begging for a meal. Some of them spent the entire day working just to afford a single supper, while others didn't even get that. There were children searching for leftover food near hotels, picking scraps from the garbage, eating whatever they could find.

"Do you see, Shaunak? We may not have everything, but we have enough. You don't have to work. Your only job is to study. And yet, you complain about your life."

Shaunak listened, but the restlessness inside him never faded. Yes, he understood he was lucky compared to many. But was he supposed to stop dreaming just because others had it worse? He didn't know the answer. All he knew was that someday, somehow, he would change things—not just for himself, but for those who never even got the chance to dream.

Shaunak's parents had always dreamed of giving him the best education—one they themselves never had. They were educated, yes, but only in the way that earned them degrees, not knowledge. They wanted something better for their son, something beyond just passing exams and getting a certificate.

So, with hopeful hearts and tired hands from endless work, they sent Shaunak to a private school in another city, far from home. It was their way of giving him a chance at a future they could never reach.

But for Shaunak, it didn't feel like an opportunity—it felt like exile.

He was too young to live alone, but fate had left him no choice. The school's hostel was already full, so he was forced to stay in a rented room, away from both his family and the comforting presence of friends. Each day, he would wake up in silence, cook whatever he could, and walk to school with a heavy schoolbag and an even heavier heart.

Loneliness wrapped around him like an oversized coat, much like the ones he still wore. There were no familiar faces to greet him, no laughter waiting for him after school. His parents worked day and night to afford his education, but he found himself wondering—was this really the price of a better life?

Shaunak's mother knew the truth—he didn't love studying. Books never fascinated him the way cricket did, nor did equations excite him like standing in front of a mirror, mimicking actors and teachers. His dreams were different, but dreams like his came with a price his family couldn't afford.

She had seen the way his eyes lit up when he talked about cricket, the way he effortlessly copied voices and made people laugh. But passion alone wasn't enough. Talent needed opportunities, and opportunities needed money—money they didn't have.

So, when Shaunak complained about studying, when he wished for a different life, she would gently remind him, **"Take risks, but never at the cost of your future or your family."**

She wasn't trying to kill his dreams. She was just protecting him from the world—the same world that crushed people who dared to dream without security. For now, education was his only way forward. And even if he didn't love it, it was the only thing that could promise him a future where dreams might one day be possible.

The classroom buzzed with nervous whispers as the teacher announced the top rankers.

First place. **Not him.** But he already knew that.

Second place. **Not him.**

Third place. **Still not him.**

Shaunak sat up a little straighter, a flicker of unease settling in his chest. He had never expected to be first, but second or third? That had seemed possible. Maybe, just maybe, he had finally done better.

But then the numbers kept rising.

Fifth. Tenth. Twentieth.

His name was nowhere.

When the teacher finally called his name, it was for the **34th rank**—out of 60 students. He walked up quietly, collected his report card, and looked at his marks. **Barely passing in every subject.**

Strangely, his mind wasn't occupied with regret or confusion. He wasn't even thinking about how he got such bad marks. He was only thinking about the fact that he *had* bad marks.

His thoughts drifted back to a few weeks ago, when the exam schedule had been announced. He had confidently challenged the topper of the other section, declaring that this year, **he would score the highest in every subject.** Now, holding his report card, his challenge seemed almost ridiculous.

As he glanced around the classroom, he saw parents hovering over their children, inspecting their marks with sharp eyes. Some scolded, some sighed in disappointment, and some demanded explanations.

But Shaunak stood alone. There was no one to check his marks, no one to ask why his grades had fallen so low. His parents were miles away, working hard to afford his education, trusting him to do his best.

And for some reason, that thought made him **happy.**

He imagined what it would be like if his parents were here. Would they have reacted like the other parents—screaming, demanding explanations? No. He was almost certain they wouldn't have asked those *idiotic questions*. They would have looked at him, tired but understanding, and simply asked, **"Did you try?"**

And maybe, that question would have hurt more than all the scolding in the world.

Shaunak held his report card tightly as he walked home, his stomach churning with unease. He wasn't just disappointed—he was embarrassed. He had expected at least *some* decent marks, something he could tell people without feeling ashamed.

Fifteen days before the exams, he had pushed himself like never before. He studied day and night, just like the class topper. He stayed up late, skipped playtime, and even ignored the geometry box he loved so much. But despite all that effort, his marks barely scraped past the passing line.

What stung more was the boy he had challenged—the one he had boldly claimed he would outscore. That boy would *ask* about his results, and the mere thought of it made Shaunak's hands tremble.

He sat at his small, rented room's table, staring at his report card. Then, without thinking much, he reached for a **red pen.**

32 became 82.

34 became 84.

One by one, he carefully altered every subject's mark, turning his failure into something he could proudly share.

Just as he put the pen down, his phone rang. It was the old, buttoned phone his parents had given him before sending him to the city. **Their call.**

His heart pounded. He hesitated before answering.

"Shaunak! How was your result?" His mother's voice was filled with hope.

For a moment, he considered telling the truth. But then he thought about how tired his parents must be, how hard they worked to send him to this school. If they knew the truth, would they feel disappointed? Would they feel like their sacrifices were wasted?

And so, with a steady voice, he lied.

"I got good marks."

His mother's joy overflowed through the phone. "**We're so proud of you!**" His father's voice in the background echoed the same happiness.

And just like that, the guilt melted away.

For the first time, Shaunak felt a strange kind of **confidence**—the confidence of telling a lie that made people happy.

That night, as he lay in bed, he made a promise to himself. **Next year, he would study with full heart and get real good marks.** He wouldn't need a red pen next time.

Because even though his parents never asked why his marks were low, he knew—**he didn't want to disappoint them again.**

It was midnight when Shaunak had a strange dream. He was alone in his rented room, searching for his parents. He wandered through endless corridors, calling out their names, but no one answered. Hours passed, yet he couldn't find them. A deep loneliness settled inside him, heavier than anything he had ever felt.

Shaunak had never been afraid of ghosts or thieves, but tonight, something felt different. The walls around him seemed to close in, pressing against his chest. He sat up in bed, his heart beating fast.

It was **1 AM.**

He wanted to call his parents, just to hear their voices. But he knew they had already gone to sleep—his family slept early, by **7 PM**, exhausted from a long day's work. Waking them up just because he felt lonely seemed unfair. Instead, he picked up his old, buttoned phone and started playing the **snake game**, distracting himself from the uneasiness in his chest.

And then—**the electricity went out.**

His fan stopped, leaving only silence. **A metallic crash echoed from the kitchen.** The sound of utensils falling.

Shaunak froze.

He looked toward the darkness but saw nothing. A chill ran down his spine, though the night was hot. His skin was damp with sweat. His first instinct was to pull the **bedsheet over his face,** as if that thin layer of fabric could protect him.

His mind raced. **What was happening?**

He tried to convince himself that it was just a coincidence. **Just the wind. Just a rat knocking over something. Just... anything but what his mind was imagining.**

But the silence pressed on, heavy and unbroken—except for the whining buzz of mosquitoes attacking his exposed skin.

"God, please... bring back the electricity," he whispered.

Minutes passed. Then an hour. Still **no power.**

The heat, the mosquitoes, the eerie silence—Shaunak couldn't take it anymore. **Enough.**

With a surge of frustration, he **threw the bedsheet aside.** He **lit up his phone's screen** and stepped toward the kitchen. His shadow flickered on the walls, stretching in the dim glow.

His hands trembled as he searched for a **matchstick,** but he couldn't find one. He grabbed a **candle** and hurried to the gas stove. With unsteady fingers, he turned the knob and used a **lighter** to ignite the burner. The flame flared up, golden and warm.

Carefully, he brought the candle close to the fire, lighting it. The **soft glow** made the room feel a little less terrifying.

He turned away, not daring to **look back into the darkness** behind him. His legs moved fast, almost running, as he **placed the candle near his bed.**

In a movie, he had once heard that **evil spirits never come near fire.** He hoped it was true.

Wrapping himself in the bedsheet once more, he squeezed his eyes shut, praying for sleep to take him away from this suffocating night.

But the mosquitoes had other plans.

CHAPTER II

The Morning of Realizations

Shaunak spent the entire night wide awake. The dim candle had burned out hours ago but sleep never came. The relentless buzzing of mosquitoes filled his ears, their tiny wings orchestrating a never-ending concert. He tossed and turned, growing more frustrated with each passing minute.

By 5 a.m., he had had enough. Instead of forcing himself to sleep in that suffocating room, he decided to step outside for a morning walk.

Wearing the same oversized clothes from the previous day, he stepped into the fresh morning air. The city streets were quieter, the sky still painted in soft hues of dawn. The crisp, cool breeze brushed against his tired face, and for the first time in hours, he felt alive.

He had expected the roads to be empty, with closed shops and deserted lanes. But as he walked farther, he saw something unexpected athletes.

Dozens of them were out jogging, stretching, and exercising. Their movements were smooth, their energy boundless.

Shaunak watched them in awe.

"What a life these athletes have," he thought. *"No exams, no grades to worry about. Just practicing their sport. And they get recognition, respect... special treatment."*

He envied them. They didn't have to struggle through textbooks, chase marks, or fear failure. Unlike a 9-to-5 job, their life seemed full of excitement and adventure.

"Who wouldn't want to play sports and make a name for themselves?" he wondered.

Lost in his thoughts, he kept walking. Before he realized it, he had wandered too far. His legs ached. He needed to sit down.

But there was no bench nearby.

He spotted a small tea stall at the corner of the street. The aroma of fresh tea filled the air. He walked toward it and ordered a cup.

At the stall, a group of elderly men sat together, lost in conversation. Their laughter and arguments blended into a lively discussion.

Some looked 80 or 85 years old, yet they seemed healthy and full of energy. One of them was deaf, while two others spoke endlessly, interrupting each other mid-sentence.

They were discussing their past jobs, debating whose struggles had been greater.

Shaunak listened curiously, absorbing every word.

One of the old men noticed him.

"Come, boy, join us!" he called out with a warm smile.

Shaunak hesitated for a moment, then nodded and pulled up a stool.

For the first time in a long while, someone had invited him to be part of a conversation.

And he was eager to listen.

This moment was a turning point for **Shaunak**. The old men at the tea stall, who had once been strangers, suddenly seemed like familiar souls.

As soon as he sat down, questions came **rushing at him** like a flood—

"Hey, boy, come here! What's your name?"
"What are you doing here at Tea Stall?"
"Where is your home? You live alone?"
"What are your goals?"
"What does your father do?"

"Which school do you study in?"

"Did you really come this far just for tea?"

"What do you want to do in life?"

"Who makes your food and washes your clothes if you live alone?"

The rapid-fire questioning didn't overwhelm **Shaunak**. He answered **calmly**, one by one, without hesitation.

The old men exchanged glances. They were **shocked**.

This was **no ordinary kid**.

Most boys his age was **watching cartoons, playing games, or daydreaming about becoming cricketers**. But **Shaunak**? He spoke with **depth**—not just words, but **thoughts beyond his years**.

They learned that **he lived alone**, that **he cooked his own meals**, and that **he had left his hometown to study**. His life was different from others his age, and it showed in the way he spoke.

They **admired his maturity**.

After a while, **Shaunakstood up to leave**. Without thinking twice, he reached into his pocket and pulled out **some money** to pay for **everyone's tea**.

The old men **laughed** and stopped him.

"Son, we are retired army officers. We've earned enough to pay for a hundred cups of tea. But the fact that you even **thought** *of paying shows what kind of person you are."*

One of them patted his back and said, *"You've got a big heart, kid."*

Another suggested, *"Take a taxi back. You walked too far."*

Shaunakshook his head.

"No need. I'll walk. I don't have much to do anyway."

As he walked away, the old men watched him go, still talking about him.

"What a boy! My grandson is his age, but all he does is play games on the phone."
"Yeah, kids these days are different. But this one... he's rare."
"May he succeed in whatever he does."
Shaunakreached his rented room.
For the first time in a long while, he felt... **nice.**
Not lonely. Not tired. Just nice.
He had always found comfort in talking to his **pets back home**, especially dogs. He used to share everything with them—how his day went, what he ate, even how he **lied about his grades.**
They never judged him.
But today was different. He had **talked to people.** And they had listened.
Tomorrow was a **holiday**, so he decided—
He would go for another morning walk.
He wanted to hear the **birds chirping again**, watch the athletes running, and just **observe life around him.**
But most importantly—
He would learn the skill of talking to people.

CHAPTER III

The Seventh Seat at the Tea Stall

That night, **the same events repeated.**

No electricity.

Mosquitoes buzzing in his ears.

The unbearable summer heat.

But this time, **Shaunak didn't feel discomfort.**

He slept peacefully, ignoring it all.

Because the next morning, he had **plans.**

As the sun **rose, Shaunak** woke up early and went for his morning walk **just as planned.**

Same road.

Same tea stall.

Same six old friends sitting at their usual spot, engaged in their **daily debates and playful arguments.**

But this time, something felt different.

They were waiting for him.

The moment **Shaunak** arrived, one of the old men **ordered tea for him without asking.**

Another pulled up a **chair for him without a word.**

He felt **welcomed.** Like he **belonged.**

That day, their conversation went deeper.

They asked him about his daily **routine**—what he did after reaching home, how he spent his time, what his goals were.

Then came the question about his **grades.**

But today, **Shaunak didn't lie.**

He **told the truth**—his **real** percentage, which was **low.**

But for the first time, he **didn't feel ashamed.**

The old men **appreciated his honesty.**

"It's good that you're not lying about it," one of them said. *"Now, just work on improving your score. You have the ability."*

Then came different opinions—

One of them insisted that **grades are important.**

But another disagreed, saying—

"Grades don't matter much. The real thing that matters is **discipline and actual learning."**

Then, an old man, a **retired IAS officer,** spoke up—

"In my 12th grade, I never scored above 45% in any subject. But I still cracked India's toughest exam with ease."

Immediately, another old man **laughed and interrupted—**

"Stop flexing about your achievement!"

And just like that, the whole group **burst into laughter.**

Shaunak laughed too.

For the next hour, they **joked, teased, and enjoyed** like old friends.

And for the first time, **Shaunak shared his own opinions—opinions that sounded more mature than even theirs.**

The next day, **Shaunak had school.**

And after two days of **long walks,** he was too **tired** to wake up early for his usual morning routine.

So, he skipped the walk and **got ready for school instead.**

As usual, he spent most of his school hours **flipping through his new textbooks,** looking at the pictures.

But something **disappointed him** this time—

There weren't as many pictures as before.

The books from **higher grades** felt **dull and monotonous** compared to the colourful ones he had in earlier years.

"So, this is what growing up feels like?" he thought.

But there was one thing that **excited him.**

This year, a **new library period** was added to the timetable.

And **Shaunak loved books.**

Not just textbooks—**but real books**. Books with **stories, adventures, knowledge beyond school subjects.**

The moment he stepped into the **library**, he felt like he had entered a **different world.**

A world where he could **lose himself in stories and ideas.**

For a brief moment, he thought of the **old men from the tea stall.**

"Will they wonder why I didn't show up today?"

"Will they miss me, the way I miss them?"

The thought lingered for a while, but soon, he was too absorbed in **books** to think about anything else.

He wished he could sit there for **hours**, listening to **stories and life lessons** just like he did with them.

"If only libraries had people like them."

As days passed, **Shaunak found himself spending more and more time in the library and on the sports ground.**

Cricket was his favourite sport.

At home, he and his **brother** used to play **all day long, sometimes without a break.**

That was one of his **happiest childhood memories—**

The sound of the **bat hitting the ball**, the **friendly fights over runs**, and the way his brother **forced him to watch cricket matches.**

His brother would **talk endlessly** about legendary players, their **skills, achievements, and legacy.**

Maybe that's where **Shaunak's love for cricket** came from—**his brother's passion.**

After a week filled with **school, homework, and routine**, the **weekend finally arrived.**

And **Shaunak had been waiting for this.**

"Tomorrow, I'll go for a walk again."

He was **excited** to see the old men, hear their **stories,** and feel **that sense of belonging again.**

He went to the tea stall, and as expected, all six of the old friends were there, just like before.

The moment they saw him, they **welcomed him warmly**, as if he was **already one of them.**

One of the old men **ordered tea for him**—without even asking, just like last time.

"So, why didn't you come back after Sunday?" one of them asked.

"We waited for you and then figured you must have school."

Shaunak **smiled and nodded.**

"Yes, school kept me busy. And this place is quite far from my home, so I couldn't come every day."

He paused for a moment and added—

"But if it were nearby, I wouldn't have missed a single day with you all."

Hearing this, the old men **exchanged glances and grinned.**

They liked this boy. **His honesty, his warmth, his presence.**

And **Shaunak felt it too.**

For the first time in a long while, he felt **genuinely welcomed, valued, and special.**

That feeling made him open up even more.

He started sharing **every detail of his week**—

How his **library period** became his new favourite, how he **missed coming here**, how he spent time on the **sports ground**, and how he was **trying to balance everything.**

The old men listened, nodding, smiling, and sometimes **chuckling at his little stories.**

They weren't just hearing him—**they were enjoying him.**

One of the old men, with a mischievous grin, suddenly asked,

"So, young man, do you have a girl in your class?"

Shaunak, sipping his tea, answered without hesitation,

"No, not even a single one. Our school has separate sections for boys and girls."

The old men chuckled.

"But do you get to talk to them at all?" another asked.

Shaunak shook his head.

"No, it's not allowed. The school strictly separates boys and girls. We barely even see them except during the assembly, sports competitions, or while walking to the library."

The men exchanged amused glances, some remembering their own school days.

"So, do you trust anyone in your life?" one of them asked.

Shaunak thought for a moment and then said,

"I never really thought about it. But in school, there's hardly any chance to build that kind of trust. The system keeps us all in our own worlds."

The conversation, which started light heartedly, took a deeper turn as Shaunak, now curious about them, started asking questions.

"What about all of you? How's life going?" he asked.

"Are you happy? Settled in life? How do your sons and daughters treat you? Do they listen to you? Do they respect your wishes?"

The old men, who had been teasing him moments ago, now found themselves reflecting.

Some smiled, some sighed.

"Life is strange, beta," one of them finally said. *"No matter how much you do for your children, in the end, you just hope they remember you with love."*

Shaunak, sensing their emotions, asked another question—one he had always been curious about.

"In Hindu dharma, there's a concept of attaining moksha—liberation from the cycle of life and death. Do you believe in it? Are you planning for it?"

The old men looked at each other, then at Shaunak, surprised at such a mature question coming from someone so young.

One of them, the retired IAS officer, chuckled and said,

"We are at that age where we must think about moksha. But let me tell you something—"

The boy leaned in, listening closely.

"Moksha isn't just about dying peacefully. It's about living without regrets, without attachments that pull you down. It's about doing what makes your soul feel light."

Shaunak nodded, absorbing every word.

The sun had risen a little higher.

Their tea was almost finished.

And yet, this conversation had **left a mark on all of them.**

One of them chuckled and waved his hand dismissively, **"Ah, I don't believe in all this. I'm an atheist. God is just an idea people created to feel secure."**

The others laughed, some shaking their heads.

Another sighed, stretching his legs, **"Forget moksha, my biggest problem is my legs. They hurt every time I walk. How will I go on any pilgrimage?"**

A third old man, who had been stirring his tea, finally spoke, **"I have been planning a spiritual journey for years. But it seems like God doesn't want me to visit. Every time**

I make plans, something comes up—family issues, health problems, or sudden responsibilities."

The fourth one smiled wistfully, "I wanted to go, but I have grandchildren to take care of. Their parents are busy with work. Who will watch over them if I leave?"

The fifth one, who had been quiet all this time, finally spoke, "I don't see the point of visiting temples and religious places. If God exists, He is everywhere, isn't He? Why should I travel miles to find Him when He is within me?"

Shaunak listened carefully, fascinated by their different views.

Then, the sixth man, the one who had visited many temples, cleared his throat and said proudly, "I have already been to every famous temple in India. I have bathed in the Ganga, Yamuna, and all the holy rivers. And let me tell you something—after visiting all those places, I was never the same."

Shaunak leaned in with curiosity.

"How did it change you?" he asked.

The old man smiled, eyes reflecting memories from years ago.

"At first, I didn't believe it would make a difference. But when I stood in front of those ancient temples, when I dipped in those sacred waters, something shifted inside me. It felt like I was washing away not just my sins, but my burdens. I realized that faith isn't about rituals. It's about finding peace. That trip became the most beautiful memory of my life."

The other old men nodded, some still skeptical, some thoughtful.

Shaunak, sipping his tea, smiled.

"So, in the end, it's not about whether you go or not. It's about what you take from the journey."

The old man patted his shoulder, "Exactly, beta. Exactly."

The tea stall buzzed with laughter and chatter again.

And in that little corner of the world, under the rising sun, seven people—six old men and one young boy—shared a conversation that spanned generations.

CHAPTER IV

Between Sips of Tea and Tales of Time

Shaunak, breathing heavily from all the walking, finally reached the tea stall. Sweat dripped from his forehead, and his shirt was slightly damp from the morning sun. The old men, who had just arrived, looked at him with surprise.

"Arre beta, what happened? Why are you so exhausted?" one of them asked, offering him a seat.

Shaunak took a deep breath, then smiled sheepishly. **"I came early today, but the tea stall wasn't open. So, I waited. Then I asked the tea stall owner about you all, and he said you go to a park. I got excited and started walking, but... I didn't listen to the address properly. I got lost and walked around for an hour before finding my way back."**

The old men burst into laughter.

"Beta, you are something else!" one of them said, shaking his head.

Another one patted his back. **"We didn't expect you to be so eager to meet us. But we're happy you came."**

Just then, one of the old men, the one who always seemed to be the most talkative, leaned forward with a mysterious smile.

Shaunak's curiosity grew as he heard the word *party*. He looked at the old men, wondering what kind of party they could be planning.

"A party?" he asked, with a puzzled expression. **"But you all are... well, quite old. What kind of party are we talking about?"**

One of the old men, who had been quiet for a while, leaned forward and grinned. "It's not just any party, beta. It's a special kind. A reunion of sorts."

Shaunak raised an eyebrow. "A reunion? With who?"

The old man who had hesitated earlier finally smiled. "Well, it's just a small gathering with some old friends. We used to work together many years ago, and now we meet occasionally to reminisce about the good old days. But it's not the kind of party with music or dancing like the younger folks enjoy."

Shaunak leaned forward; his curiosity piqued. "I don't mind at all! I think I'd love to hear those stories, the ones you guys keep mentioning. You know, about your work, and how things used to be. I'm sure it'll be interesting."

A few of the old men hesitantly said, "It's such a boring party for old people. Young ones like you will get bored."

Shaunak immediately shook his head, his voice firm yet filled with warmth. "No, I will not get bored. Wherever you guys are, it will always be fun for me. I miss you even during my school hours. I wish you were my age so we could spend our whole days together—in school, the library, and the sports grounds. You guys mean a lot to me."

The group fell silent for a moment, taken aback by the boy's sincerity. Shaunak's eyes glistened as he continued, "I don't have any friends. Even if I try to make some, nobody includes me in their groups. They talk about cartoons, movies, computer games, and indoor activities, but I do not enjoy any of those. I like talking about life, about real things. But they think I'm strange for that."

The old men exchanged glances. They had spent years reminiscing about their youth, longing for a time when they were surrounded by friends, but here was a boy—so young, yet carrying the same loneliness they sometimes felt.

One of them, an elderly man with deep wrinkles and kind eyes, placed a hand on Shaunak's shoulder. "You don't have to worry about that, son. You are already one of us."

Shaunak smiled faintly, but inside, a small fear lingered. At first, he had felt like he was finally a part of something, but now, even these old men seemed to be excluding him from their gathering. Was he truly welcome, or was this just another group where he would always be on the outside?

One of the old men placed a hand on Shaunak's shoulder and said with a warm smile, **"You're not excluded, son. We just thought you might not enjoy it. But hearing you say all this... it means a lot to us."**

Another one chuckled, **"If only we were your age, we'd be running around with you in the sports ground, debating over books in the library, and maybe even getting scolded by teachers together!"**

One of the old men sighed and placed a hand on Shaunak's shoulder. "Listen, son, we enjoy your company too. You have become one of us in such a short time," he said with a warm smile.

Another elder nodded. "But this gathering... it's not something meant for you. We're planning a liquor party, and you are not even eighteen yet."

Shaunak's expression fell slightly. "So what? I don't drink, and I won't. I just want to be with you all," he protested.

One of the men chuckled. "That's exactly why, Shaunak. We don't want you to pick up a habit that is not good for you. You are just like our grandchildren, and we would never want them to be around this."

Shaunak looked at them, understanding their concern. He felt a warmth in his chest—this was not about excluding him. It was about protecting him. For the first time in his life, he felt truly cared for by someone outside his family.

Here's an extended version of the story, adding depth to the debate, the emotions, and Shaunak's thoughts.

That day, Shaunak stood his ground, his eyes filled with determination. "I understand your concerns," he said, looking around at the six old men who had become like a family to him. "But I do not want to be left out. I do not have anyone else, and spending time with you all means a lot to me. I promise I will not drink or pick up any bad habits."

The old men exchanged glances, their faces lined with worry and thought.

One of them, a retired school principal, shook his head. "Shaunak, we don't doubt your intentions. But certain things, once familiar, do not remain just 'things.' They become temptations. It starts with one gathering, one casual sip—before you know it, you don't even realize when you've fallen into the habit." He sighed deeply. "When I was your age, I had no interest in drinking. But my friends did. I only accompanied them, just like you are asking to do now. At first, I only sat with them, then one day I took a sip out of curiosity, and then another. Years later, I found myself unable to say no. It cost me my health... and almost my family."

Another man, an ex-army officer, shook his head and disagreed. "That's not always true. Not everyone who drinks gets addicted. Look at me—I drink occasionally, but I never let it control me. Alcohol, in moderation, does not harm. In fact, some say it's even good for the heart."

The debate sparked among the group, each man adding his own perspective.

"I still don't think it's right," said the eldest among them, his voice gentle yet firm. "Shaunak is young. There's no need for him to see this side of life so soon."

"But isn't he mature for his age?" countered another. "He speaks more wisely than most adults. If he's smart enough to understand what's right and what's wrong, why should we exclude him? If we push him away today, it might hurt him more than including him would."

Shaunak listened carefully; his hands clenched into fists at his sides. He wasn't a child. He knew the difference between right and wrong. More than anything, he didn't want to feel abandoned again.

"If I promise to never drink before completing my college," he said slowly, "will you let me come? I just want to be there. I don't want to be left behind. You all are the only ones I have."

The six men fell silent. They looked at each other, then at Shaunak.

Finally, the ex-army officer smiled. "Alright, son. But on one condition—you keep your promise. No drinking until you finish college."

Shaunak nodded eagerly. "I swear."

The eldest of the group sighed but smiled. "Fine. But remember, Shaunak, life is full of choices. Sometimes, the hardest ones define who we become. I hope you always make the right ones."

That evening, Shaunak walked beside them, feeling a mix of excitement and nervousness. He was not just a boy tagging along with elders—he was truly part of their group now. And though the night ahead was unfamiliar, he knew one thing for certain: he had earned their trust. And he would never break it.

CHAPTER V

When the Glasses Clink, the Hearts Speak

Shaunak could hardly contain his excitement. This was the first time he would see the real side of the old men—the version they never showed during their morning tea discussions or casual walks in the park. He had always heard that alcohol had a way of bringing out the truth in people. In movies, he had seen characters reveal their deepest secrets after a few drinks, and he wondered if that would happen tonight. Would they open up about their past? Would he get to know the untold stories of their youth?

The plan for the day was simple. They all had lunch together at one of the men's homes, where his daughter-in-law had cooked a delicious meal. While they ate, the old man asked Shaunak about his school. He even threw a few mathematics questions his way, testing his knowledge. Shaunak answered every single one correctly, earning a nod of approval from the group.

"You're a smart boy," one of them remarked, smiling. "Keep it up, and you'll go far."

After lunch, they all rested for a while before heading out to the place they had decided on earlier. The journey itself felt like an adventure—Shaunak walking alongside his six elderly friends, his mind racing with curiosity.

When they reached their destination, Shaunak noticed how well-prepared they were. One of the men had brought ten packets of snacks—mixtures of peanuts, chips, and namkeen. Another had carefully selected bottles of liquor, about thirteen in total. It was clear that this wasn't their first time doing this.

Instead of spreading out into separate rooms, all seven of them gathered in a single space. The air buzzed with a different kind of energy—one that Shaunak hadn't felt before. There was laughter, warmth, and a strange sense of freedom among them. These men, who were usually reserved in public, were suddenly relaxed, almost like young boys again.

Shaunak, sitting cross-legged on the floor, couldn't hold back his curiosity. "So, how often do you celebrate like this?" he asked.

One of them chuckled. "Not too often. Only when one of us feels the need to... escape."

"Escape?" Shaunak frowned.

"Yes," another old man said, pouring a drink into his glass. "You see, Shaunak, we're not addicted to alcohol. It's not the liquor we seek—it's the freedom to speak, to express. Life, as you grow older, becomes heavy. We carry memories, regrets, joys, and sorrows, but society doesn't always allow us to share them openly. Drinking gives us that space. It's like pressing a pause button on life."

Shaunak listened intently. He had never thought about it that way. He had always assumed people drank just for fun or out of habit. But here, it was different. These men weren't drinking to forget—they were drinking to remember, to share, to feel lighter.

"But why do you need alcohol for that?" Shaunak asked. "Why not just talk openly, like you do every morning at the tea stall?"

There was a moment of silence before one of them spoke.

"Because, my boy," he said, "society has taught men to be strong, to keep emotions buried. Even among friends, it's hard to just sit and say, 'I'm feeling lonely,' or 'I miss my youth,' or 'I regret the things I never did.' Alcohol is just an excuse. It gives us permission to say what we otherwise wouldn't."

Shaunak absorbed their words. He realized that this gathering wasn't about the drinks at all. It was about companionship, about finding a safe space to be vulnerable.

As the night went on, the stories began to flow. One old man talked about the girl he had loved but never confessed to. Another spoke of his dreams of traveling the world, dreams that had faded under the weight of responsibilities. Someone else reminisced about childhood mischief, while another laughed about how terrible he had been at studies but somehow made it through life.

Shaunak sat there, listening, learning, and understanding. He saw a side of adulthood he had never imagined—a side that carried longing, nostalgia, and an unspoken desire to relive the past, even if just for a night.

Here's an extended version of the scene, adding depth to the emotions and capturing Shaunak's realization.

Shaunak, filled with curiosity, looked around the room where laughter had suddenly faded into an unusual silence. The cheerful banter from moments ago had disappeared, replaced by an awkward stillness. He had been observing them all evening, noticing how they laughed a little too loudly, how their smiles carried a weight he couldn't quite understand.

Sensing something deeper, he finally asked, "Whose party is this dedicated to? What's the occasion? Is it a celebration or... something else?"

The room remained silent. No one met his gaze.

He could feel the air shift—thicker now, heavier. The silence was not just awkward; it was filled with something unspoken. Something painful.

Then, one of the old men, a frail but dignified figure with deep lines of wisdom etched on his face, leaned in close to Shaunak's ear and whispered softly, "It's for him."

Shaunak turned to see where the old man was pointing. Across the room, sitting in a quiet corner with a faint, tired smile, was a retired officer—his hands wrapped around a glass he hadn't even sipped from yet. His eyes, usually sharp and commanding, seemed distant, lost in a world far away from the noise in the room.

The whisper continued, "His wife passed away a few days ago."

Shaunak felt a chill run down his spine.

"That's why we are here today," the old man added, his voice laced with sorrow. "Not to celebrate... but to remind him that he is not alone."

Shaunak's mind reeled. Just moments ago, he had assumed this was just another casual gathering—a night of shared stories and laughter. But now, everything made sense. The forced smiles, the loud laughter, the occasional distant looks. This wasn't just a party. It was their way of grieving, of comforting a friend without making it obvious.

Shaunak's eyes shifted back to the retired officer. He imagined the weight of his loss—the empty house, the absence of a voice that once filled his days, the silence that now followed him everywhere. A man who had spent his life in discipline, in service, in control—now left helpless against the one thing he couldn't fight: time.

The old man continued, his words barely above a whisper, "We don't know how to grieve, Shaunak. We were never taught. We only know how to be strong. So, instead, we sit together, we drink, we talk, we laugh—because that's the only way we know how to say, 'We're here for you.'"

Shaunak felt something heavy settle in his chest. He had always thought of these men as his friends. He had admired their wisdom, their humour, their ability to turn every moment into something meaningful. But now he realized—they were not just his friends.

They were survivors.

Survivors of time, of love lost, of friendships faded, of memories that haunted them. They were not living with friends. They were living with ghosts.

And tonight, they were not just drinking for themselves.

They were drinking for the one among them who had just lost another piece of his past.

Shaunak sat there, the weight of realization settling heavily on his shoulders. These men, whom he had grown so fond of, whom he had started to call his own, were just like everything else in life—temporary. He had finally found a group where he felt included, where he felt seen, where he belonged. But time, as always, had its own cruel ways. These friendships too, like everything else, would one day slip away.

Sensing the shift in his mood, one of the old men placed a hand on his shoulder. His voice was calm yet firm, carrying the wisdom of years.

"Shaunak, life is a river. Everything flows; nothing stays. The sooner you learn detachment, the lighter your heart will feel."

Another one chuckled softly, taking a sip from his glass. "You are too young to be worrying about the future. Just live in the present, my boy. We are here today, laughing together, and that's what matters."

Shaunak nodded, but the ache inside him didn't disappear. He wanted to believe in their words, but how could he? He had spent his entire life searching for friendships, for bonds that wouldn't break. And now, when he finally found them, he was being asked to prepare for their loss.

One of the old men, who had been silent all this time, suddenly lifted a bottle of beer and handed it to Shaunak. A mischievous smile played on his lips.

"Alright then, let's see if you're really as mature as you say you are," he said, eyes twinkling. "Take a sip."

The others watched him closely, their expressions unreadable. Was this a joke? A test?

Shaunak looked at the bottle in his hands. The golden liquid inside reflected the dim lights of the room. He had promised them he wouldn't drink before completing his college. He had promised himself.

Without hesitation, he placed the bottle back on the table and pushed it away.

"I don't need this," he said firmly, looking at each of them. "Not today, not ever."

Silence.

And then, slow claps.

The old men burst into laughter, nodding their heads in approval.

"He passed," one of them said, grinning.

"He's one of us," another added with a proud smile.

Shaunak smiled too, but his heart still felt heavy.

Shaunak accepted the packet of mixture and a bottle of coke, settling comfortably among them. The old men, now in their relaxed state, leaned back in their chairs, sipping from their glasses and reminiscing about their past.

The room, once filled with laughter, now carried a different kind of warmth—a nostalgic silence, broken only by the occasional clinking of glasses and the soft rustling of the evening breeze through the slightly open window.

One of the old men, the retired officer whose wife had passed away recently, cleared his throat, and spoke first.

"You know, Shaunak, there was a time when I was just like you," he said, staring at the ceiling as if reliving his youth. "I was full of dreams, full of energy. Life felt like an endless road. I thought I had all the time in the world..." He sighed. "And yet, here I am. Looking back, I realize that time is the fastest thing in this world. It slips through your fingers before you even know it."

Another man chuckled, shaking his head. "He's getting emotional again," he teased. "But he's right. We were all young once. We had love, we had ambitions, we had struggles. And now, here we are, sitting in this room, sharing whatever little remains of our past."

Shaunak listened intently, taking small sips of his coke. He felt as if he had traveled back in time with them, seeing glimpses of their youth through their words.

One of them, the man who had once cracked one of the toughest exams in the country, spoke next. "You know, Shaunak, I was never a bright student in school. Never scored more than 45% in my subjects. But I never stopped learning. Life doesn't care about marks; it cares about discipline and consistency."

Shaunak nodded, remembering how they had talked about this before.

Then, the oldest of the group, the one who rarely spoke, leaned forward. "Tell me, boy," he said, his voice softer than the others. "What is it that you want from life?"

Shaunak was caught off guard. No one had asked him this so directly before. He looked down at his bottle of coke, rolling it between his fingers.

"I... I do not know," he admitted. "I want to be someone. I want to do something meaningful. But sometimes, I feel like I do not belong anywhere. Like I am always searching for something, but I do not even know what it is."

The old men exchanged glances and smiled knowingly.

"That's the beauty of youth," one of them said. "You are supposed to be lost. That's how you find your way."

CHAPTER VI

Tales Told Over a Drink

The oldest among them, Subedar Bhaskar, took a deep sip of his drink, his wrinkled hands trembling slightly as he smiled. His eyes, heavy with the weight of time, glistened under the dim yellow light of the room. Shaunak, who had been listening to their stories with quiet fascination, leaned in slightly as Bhaskar cleared his throat.

"Let me tell you a love story, boy," he said, his voice carrying the weight of memories, rich and full of longing. He looked into the distance as if watching the past unfold before his eyes, a silent film only he could see.

"When I was a young soldier, barely your age, I fell in love with a girl named Meera. She was not just beautiful—she was poetry in motion. Her laughter was like the first rain after a long summer, her presence as soothing as a river flowing through the hills. Every morning, as I walked to the barracks, I would see her watering the plants outside her house. And every time, she would smile at me. That smile, Shaunak, was my sunrise."

Bhaskar chuckled softly, shaking his head as if laughing at his younger self. "I was a fool, you know? I used to slow down my steps just to steal a few extra seconds of looking at her. Some days, I'd pretend to fix my shoe or adjust my uniform just so I could stay there a little longer. And then one day, I finally gathered the courage to talk to her. I still remember how my hands trembled, how my heart pounded like war drums. But Meera... she blushed, but she didn't look away. That day, my world changed."

They started meeting secretly—by the lake, in the narrow streets, and sometimes, just in stolen glances. The universe conspired for them, it seemed, making the wind carry their whispered words and the stars twinkle in their secret meetings. She would tie a small red thread around his wrist before every mission, whispering, *'Come back to me.'*

"But love, my boy," Bhaskar sighed, his smile fading, "it isn't always fair."

Shaunak held his breath, sensing that the story was about to take a turn.

"One evening, as we planned to run away and start a life together, a telegram arrived. My deployment orders. The war had come knocking on my door. I had to leave the very next day. Meera cried, holding onto my hands as if she could stop time itself. But duty calls, and a soldier cannot refuse. That night, under the banyan tree where we often met, she tied one last red thread around my wrist, saying, *'Even if the world forgets, this thread will remember.'* I promised her I would return. I swore it on my life."

The room fell silent, the old men looking down at their glasses, lost in their own pasts. Shaunak sat frozen, already dreading the next part of the story.

"Wars don't just take lives, Shaunak. They steal time, they erase memories, and they change people in ways they never imagined. Years passed. Battles were fought. Friends were lost. I wrote letters, dozens of them, but none were answered. Hope kept me alive, the thought of Meera waiting for me, of her smile greeting me when I returned. But fate had its own plans."

Bhaskar took a deep breath, steadying himself. "When I finally came back, after what felt like a lifetime, I ran to her house. My heart was pounding, my legs weak from exhaustion and excitement. But when I reached, I found an old woman sitting outside, her eyes filled with a quiet sadness. I asked for Meera, my voice barely a whisper."

The woman smiled softly, a kind but sorrowful smile. 'She waited, Bhaskar. She waited till the end. She never married. Every morning, she tied a red thread on the banyan tree, whispering your name, hoping the wind would carry it to you.'

Bhaskar swallowed hard, his eyes glistening with unshed tears. "I asked, 'And then?'

The old woman sighed, looking away. 'Then one morning, she didn't wake up.'

The silence that followed was deafening. Shaunak felt a lump form in his throat, his chest tightening with unspoken sorrow. He watched as Bhaskar untied a faded red thread from his wrist—the same one Meera had tied decades ago. His hands trembled, his lips pressing together as he traced the fragile strands with his fingers.

"Love, boy," Bhaskar said, his voice cracked and raw, "doesn't grow old. Only we do."

He took another sip of his drink, his eyes lost in the shadows of a love that never faded, a promise that outlived lifetimes. The other old men looked away, pretending to be occupied with their glasses, their own hearts burdened by memories of loves lost and regrets unspoken.

Shaunak sat there, feeling the weight of those words settle deep within him. He had heard many love stories before, seen countless romantic films, but none had ever touched him like this.

And as the night stretched on, Shaunak realized that some loves never die. They live on, in whispers of the wind, in the rustling of leaves, and in the fragile threads that refuse to break, no matter how many years pass.

Captain Mehta took a deep sip of his drink, his voice lowering as the others leaned in closer. "This isn't just a story, Shaunak," he said. "It's something my own eyes have seen."

He placed his glass on the table and began.

"It was 1999, the Kargil War. Our battalion was pushing through the frozen cliffs, and that's when we lost Rajbir. He was the best among us—sharp, fearless, always the first to volunteer. But one night, during an ambush, we were forced to retreat. Rajbir was the last man covering us. When we looked back, he was gone. No body, no sign of a struggle—just... gone."

The room fell silent except for the distant sound of a stray dog howling outside. Captain Mehta continued.

"Years passed. His name was engraved on the war memorial. And then, one winter, something strange happened. Our regiment was stationed near the same mountains. It was a bitterly cold night, the kind that freezes your breath before it leaves your lips. Our patrol team reported seeing a lone figure in the mist—standing perfectly still, holding a rifle, watching over the valley.

At first, they thought it was an enemy scout. But when they aimed their weapons, the figure simply turned and walked deeper into the fog, vanishing without a sound. No footprints. No trace. Nothing."

Shaunak shivered. "And you think... it was Rajbir?"

Captain Mehta's expression darkened. "We did not believe it at first either. But then, something happened that no one could explain. One night, a soldier named Vikrant was on patrol when he got lost in the thick fog. His radio failed, and his torch flickered out. That is when he saw him."

Mehta leaned in, his voice just above a whisper.

"Rajbir. Standing there. His uniform old, his boots caked in ice, his eyes glowing in the dark. Without a word, he motioned for Vikrant to follow. Too scared to resist, Vikrant obeyed. Step by step, Rajbir led him through the mist, taking a path none of us had ever used before. When Vikrant finally emerged near the camp, he turned back to thank him... but Rajbir was gone."

He paused, his fingers tapping the table.

"To this day," Captain Mehta murmured, finishing his drink, "when the fog rolls in over those mountains, soldiers say they still see him. Watching. Guarding. Protecting. Because some soldiers... never leave their post."

Havaldar Khan, the jolliest of the six, chuckled as he poured himself another drink. "Enough of these ghost stories and heartbreaks," he said, waving his hand. "Let me tell you something lighter. A story of how I once captured a spy... by accident."

The group leaned in, intrigued.

"This was during my posting in a remote border village. We had intel that an enemy spy was lurking around, disguised as a civilian. Every night, we patrolled, trying to catch him, but the bastard was too smart. He blended in so well that even the villagers had no clue who he was."

He took a sip of his drink and grinned. "Then one fateful night, I got drunk."

The group laughed. Shaunak raised an eyebrow. "And?"

"And I lost my way back to the barracks. So, I stumbled into a random house, thinking it was my own quarters. The moment I entered, I saw a man sitting there, looking shocked as hell. He had a long beard, a suspicious bag, and eyes that screamed, 'I don't belong here!'"

"Wait, so it was the spy?" Shaunak asked.

Havaldar Khan smirked. "Patience, boy. I was too drunk to think straight. So I sat down, pointed a finger at him, and said—get this—'Acha, toh tu hi hai wo jasoos!'" ("Ah, so you're the spy!")

The man froze. His face went pale. And before I could even blink, he lunged at me!"

The group gasped.

"Now, mind you, I was too drunk to fight properly. So I did the only thing I could—I fell. Right on top of him! We both crashed to the ground, me on top, him struggling beneath me." Khan wiped a tear of laughter from his eye. "Next thing I know, my fellow soldiers burst in and see me pinning this man down. They pull him up, search his bag, and boom! Maps, codes, fake IDs—the whole damn kit!"

"You just guessed and it turned out to be true?" Shaunak asked in disbelief.

"Exactly! I had no clue who he was. I was just too drunk and too cocky!" Khan laughed. "And guess what? The next morning, my superior commended me for my 'keen observation skills and sharp instincts.'"

The group burst into laughter as Khan raised his glass.

"And that's how I, a drunken fool, caught a spy... with nothing but dumb luck and a big mouth."

The night was thick with laughter and the warmth of old friendships. Shaunak sat among them, listening intently, his eyes wide with wonder as he soaked in every word.

Then, suddenly, Subedar Bhaskar placed a cold beer bottle in front of him. The golden liquid inside glowed under the dim light.

"Here, boy," Bhaskar said, his voice steady but testing. "Take a sip."

The laughter around the table quieted. The other five old men exchanged knowing glances, waiting for Shaunak's reaction.

Shaunak looked at the bottle, then at Bhaskar, and then at the others. He could see it in their eyes—they were testing him. He knew this wasn't about drinking. It was about something much bigger.

He leaned back, crossed his arms, and smiled. "I know what you're doing."

Bhaskar raised an eyebrow. "Oh? And what's that?"

"You made me promise that I wouldn't drink before the right age," Shaunak said confidently. "And that I'd never drink when I was alone or sad. That was the condition to be part of this group, remember?"

A smirk played on Bhaskar's lips, but he did not say anything.

Shaunak pushed the bottle slightly away. "And besides, I don't like the smell of beer anyway. Even if you had not made me promise, I wouldn't drink it. No one in my family drinks, and I'm not the exception."

For a moment, there was silence. Then, Captain Mehta let out a deep, satisfied laugh.

CHAPTER VII

A Question That Never Leaves

The old men fell silent as Shaunak took a deep breath. The warm glow of the room light flickered over his face, and for the first time that night, the laughter had faded.

"I don't need alcohol to tell my story," he said, his voice steady. "But I want to share something I've never told anyone. Because you all feel like family to me now."

The six old men nodded; their faces now serious, ready to listen.

"I had a brother. My uncle's son. By relation, my cousin, but to me, he was more than that. He was my role model, my guide, my friend. He was the kind of person who always put others before himself. If someone needed help, he would be the first to offer. If someone was struggling, he'd share their burden, no matter how heavy."

Shaunak's fingers tapped lightly against the table as he continued.

"He had a great life. A good job, loving parents, and a passion for riding. He travelled solo, covering almost every state in the country on his bike. The road was his escape, his meditation. But even with all that adventure, he always stayed grounded. His heart belonged at home, with his family."

He paused, looking at the beer bottle in front of him before pushing it aside.

"But then, he fell in love. And that was his downfall."

The old men exchanged glances but said nothing.

"He loved her deeply. Planned his whole life with her. Every dream, every decision—she was at the centre of it.

And then, one day, he found out the truth. She was cheating on him. At first, he refused to believe it. He thought maybe it was a misunderstanding, maybe someone was trying to poison his mind. But when he confronted her... the truth hit him harder than any betrayal ever could."

Shaunak's voice grew heavier, but he didn't stop.

"She wasn't just cheating on him with one guy. There were many. And the worst part? She told them all the same story. The same dreams, the same promises, the same 'forever' that she had whispered to him."

The night air grew colder as silence settled around them. Even the distant hum of the city seemed to fade.

"And that broke him," Shaunak said, his voice barely above a whisper. "Not just his heart, but his spirit. The man who always thought of others, who always put his family first, who was strong enough to travel the whole country alone—suddenly, he felt lost. Like nothing in the world made sense anymore."

Havaldar Khan let out a slow sigh, rubbing his temple. "And what happened to him, boy?"

Shaunak looked up, his eyes reflecting a deep sadness.

"He stopped riding. Stopped talking. Stopped being the person he once was. He was not just heartbroken... he was shattered. And the worst part? The girl moved on like nothing ever happened."

The group sat in silence for a long time. Then, Captain Mehta spoke.

"Love is like war, Shaunak," he said, his voice calm but firm. "Some battles you win, some you lose. But the real fight is after the war—learning how to live again."

The air grew heavier as Shaunak continued. The old men, who had been through wars and heartbreaks of their own, listened intently. There was no laughter now—only the quiet hum of a story that carried a weight none of them could ignore.

"But that wasn't the end," Shaunak said, his voice quieter now. "The worst was yet to come."

The old men leaned in.

"He tried to move on. He told himself he would heal, that time would make things better. But no matter how much he tried, the pain never faded. It lingered like a wound that refused to close. And instead of blaming her... he started blaming himself."

Havaldar Khan shook his head knowingly. "That's a dangerous road, lad."

Shaunak nodded. "He kept thinking—*What did I do wrong? Why wasn't I enough?* And the more he thought, the more he believed it was his fault. He started punishing himself in ways no one should. He stopped eating properly, stopped taking care of himself. And the worst part? He wanted to go back to her."

Captain Mehta let out a deep sigh. "Even after what she did?"

"Yes," Shaunak said, his jaw tightening. "He thought if he just begged enough, if he changed himself, if he proved his love again, maybe she'd take him back. But she never did. She didn't even care."

Silence settled for a moment before Shaunak continued.

"And that's when he lost himself completely. He started drinking, picking fights over the smallest things, lashing out at people who had nothing to do with his pain. The kind and selfless person he once was... disappeared. He became someone even he didn't recognize."

Subedar Bhaskar, who had seen too many young men destroy themselves, exhaled sharply. "And did he realize what he was becoming?"

Shaunak looked at him. "Yes. That was the worst part. He knew. He knew he was walking down the wrong path. He could see himself turning into a person he never wanted to be. But he couldn't stop. It was like he was trapped in his own misery, and no matter how much he tried to escape, he kept getting pulled back in."

The group remained silent, absorbing the weight of the story.

Then, Captain Mehta spoke again. His voice was softer now, but firm. "Pain can make a man or break him. It all depends on what he does with it."

Shaunak looked down at the table, lost in thought.

"And what about now?" Havaldar Khan asked. "Where is he?"

Shaunak clenched his fists. "Still fighting his demons."

Shaunak's voice had become heavier, his words slower, as if each syllable carried a weight too painful to bear. The old men, who had seen wars, loss, and heartbreak, now sat in complete silence. The night air, once filled with stories and laughter, now felt colder, heavier.

"One day," Shaunak continued, his gaze fixed on the table, "he came to me. He looked different—not like the brother I had known. There was something missing in his eyes. Like he was there, but not really. And then he said something that shook me to my core."

He swallowed hard before speaking again.

"I am struggling to live. I don't know how to continue like this. I'm thinking of going somewhere far away, where no one will ever find me. Do you know... if I die, everyone will love me? Even she will."

A chill ran through the old men. None of them moved.

Shaunak took a deep breath and continued, "Then he said something even worse."

"I am still alive only because I don't want my mother to hear that her son committed suicide. I don't even know why I'm telling you this. I just came to wish you love and luck."

Shaunak clenched his fists. "And then... he asked me something no one had ever asked before."

"How can I do it? How can I end it all, with the least pain, in a way that no one ever knows it was suicide?"

He looked up, his eyes glistening with something raw, something unspoken. "I was speechless. I had no words. This was the man I had always respected, always looked up to. And now... he was slipping away, right in front of me."

Subedar Bhaskar sighed, rubbing his temples. "And what did you say?"

Shaunak exhaled slowly. "Nothing. I couldn't say anything. I just... stared at him. I should have stopped him. I should have told someone. But I was too small for that. I didn't know how to handle something so big."

He paused. And then, with a voice barely above a whisper, he said, "The very next day, we heard the news."

The old men knew what was coming, but they still held their breath.

"He had a road accident."

Shaunak let those words sink in before continuing.

"We lost him. Everyone said it was an accident. But was it? I do not know. And that question... it haunts me like hell."

The old men sat still; their expressions unreadable.

"What if I had said something? What if I had given him some advice that made him rethink? What if I had told his parents? Could I have saved him?" Shaunak's voice cracked, the pain he had held inside now spilling out. "Or am I just overthinking? Was it really just an accident?"

No one spoke for a long time. Then, Captain Mehta, the oldest among them, placed a firm hand on Shaunak's shoulder.

"You were just a boy, Shaunak. You were not responsible for his choices. A man who has lost the will to live... sometimes, no matter how much we try, we cannot pull them back."

"But I miss him," Shaunak whispered. "Every single day."

Mehta nodded. "And you always will. But instead of drowning in guilt, honour him. Live the way he once did—before the pain took over. That's how you keep him alive."

Shaunak stared at the table for a long time before finally nodding.

The fire crackled softly, casting flickering shadows on the old faces gathered around Shaunak. The night, once filled with laughter and drunken stories, had taken a solemn turn.

Shaunak's voice, steady yet heavy, continued.

"I didn't tell my uncle and aunt because I didn't want to hurt them. And I didn't tell my parents because I knew they might reveal this secret in some way or another. Or maybe... maybe my brother didn't want the girl's name to come out. He didn't want her to be blamed, even after everything she had done to him. Maybe he didn't want our family name to be dragged into this mess either."

He looked at the old men, his gaze unwavering. "So, I kept it inside. Alone."

A silence stretched between them. Not an empty silence, but one heavy with thoughts, with unspoken respect.

Subedar Bhaskar finally exhaled, shaking his head. "At your age, I wouldn't have lasted a day with a secret like that.

I'd have run straight to my father."

Captain Mehta gave a slow nod. "Even now, at this age, I don't think I could've held onto something that big."

The others murmured in agreement.

"But you," Havaldar Khan said, studying Shaunak like he was something rare, something unheard of, "you carried it alone. And you still carry it, don't you?"

Shaunak swallowed, his throat dry. "Yes."

The old men exchanged glances. They had seen war. They had lost comrades. They had buried friends. But what this boy had done...

"You know, lad," Captain Mehta finally said, leaning forward, "secrets like these—they don't just sit inside you. They grow. They change you. They make you question everything, including yourself."

Shaunak clenched his fists. "I do question myself. Every day. What if I had spoken up? What if I had done something differently? Maybe he would still be here."

"But maybe not," Subedar Bhaskar said. "Maybe he was already too far gone."

Shaunak looked down. "But what if he wasn't?"

The fire crackled again, filling the space where no answer could.

And then, Havaldar Khan spoke. "You know what I think?"

Shaunak met his eyes.

"I think your brother wouldn't want you to carry this guilt. He made his choice. Right or wrong, it was his. And you—you were just a kid trying to do what you thought was right. Hell, even at our age, we cannot always tell what's right and what's wrong. But I'll tell you this," he said, his voice firm. "If you keep carrying this alone, one day, it'll break you too."

Shaunak looked at him, really looked at him, and for the first time in years, something inside him shifted.

"You don't have to forget him," Captain Mehta added. "But don't let his story become the reason you stop living your own."

The night had settled into a deep, reflective silence. The warmth of the dwindling fire barely reached their hands, but the heat of Shaunak's words still lingered. The old men, who had seen life in its rawest forms, sat with keen eyes, their drunken haze momentarily lifted by the gravity of his story.

Then, Havaldar Khan leaned forward, breaking the silence. "So, what about now?" he asked, his voice laced with curiosity. "After everything—after seeing what love did to your brother—has your perception changed?"

Shaunak looked at him, his expression unreadable.

"Let me ask you something straight," Khan continued. "Do you still believe in love? Would you ever trust it blindly again? Do you even believe in soulmates anymore?"

A slow breath escaped Shaunak's lips. He ran a hand through his hair, his fingers tightening for a moment before he spoke.

"Yes," he said firmly. "I believe in love. And I believe in soulmates."

The old men exchanged glances, surprised. They had expected bitterness, cynicism—maybe even anger. But instead, there was certainty.

Shaunak continued, his voice steady. "Even before my brother changed because of love, I believed in it. And nothing has ever shaken that belief. Not his pain, not his betrayal, not even his death."

Captain Mehta, intrigued, leaned in. "Why?"

A small smile played at the corner of Shaunak's lips, one that carried both warmth and mystery. "I don't know why, but from childhood, I've always felt like... there is someone made for me. Someone who exists in this world, waiting, just as I am. I don't know where she is, or when I will meet her. But someday, she'll come into my life, and everything will change."

The old men fell silent again, absorbing his words. There was something about Shaunak's conviction that made them believe, even if just for a moment, that fate might have a plan after all.

Subedar Bhaskar chuckled, shaking his head. "You're a strange one, kid. Most people, after witnessing such tragedy, would give up on love altogether. But you? You're waiting for it."

Shaunak shrugged. "Maybe that's what makes it worth waiting for."

"You know," Shaunak continued, "I've always been drawn to love stories. Whenever I see a newspaper column or an article about love, I cannot help but read it. It does not matter if it's real or fiction—I just love the idea of loving someone and being loved in return. It's like... the purest feeling in the world."

Subedar Bhaskar raised an eyebrow. "Even after what happened to your brother?"

Shaunak nodded without hesitation. "Especially after that. His story was tragic, yes, but love itself was not the villain. The wrong person was. That doesn't mean true love doesn't exist."

He took a deep breath before continuing, his voice soft but filled with an unmistakable longing.

"Just yesterday, I read an article about a couple. The woman's kidneys had failed, and she was on the verge of death. Without hesitation, her partner donated one of his own to save her. And do you know how their story began?"

The old men shook their heads.

"In a train," Shaunak said, a small smile playing on his lips. "They met by chance—two strangers, sharing a journey. They talked, laughed, and by the time the train reached its destination, something had changed between them. A connection had formed, one neither of them could ignore. Over time, they fell in love, built a life together, and when the ultimate test of love came, he gave her a part of himself—literally."

The group remained silent, absorbing his words. Even the most battle-hardened among them felt a strange warmth in their chests.

Shaunak looked at them, his expression open, vulnerable. "I want that kind of love. The kind that does not hesitate. The kind that is not bound by conditions. The kind where two people are willing to give their all for each other, no matter what."

Captain Mehta chuckled, shaking his head. "You've got the heart of a poet, kid. The world needs more people like you."

Shaunak smiled. "Maybe. Or maybe I'm just someone who still dares to believe in love, even when the world tells me not to."

CHAPTER VIII

The Boy Who Stayed Awake

The night had grown heavy with silence, each man sinking into the weight of the stories they had heard. One by one, their eyes closed, their breathing slowed, and soon, the only sounds left were the distant rustling of trees and the occasional crackling of the dying fire.

But one man remained awake.

He was the reason for the gathering—the one who had lost his wife. The party, meant to lift his spirits, had become a night of deep confessions, laughter, and pain. Yet, through it all, he had stayed silent, letting others pour out their hearts.

Now, as his friends and Shaunak slept soundly around him, he took a deep breath and began his story.

"She was my everything," he whispered to the night. "I met her when I was just a reckless young soldier, full of pride and fire. She was nothing like me—gentle, kind, patient. I was the storm; she was the calm. And somehow, she chose me."

He looked around, knowing that no one was listening. But for the first time, it felt easier to speak. No eyes to judge him, no interruptions, no questions. Just him and the memories of his wife.

"She waited for me through war, through long deployments, through endless letters that never came fast enough. She built our home with her own hands, filled it with laughter and warmth. And every time I came back, she was there at the doorstep, smiling, as if no time had passed at all."

His voice trembled slightly, but he kept going.

"She grew old before my eyes. Her hair turned silver, her hands wrinkled, but her love never changed. Even when her body became weak, even when she forgot where she kept her glasses or what day it was, she never forgot me. Not once."

He sighed, staring into the fading embers.

"And now, she's gone. And I... I don't know who I am without her."

A single tear slipped down his weathered cheek, but he wiped it away, chuckling softly.

"Look at me, talking to a bunch of sleeping fools," he muttered. "But maybe this is the best way. No interruptions. No sympathy. Just me, telling her story."

He kept speaking, whispering memories into the night, as if his wife were still there, listening.

By the time the first rays of dawn touched the sky, his eyes grew heavy. He finally felt light, as if he had unburdened something he had carried for too long.

As his friends stirred awake, stretching and groaning from their night's rest, the old man finally closed his eyes and drifted into the most peaceful sleep he had had in years.

None of them knew what he had shared.

And he did not mind.

The morning after their unforgettable night, the old men and Shaunak spent the entire day together at a small hotel, sharing laughter, old memories, and untold stories of their past. The atmosphere was light, filled with the kind of warmth only true companionship brings.

For Shaunak, something had changed. The weight he had unknowingly carried—the confusion, the doubts, the silent pain—felt lighter. The stories he had heard, the lessons he had absorbed, had given him a fresh perspective on life.

As the evening fell, they all parted ways, each returning to their own lives. But something lingered—a bond that would never fade.

The next morning, Shaunak returned to his usual routine, but nothing felt the same. School, which once felt mundane, now seemed full of possibilities. He found himself more attentive in class, eager to participate. For the first time in a long while, he raised his hand to answer questions, surprising even his teachers.

But where he truly shined was on the field.

Shaunak had always been good at sports, but now, he approached it with newfound passion. Cricket had always been his love, but now he played not just for fun, but with purpose, with drive. His dedication did not go unnoticed.

As the interschool cricket tournament approached, Shaunak gave it everything he had. With his skill and leadership, his school clinched victory, marking their name in the competition. The applause, the cheers—it all felt surreal.

Winning the interschool cricket championship as a captain had changed everything for Shaunak. His name echoed in the school corridors, whispered in admiration. The boys respected him, the teachers acknowledged him, and even the girls—who had never noticed him before—now knew his name.

He enjoyed the attention. Every match felt like a festival, and he made sure to make the most of it. Whenever there was a game, he subtly adjusted his fielding position to be near the section where the girls sat. The sound of them cheering his name filled him with an indescribable thrill.

At first, it was innocent fun. But soon, it became something more.

He started recognizing familiar voices in the crowd, noticing the same faces clapping every time he played a shot. Girls he had never spoken to were suddenly smiling at him in the hallways. His confidence soared.

But what truly set him apart was his leadership. Despite being from a lower grade, he now found himself guiding senior players, telling them how to position themselves, when to go aggressive, when to hold back. They listened. They respected his strategies.

With every match, his reputation grew. He was not just a player anymore—he was becoming a legend in his own school.

After another victorious match, as Shaunak basked in the cheers and handshakes, something unexpected happened.

A girl walked up to him.

"Congratulations," she said with a smile before turning and heading back to her class.

Shaunak stood frozen. His heart raced. He had never spoken to a girl before—at least, not like this. The way she had looked at him, the casual yet confident way she spoke, left him stunned.

For the rest of the day, he could not focus. His mind kept replaying that moment, her voice echoing in his ears. Who was she? Why did she come up to him? Did she—no, that could not be.

That evening, as he sat on his bed, still lost in thought, one of his teammates mentioned her name.

"She goes to Sir Rajan's coaching class," the boy said casually. "She's the most beautiful girl in our school, man. But she's terrible at studies."

Shaunak listened carefully, absorbing every word.

So, she was not just beautiful—she was confident. She had walked up to him while he could not even gather the courage to respond. That thought alone made him smile.

For the first time in his life, Shaunak felt something he could not explain. A strange excitement, a curiosity, a pull toward someone he had barely spoken to.

Shaunak had never felt this way before—anxious yet excited, nervous yet determined. The moment she had congratulated him after the match had ignited something in him, and now he wanted to talk to her.

The next morning, he planned. He reached school early and positioned himself near the entrance, waiting for her to arrive. His mind rehearsed the conversation repeatedly—
"I will start with a simple thank you... then maybe ask her name, or should I act like I already know? No, that will be weird. Maybe compliment her confidence? No, that's too much."

Minutes turned into hours, but she never showed up.

Maybe she was absent? He told himself it was just bad timing.

The next day, he tried again. Same plan, same spot. But once again, she was nowhere to be seen in the morning. Disappointment crept in, but he refused to give up.

Then, during dispersal, as he was about to leave, he finally spotted her.

His heart pounded. His hands clenched into fists, trying to stop them from shaking.

"This is it. I have to talk to her today."

His words were ready, carefully crafted in his mind. He was going to thank her for congratulating him, make a small joke, and maybe even ask if she watched the whole match.

But as he took a step forward, doubt crashed into him like a wave.

"What if she doesn't remember me? What if she thinks I am weird? What if I freeze again and embarrass myself?"

He hesitated.

And in that hesitation, she walked past him, completely unaware of the battle raging in his mind.

Shaunak just stood there, watching her go, cursing himself for missing his chance again.

After failing to talk to her outside school, Shaunak gave up the idea of meeting her by chance. But the thought of her never left his mind.

That weekend, he met his six old friends and shared everything—the failed attempts, the nervousness, the way he had frozen when she walked past him.

The old men listened patiently. Then, one of them chuckled and asked, "Okay, apart from all this, how are your studies going?"

Shaunak straightened up. "Good," he replied.

One of the men smirked. "Then why don't you join the same private coaching class where she studies?"

Shaunak's eyes widened. He had not thought of that.

It was the perfect plan. He would not have to wait outside school or worry about missing his chance—he could just naturally be around her.

The idea excited him, but there was a problem—convincing his parents. He was already a top student. He never needed extra coaching.

That night, he sat with his parents and said, "I want to do even better in my studies. I think joining a coaching class would help."

His parents exchanged surprised glances. His father smiled. "You're already doing well, but if you think it will help, we support you."

His mother was even more impressed. "We're proud of you for taking your studies so seriously."

Shaunak forced a smile, feeling a pang of guilt. The truth was, he did not need coaching at all. The library was enough for him to ace his exams. But this was not about studies—it was about seeing her again.

And so, despite knowing he did not need it, he joined the coaching class.

CHAPTER IX

When Hi Meant Hope

The first day at coaching class, Shaunak saw her approaching. His heart pounded, but he forced himself to speak.

"Hi," he said.

She glanced at him, a bit surprised, and replied, "Hello."

There was a pause before she asked, "What?"

Shaunak, struggling to keep his composure, simply said, "I just came to say hi," and quickly walked into the classroom before his nervousness betrayed him.

From that day, it became a routine. Every day, he arrived on time—just to say "hi." Slowly, she started expecting it. Their interactions grew longer, and she began seeing him as a friend.

Shaunak, on the other hand, had already started feeling something more.

For no reason, he would ask her for extra pens, borrow her notebook, and even pretend to struggle with diagrams just so she could help him. These little excuses kept bringing them closer.

She had many guy friends, and every time she laughed or talked to one of them, Shaunak felt a pang of jealousy. He knew he had no right to feel that way, but he couldn't help it.

To win her attention, he started bringing her chocolates. He volunteered to do her homework and patiently helped her with mathematics, even though he knew she wasn't really interested in studying.

Day by day, their bond strengthened. But deep inside, Shaunak was unsure—was he just a helpful friend to her, or was there something more?

One day, while they were sitting in the library, Nancy suddenly turned to him and asked, "Shaunak, why are you always so nice to me?"

Her question caught him off guard. He chuckled nervously and said, "Because you're my friend, of course."

She smiled, seemingly satisfied with the answer, but deep inside, Shaunak knew it wasn't the whole truth.

The months passed, and coaching classes became the highlight of his day. He found himself drawn to every little thing about her—the way she absentmindedly twirled her pen while thinking, the way she scrunched her nose when confused, and the way she smiled at him when he explained something in the simplest way possible.

One evening, as they walked out of class together, Nancy was unusually quiet. She seemed to be lost in thought. Finally, she said, "Shaunak, do you ever feel like some friendships are more than just friendships?"

His heart skipped a beat. Was she thinking what he was thinking? He wanted to ask, to confess, but fear held him back.

Instead, he said, "Maybe. Sometimes, things just happen."

Nancy nodded but did not press the matter. As they reached the crossroads where they had to part ways, she hesitated before saying, "I'm glad we met."

Shaunak smiled. "Me too."

But deep inside, the question remained—was he just a good friend, or did Nancy feel the same way he did?

One evening, as Shaunak was returning from coaching, he saw her standing with a guy. His heart skipped a beat, but he forced a smile and casually approached.

"Hi," he greeted her.

She turned, briefly met his eyes, and replied, "Hello."

Then, without saying anything more, she and the guy walked away. Shaunak stood there, feeling a strange heaviness in his chest. He told himself it was nothing—but deep inside, it hurt.

The next day, one of her friends casually mentioned, "You know, she was laughing yesterday, saying you're mad. That you randomly showed up when she was with her boyfriend."

Shaunak felt his world crack. The warmth he had felt in their friendship suddenly turned cold.

That evening, he met his old friends at the tea stall and told them everything. He waited for their advice, hoping for some wise words to fix this mess.

The old men listened carefully. Then one of them, the most experienced among them, sighed and said, "Son, leave the coaching class. Forget about her. Some people are just not meant to stay in your life."

The others nodded in agreement.

"But... I liked her," Shaunak whispered, struggling to accept their words.

One of the men patted his shoulder. "Liking someone is not enough. If she doesn't respect your presence, she's not worth your time."

Shaunak sat there, staring at his cup of tea, realizing for the first time what unrequited feelings truly felt like.

That same evening, Shaunak made his decision—he left the coaching class. He knew he didn't need it anyway. But there was another issue—his parents were giving him extra money every month for tuition. If they found out he wasn't attending, they might stop giving him the money or, worse, ask him to leave school and help his father in business.

So, instead of wasting it, Shaunak found a better purpose. He joined a cricket academy, something he had always wanted to do but never had the chance. Every rupee his parents gave for tuition now went into training, new gear, and match fees.

At home, he pretended everything was normal. He still left at the same time as his coaching class and came back at the usual hour, but instead of sitting in a classroom, he was out on the field, sweating, training, and pushing himself harder than ever.

Cricket became his escape. Every time he hit the ball, it felt like he was smashing away his past. Every time he ran between the wickets, it felt like he was running toward a new future. The pain of betrayal, the sting of her words—all of it started fading as he focused on his game.

Shaunak had never imagined this moment. The girl he once admired, the one he had left coaching for, was standing right in front of him—cigarette in hand.

As soon as he saw her, he wanted to disappear. He quickly tried to hide, but the tea stall owner unknowingly exposed him, mentioning that his old friends had gone for their morning walk and would return soon.

She spotted him. "Hey, Shaunak!" she called out.

There was no escape now. He turned toward her, forcing a smile. "Hi," he replied.

"Where have you been? Why did you leave the coaching class?" she asked, a hint of concern in her voice.

His heart wavered for a moment. He wanted to tell her the truth—that he had left because of her, that he had poured his pain into cricket, that he was trying to move on. But instead, he lied. "I wasn't feeling well," he said casually.

She looked at him with slight worry. "What happened?"

For a second, he almost melted. The concern in her voice, the way she looked at him—it was everything he had wanted once. But he knew better now.

The tea stall owner brought two cups of tea. She handed one to him, but then, with a smirk, she extended her cigarette toward him. "Want one?" she asked playfully.

Shaunak hesitated. He hated smoking—the smell, the habit, the way it consumed people. He had always despised smokers. But for her, all those thoughts disappeared. He wanted to impress her, to seem cool, to not look weak in her eyes.

He took the cigarette, hesitated for a second, then took a puff.

Instantly, his throat burned, and he coughed violently. His eyes watered, his lungs protested, but he forced himself to recover quickly.

She laughed. "You don't smoke, do you?"

He wiped his mouth and shook his head. "I do... just not today. My health isn't great."

She smirked but did not question further. He felt ashamed, but he also felt something else—he was slipping. Slipping into something he had promised himself he would never become.

And the worst part? He did not even care.

The tea stall owner had seen everything—the hesitation, the cough, the forced lie. But before his old friends arrived, Shaunak leaned in and whispered, "Please, don't say a word about this to them. I don't want them to know."

The old man at the stall looked at him with wise, tired eyes. "Some things you can hide from others, but not from yourself, beta," he said.

Shaunak ignored the words and extended his hand. "Promise me," he insisted.

The old man sighed and nodded. "Fine. I won't say anything."

A few minutes later, the girl left, disappearing down the street. Shaunak exhaled, feeling both relieved and restless. He sat at the stall, sipping his now-cold tea, waiting.

Soon, his old friends arrived, laughing and chatting about their morning walk.

"Arre, Shaunak! When did you come?" one of them asked, patting him on the back.

"A while ago," he said casually. "Had some free time, so I thought I'd meet you all."

They sat together, ordering tea. As they talked about their day, Shaunak listened, but his mind was elsewhere. He kept glancing at the tea stall owner, wondering if he would accidentally slip something. But the old man kept his promise.

Trying to distract himself, Shaunak changed the topic. "So, what's new with you all?" he asked.

One of the older men chuckled. "Same old stories, beta. But tell us, what's new with you? You seem... different."

Shaunak forced a smile. "Nothing much. Just busy with cricket."

But deep inside, he felt a storm brewing. He had lied to his friends, just like he had lied to himself.

CHAPTER X

The Smoke Between Us

That night, after returning home, Shaunak could not stop thinking about Nancy. The moment replayed in his mind—the way she casually offered him a cigarette, the very same one she had been smoking. Technically, he thought, he had touched the cigarette that she had touched.

Something about that thought sent a strange thrill through him. Acting on impulse, he went to a nearby shop and bought an entire pack of cigarettes. Sitting alone in his room, he lit one, trying to mimic the way she had held it between her fingers, the way she had exhaled the smoke effortlessly. Coughing through his first few attempts, he kept going, determined to make it feel natural.

The next evening, at the same time, he went back to the stall, almost hoping to see her there. And as if the universe had planned it, Nancy was already standing by the counter, cigarette in hand.

As the smoke curled around them, Shaunak felt something strange—an odd sense of closeness, as if they were sharing a secret world that no one else could enter. The cigarette between his fingers no longer felt foreign. Instead, it felt like a bridge, a silent connection between him and her.

She smirked as she took the cigarette from his hand. "Look at you," she teased. "Acting all grown up now."

He chuckled, trying to hide the nervous excitement bubbling inside him. "Maybe I am," he said.

They sat on the broken bench near the tea stall, smoking in rounds, lost in their own little universe. The stall owner stole glances at them but said nothing.

"So," she said, exhaling smoke, "why did you really leave the coaching class?"

Shaunak hesitated. He could tell her the truth—that he could not bear to see her with someone else. That every time he looked at her, he felt like the world was spinning too fast. But instead, he shrugged and said, "Got busy with other things."

She nodded, as if she understood something he was not saying. "You know," she said, "you're different from the other guys I know."

His heart skipped a beat. "How?"

"You don't try too hard," she said simply. "And you don't ask too many questions."

Shaunak laughed. "Maybe I should start asking more."

She leaned back, looking at the sky. "Maybe you shouldn't."

They smoked in silence for a while, the unspoken words hanging between them like the smoke drifting into the sky.

That night, as Shaunak lay in bed, he thought about her again. The way she held the cigarette, the way she looked at him, the way she made him feel like he was someone important, someone special.

For the first time in his life, he was not just thinking about love stories in books or newspaper columns.

He was living one.

Shaunak did not even think twice before giving her whatever she asked for. Every time his phone buzzed with her message; his heart raced. She needed him—that was all that mattered.

"Shaunak, can you recharge my number? It is urgent."

"Shaunak, I need   ₹500. I will return it soon."

Each time, he told himself she would return the money. But deep down, he knew she would not. It did not matter. The way she smiled at him when he helped her—that was enough.

His friends noticed the change. He started skipping practice, arriving late at their usual meetup spots, always distracted. The cricket academy fees he once saved carefully were now being spent on her recharges, her small "emergencies."

One day, after practice, one of his teammates pulled him aside.

"You've changed, Shaunak," he said. "You don't even care about cricket anymore."

Shaunak forced a smile. "It's not like I was ever going to make it to the state team anyway."

"That's not the point," his friend insisted. "You loved playing. Now, you just... exist."

Shaunak shrugged it off. But late at night, lying in bed, the words echoed in his head. Had he really changed that much?

The next time she asked for money, he hesitated for a second. But then he looked at her message:

"You're the only one I can ask, Shaunak. You're different from everyone else."

His hesitation disappeared.

She needed him.

And he needed to matter to her.

The scene at the tea stall had turned chaotic. The girl's father, red with fury, kept hurling abuses at Shaunak, blaming him for leading his daughter astray.

"You think you can ruin my daughter's life?" he shouted, raising his hand again.

Shaunak didn't retaliate. He simply stood there, silent, accepting every slap, every punch. Deep inside, he knew the truth—he wasn't innocent, but he wasn't the only one responsible either.

The girl, still crying, didn't utter a word to defend him. That hurt more than the beating.

Just then, Shaunak's old friends arrived. The tea stall owner had sent word about the commotion. The group of old men quickly assessed the situation.

One of them, the same man who always gave him life lessons, stepped forward and placed a firm hand on the angry father's shoulder.

"Enough," he said in a calm but authoritative voice. "Shaunak is not solely to blame. Your daughter was there with him, wasn't she? She was smoking too, wasn't she?"

The father hesitated. His anger flickered for a moment.

Another old man spoke up. "Punishing him like this won't fix anything. Maybe instead of beating him, you should ask your daughter why she was there in the first place."

Shaunak looked at the girl, hoping—just hoping—she would say something in his defence. Maybe just one word.

But she lowered her gaze and stayed silent.

His heart sank.

The old men diffused the situation, telling the father that violence would not solve anything. Begrudgingly, the man left, dragging his daughter away.

Shaunak stood there, still processing everything. The people he had spent his money on, the girl he had trusted—none of them stood up for him.

One of his old friends patted his shoulder. "Let's go," he said. "You need to clear your mind."

Shaunak stood frozen, his ears ringing with the weight of her words.

"She blamed me?"

His heart pounded, but he did not say a word. He just watched as she walked away with her father, never once looking back at him.

The tea stall owner sighed and muttered, "I saw everything, beta. You never forced her. But the world believes what it wants to."

Shaunak did not respond. He felt numb. Everything—the money he spent on her, the moments he cherished, the sacrifices—meant nothing now. In a single moment, she erased him from her life, painting him as the villain.

The old men, his only true friends, watched him in silence. One of them finally spoke, "Shaunak, do you realize what just happened?"

He nodded slowly. "I was just a fool."

"No," the old man said. "You just loved the wrong person."

Shaunak stood silently; his head lowered as the old men scolded him. Their voices carried the weight of disappointment, but beneath it, there was concern—deep, genuine concern.

"You think we are just some old fools who sit around telling stories?" one of them said. "We have lived through more than you can imagine, boy! And yet, you did not come to us when you needed us the most."

Another shook his head. "The worst thing you did was not smoking, spending money, or getting involved with that girl. The worst thing was losing yourself. Becoming someone, you are not."

Shaunak clenched his fists. He knew they were right. He had allowed himself to be manipulated, to drift away from his principles. And for what? A love that was never real? A friendship built on lies?

"I messed up," he admitted, his voice barely above a whisper. "I should have come to you all earlier. I will not let this happen again."

The old men exchanged glances. They could see he was hurting, but they also saw something else—a flicker of realization.

"You're young," one of them finally said, his tone softer now. "You will make mistakes. But the real question is—will you learn from them?"

Shaunak took a deep breath. "I will."

And for the first time in a long while, he meant it.

For the whole week, Shaunak avoided the tea stall. The memory of that evening—her father's rage, the accusing stares, the hushed whispers—was too fresh, too humiliating. He could not bear the thought of facing those people again. Even his old friends, the ones who had always stood by him, felt distant now. He didn't know if it was guilt or shame keeping him away, but he could not bring himself to meet them.

Instead, he spent his time alone, replaying everything in his mind. He had sent her a message, asking if she was okay. She had replied with a simple "I'm fine." No apology, no regret, just two empty words. But he held onto them like they meant something.

Days passed, and Shaunak buried himself in his cricket practice. A big match was coming up, one that would be played near her home. His team needed him at his best, but his heart was elsewhere. He kept thinking about her—about how she had turned against him so quickly, how she had let him take the blame. And yet, despite everything, he still wanted her there.

So, he messaged her.

"I have a match near your house. Will you come?"

She did not reply immediately. He waited, staring at his phone, hoping to see those three dots appear. Finally, she responded:

"Maybe."

Maybe. It was not a yes, but it was not a no either. It was enough to keep his hopes alive.

Every day leading up to the match, he reminded her.

"Don't forget, my match is tomorrow."

"I will be playing near your house. Hope you come."

"I'd love to see you there."

Each time, she responded with vague, non-committal answers. But Shaunak convinced himself that deep down, she wanted to come. That she still cared.

The day of the match arrived. His team gathered at the ground, stretching, strategizing, preparing for battle. But his eyes kept drifting to the sidelines, scanning the crowd. Was she here? Would she come?

As the match started, he forced himself to focus. He had to play well, to prove himself, to regain the respect he had lost. But no matter how hard he tried, a part of him was still searching, still waiting for her to show up.

There was still a probability that she might be there. That thought alone pushed him to give his absolute best. As he walked onto the field, gripping his bat tightly, he told himself— *this match is not just a game; it's a moment, a chance.* A chance to make her notice him again, to make her see the boy she had once congratulated with a shy smile. Maybe, just maybe, after this match, she would walk up to him again, just like the first time, and say, *"Congratulations."*

With that thought fuelling his spirit, Shaunak played one of the best innings of his life. Every shot, every stroke, every run—he poured his heart into it. He wasn't just playing; he was proving something—to himself, to her, to the crowd. His bat spoke louder than his words ever could. The ball flew to the boundary multiple times, and the sound of applause filled the air. But amongst all the noise, he was searching for just one voice, one cheer—hers.

During the fielding session, he intentionally positioned himself near the area where the girls' crowd had gathered. His teammates didn't question it, assuming it was just his strategic choice. But only he knew why he chose that particular spot. *She might be watching.* Maybe she would see how good he had become; how much he had grown. Maybe, just like before, she would call out his name and cheer for him.

But as he stood there, hands on his knees, scanning the faces in the crowd, there was no sign of her. He kept glancing towards the stands, hoping, waiting. In every interval, while the team gathered around the coach for strategy discussions, his eyes wandered, searching for her presence.

When he walked back to bat again, he imagined her watching. He hit harder, ran faster, played smarter. Every time the ball connected with his bat and raced towards the boundary, he imagined her standing somewhere in the crowd, watching him, impressed by him.

The match was intense, the scores were close, but Shaunak's performance helped his team stay ahead. The final overs arrived, and the tension in the air was thick. His teammates cheered him on, the crowd was on edge, but his mind was fixated on only one thing—*Is she here? Will she come to me after the match? Will she say something?*

Anything?

Finally, the last ball was played, the match ended, and Shaunak's team emerged victorious. His teammates rushed towards him, lifting him in celebration. The crowd erupted in cheers, and people clapped and whistled for him. He had done it. He had won the game.

But amidst all the cheers and celebrations, his heart was still waiting. His eyes darted towards the crowd, scanning every face, hoping to see her walking towards him. He stood there, catching his breath, drenched in sweat, waiting.

But she never came.

Minutes passed, his teammates left the field, the crowd started to disperse, but she was nowhere to be seen. His heart sank.

Still, he refused to give up hope. Maybe she was waiting outside. Maybe she was shy. Maybe she would message him later.

With that flicker of hope, he picked up his bag and walked out of the ground, expecting to see her standing somewhere, waiting for him.

But she was not there either.

He checked his phone. No messages. No calls. Nothing.

For the first time, the victory felt hollow. The match he played with all his heart suddenly felt meaningless. He had thought that winning would bring her back into his life, that she would see him the way he wanted her to. But she had not even cared enough to show up.

CHAPTER XI

The Ones Who Stayed

The time for the prize distribution arrived, a moment that should have been filled with excitement and pride. Shaunak had worked so hard, given his best, and now his efforts were being recognized. But as he stood backstage, waiting for his name to be called, a deep sadness settled over him.

The crowd was buzzing with applause for other winners, their families cheering them on, clapping, taking pictures. He looked around, but there was no familiar face, no one there just for him. He wished, at the very least, that his parents had been present to see him achieve this. But they had never supported his love for cricket. In their eyes, it was just a distraction from studies, a waste of time. If they had known about this event, they might have scolded him rather than congratulated him.

A bitter thought crossed his mind—*Even she isn't here.* The one person he had played his heart out for didn't even care enough to come. He clenched his fists, forcing a smile, not letting anyone see the turmoil inside him.

"Shaunak Sharma!" the announcer's voice echoed across the field.

Taking a deep breath, he walked up to the stage. The crowd clapped, some teachers nodded in approval, but he barely heard any of it. His mind was clouded with too many thoughts. *What am I doing this for? Who am I proving anything to?*

As he took the trophy in his hands, a sudden cheer from the back caught his attention. A group of voices rose above the rest—loud, genuine, full of pride.

He turned his head and saw them—his old friends. The very people he had ghosted for a week. The ones who had always looked out for him, guided him, and scolded him when he lost his way.

He never told them about this match, never even mentioned the event. And yet, here they were. Somehow, they had found out and had come just for him.

At that moment, all his sadness vanished. A warmth spread through his chest, replacing the loneliness he had felt moments ago. He had spent so much time chasing after someone who didn't care, but here stood the people who truly did.

As he stepped down from the stage, he didn't think twice. With the trophy and cash prize in his hands, he walked straight to them. Without hesitation, he bent down and touched their feet—something he had never done before.

The old men were startled for a second, but then their expressions softened. One of them patted his head, another squeezed his shoulder proudly.

"You played well, boy," one of them said with a smile. "We knew you had it in you."

Shaunak looked up at them, his eyes slightly misty. He had been so lost, so caught up in seeking validation from the wrong people, that he had forgotten who truly mattered.

For the first time in weeks, he felt at peace. He had won something far more valuable than a cricket match—he had won back himself.

As Shaunak walked back, still basking in the warmth of his friends' presence, he caught sight of something—or rather, someone.

She was there. The girl who had once occupied every thought in his mind, standing just a few feet away. But she wasn't alone.

She was laughing, completely immersed in a conversation with another guy. They seemed comfortable together, as if they had known each other for a long time. The way she looked at him, the ease in her body language—it was enough for Shaunak to understand.

She had moved on. Maybe she had never even considered him more than an acquaintance.

For a moment, his steps slowed. A familiar ache tried to rise in his chest, but this time, it didn't take over.

He didn't feel the same sting he had expected. No jealousy, no regret, no anger. Just a quiet realization—*I was never a part of her world, and maybe I was just forcing myself into it.*

Without a second glance, he turned back toward his friends and kept walking, a genuine smile forming on his face.

His friends, oblivious to what had just happened, were busy debating what to do with his prize money.

"Let's have a grand party!" one of them suggested, throwing an arm around his shoulder. "You owe us, man!"

Another one chimed in, "Yeah, you ghosted us for weeks! Consider this a fine."

Shaunak chuckled, shaking his head. "Fine, fine! But no luxury party, we'll just go to our usual place."

They all laughed, playfully arguing about where to go, what to eat, and who was the worst dancer among them. The easy banter, the carefree jokes—it was a reminder of how simple happiness could be.

As they reached their usual tea stall, the old vendor greeted them with a knowing smile. "Looks like the winner's finally back."

Shaunak smirked, handing over a few notes from his prize money. "Give us tea, the strongest you have."

The vendor chuckled. "Celebration?"

"More like a reunion," one of the friends replied, nudging Shaunak.

They all sat down, sipping their tea, talking about everything and nothing. The conversation drifted from cricket to school, from upcoming exams to future plans.

For the first time in weeks, Shaunak felt free. He wasn't worried about a text that wouldn't come, wasn't trying to impress someone who never noticed. He was just himself, surrounded by the people who had always been there.

As the night deepened, one of his friends looked at him seriously and said, "You've learned your lesson, right?"

Shaunak smirked, taking a slow sip of his tea before replying, "Yeah. Next time, I'll spend my money on better things... like bribing you guys to keep quiet about my stupid mistakes."

The group burst into laughter, and just like that, the past was behind him.

Because in the end, some people come into your life as lessons, and others as blessings. And tonight, Shaunak knew exactly which ones mattered.

Shaunak had settled into a peaceful routine. No longer distracted by fleeting affections, he focused on his studies, his game, and the quiet comfort of books. Even when some girls tried to strike up conversations with him, he remained distant, unwilling to be drawn into another meaningless attachment.

Most of his time was divided between the library, sports ground, and the old friends who had always stood by him. Their bond had deepened after everything he had gone through, and he cherished their company more than ever.

But fate, as always, had its own plans.

One evening, while returning from the library, Shaunak saw a few of his old friends gathered outside their usual tea stall. Their expressions were grim, their voices hushed. As he approached, one of them looked up and said, in a voice that was barely a whisper, *"He's gone."*

Shaunak frowned, confused. "Who's gone?"

The silence stretched unbearably before another friend spoke. *"The old man... the one whose wife had passed away. He left us today."*

For a moment, Shaunak just stood there, the words not fully registering. The same old man who had shared his story that night, the same one who had laughed and scolded them like a father figure, the one who had silently listened when others were too tired to stay awake—he was gone.

The memory of that night came rushing back. How he had talked while everyone else slept, pouring his heart out in the darkness. And now, that voice was silenced forever.

Shaunak felt a lump rise in his throat, but he swallowed it down. The others were quiet too, lost in their own thoughts.

One of the friends finally spoke. *"We should do something for him."*

Shaunak nodded. *"We will. We owe him that much."*

The next day, they all gathered at the old man's small home, where his relatives had assembled for the final rites. Unlike the grand farewell his wife had received, his departure felt quieter, almost unnoticed by the world.

Standing there, Shaunak realized how much the old man had meant to them—not just as a friend, but as someone who had been their guiding light, even in his grief.

That evening, after the rituals were done, the group sat by the river, just as they used to. But this time, there was an empty space among them, one that could never be filled.

Shaunak stared at the water, lost in thought.

"We should remember him the way he would have wanted," he finally said. *"With stories, with laughter. He didn't get to share his pain when his wife died. But he shared it with us in the end. That meant something."*

One of the friends sighed. *"He always used to say, 'Memories are all we leave behind.'"*

Shaunak looked up at the sky, at the countless stars twinkling above.

"Then let's make sure we don't forget."

The evening after the old man's final rites, Shaunak and his friends gathered at their usual tea stall, their hearts heavy with loss. The tea stall owner, who had silently witnessed their many gatherings, approached them with an old envelope in his hands.

"He left this for you all," the tea stall owner said, his voice quiet.

The envelope was slightly crumpled, the ink faded in some places, but the handwriting was unmistakably his—the old man's. One of the friends carefully opened it, revealing a letter written with shaky yet deliberate strokes.

To My Friends,

"Life gave us moments, some happy, some sad. But what I cherish most are the ones I spent with you all. I have no grand wealth to leave behind, no great legacy to pass on, but I do have memories—our memories."

"I wish we had met Shaunak earlier. In such a short time, he became one of us, as if he was always meant to be here. But maybe that's how life works—we meet people at the right time, not a moment sooner or later."

There was a pause as everyone glanced at Shaunak. He swallowed hard, his eyes fixed on the letter.

To Shaunak,

"I see a lot of myself in you, boy. A heart too deep, love too unconditional, and pain too silent. Don't change that. The world may not always understand it, but love never goes to waste. It finds its way back to you—maybe not from the person you gave it to, but in other ways, through other people."

"Never stop trusting. Never stop loving. But also, never let anyone take that love for granted. You are young, and the world will test you, but I hope you remember this—losing faith in people is easy, but believing despite the pain is what makes a good soul."

The letter ended there. Silence stretched between them as Shaunak lowered his head, gripping the paper tightly. He had spent so much time wondering if he had been foolish to trust, if his love had been wasted, if he should have guarded himself more. But here was a man who had lived longer, seen more, and still believed in love's return.

Shaunak closed his eyes, taking a deep breath.

"You okay?" one of the friends asked.

He looked up, a faint smile forming. *"Yeah. I am."*

CHAPTER XII

When the Glue is Gone

Days turned into weeks, and Shaunak could feel the change. The tea stall, once buzzing with laughter and endless discussions, now felt emptier. The old man who had passed away was not just a friend; he was the glue that held them all together.

Before, if someone missed a meeting, he would call them ten times until they showed up. If two friends fought, he would sit them down and settle things, ensuring no grudges lasted long. If someone tried to avoid the gathering with excuses, he would curse them affectionately, dragging them back into the group.

Now, without him, things were different.

The first weekend after his passing, most of them came out of habit, but the atmosphere was heavy. They sat in silence, sipping tea, struggling to fill the void he left behind. They left early that day, unable to pretend everything was normal.

The next weekend, even fewer showed up. Some blamed work, others simply didn't feel like coming. The absence of that one persistent voice calling them back made it easy to drift apart.

Shaunak noticed it more than anyone. He had seen this group as a unit, inseparable, strong. But now, cracks were forming. It wasn't that they didn't care—it was just that without someone holding them together, life slowly pulled them in different directions.

One evening, Shaunak sat alone at the tea stall, watching the empty chairs. The tea stall owner, who had witnessed their bond over the years, sighed.

"It's strange, isn't it?" he said, placing a cup in front of Shaunak. *"One person leaves, and suddenly everything changes."*

Shaunak nodded. He had never imagined a time when this group wouldn't be the same. He thought about all the moments they had shared—the stories, the laughter, the scoldings.

Then, he made a decision.

He picked up his phone and called one of the friends. *"Come to the tea stall. Now."*

"Why? Who else is there?" the friend asked.

"Does it matter? Just come."

Then he called another. And another. Some didn't pick up, some hesitated, but he kept calling—just like the old man used to do.

That evening, a few of them showed up. The next week, a few more. Slowly, the habit returned. Shaunak wasn't trying to replace the old man—no one could—but he realized something important: bonds don't stay strong on their own. Someone has to make the effort.

And this time, it was his turn.

Days passed, and life kept testing their bond.

One of the old friends announced that his family was shifting to another city. It wasn't an easy decision for him, but work and family responsibilities left no choice. The farewell wasn't grand—just a quiet evening at the tea stall, remembering old times. They all laughed, but deep down, everyone knew things would never be the same again.

Then came an even bigger blow. One of the remaining friends suffered a stroke, leaving him paralyzed. The once lively man who used to crack jokes and scold them for being careless could no longer walk. He tried to smile through it, but Shaunak could see the pain in his eyes.

From six, they were now down to three.

At the tea stall, the empty chairs became a constant reminder of those who were missing. Conversations grew shorter. The laughter, once loud and endless, now faded too soon.

Shaunak, however, refused to let this be the end. He and the two remaining friends made sure to visit the paralyzed friend often. They sat by his bedside, updating him about life outside, about cricket matches, about the weather—anything to make him feel involved. They even convinced the tea stall owner to deliver tea to his home so they could continue their habit, even if it wasn't at the same place.

But deep inside, Shaunak felt the weight of change.

Fate was pulling them apart, one by one. And for the first time, he wondered—was this how life worked? No matter how strong a bond is, time finds a way to loosen it?

Yet, he also remembered the words from the old man's letter—*"Love never goes to waste. It always returns in some way."*

Maybe, just maybe, the love and friendship they had shared would find a way back into their lives again.

As Shaunak stepped into class 10, he realized how much he had changed.

The classroom was filled with the usual chatter, students talking about movies, trends, and social media. But none of it interested him. He had spent so much time with his old friends, listening to their life stories, understanding emotions on a deeper level, that he couldn't relate to kids his age anymore.

They talked about temporary things—new gadgets, social media followers, and gossip. He craved real conversations—about life, love, and trust. About the meaning behind actions, the depth of emotions.

He found himself alone, but not lonely. He did not mind sitting in the last row, observing the world rather than trying to fit in. The bond he had with those old men had changed him forever. He was not like the others—his heart still craved unconditional love, respect, and deep conversations.

But the world did not seem to work that way anymore.

People his age did not believe in unconditional love; they believed in conditions. They did not care about trust; they cared about temporary fun. They did not want to listen; they wanted to be heard.

Shaunak, however, still believed.

He believed in love that expected nothing in return. In respect that didn't depend on status. In trust that was not shaken by doubt. And no matter how much the world changed, he was not ready to let go of that belief.

Even if it made him different.

Shaunak sat alone on the terrace of his house, staring at the night sky, lost in deep thought. The question of his future weighed heavily on him. What career should he choose?

Every time the old men at the tea stall asked him what he would do when he grew up, he had always answered sarcastically, brushing the question aside. But now, standing at the crossroads of his life, he had no definite answer.

His heart told him to follow his passion—cricket. He loved the game, lived for it, and felt alive whenever he held the bat. But he wasn't naive. He knew how difficult it was to make it in professional cricket. Talent alone wasn't enough. There was favoritism, politics, and a luck factor that he couldn't control.

If he could just secure a place in the state team, he would be happy. He didn't need international fame—just the satisfaction of playing the sport he loved. But even that seemed far-fetched. He was still stuck in the district team, with no proper guidance, no coach who genuinely cared about his growth, and worst of all, no family support.

His parents had already sacrificed a lot to provide him with a good education. They never supported his dream of cricket. To them, it was just a game, a distraction from studies, not a career. They expected him to choose a safe, stable job—one that would help him take care of the family, not chase an uncertain dream.

The responsibility of his family's struggles weighed heavily on him. He couldn't afford to disappoint them. He knew how hard it was for them to keep him in school, to pay for his tuition, to make ends meet. Could he really be selfish and choose a path that had no guaranteed future?

Confusion clouded his mind. Passion or responsibility? Dreams or reality? Heart or mind?

For the first time in his life, Shaunak had no answer.

Shaunak pushed aside all thoughts about his future for now. The most immediate challenge ahead was his board exams. In his society, board exam results were everything. No matter what someone planned for their career, the first question anyone asked was, *"Kitne marks aaye?"*

In his family, academic excellence was the norm. His siblings and cousins were all brilliant students, topping their classes and making their parents proud. Compared to them, Shaunak had always been an average student. He wasn't weak in studies, but he never excelled either.

Despite this, he had received more privileges than most of his relatives' children. His parents ensured he got the best facilities—good books, private tuition, and everything he needed to study well. But with that came a burden of expectations. Everyone assumed that since he had received better resources, he *had* to score high marks.

The pressure was immense. He was not afraid of failing, but he was afraid of disappointing his family. He did not want to be the only one in the family with an average result.

Until now, he had always managed to get decent marks in school because his teachers knew him well. They admired his good behaviour, respected him for his achievements in cricket, and often gave him extra marks in internal exams. But this time, the board exams wouldn't be checked by teachers who knew him. There would be no extra marks for his kindness, no appreciation for his cricket skills.

The only thing that mattered now was how much he actually knew.

For the first time in his life, Shaunak felt truly free from competition. He wasn't trying to outdo anyone, nor was he comparing himself with his cousins or classmates. His only goal was to do his best, and that was enough.

One evening, as he was returning from his coaching class, he ran into *her*—the girl who once called him mad, the same girl who had blamed him at the tea stall. She smiled at him as if nothing had ever happened.

At first, he thought she just wanted to chat, but then she hesitated before speaking. "Shaunak, I need a Favor."

He didn't react, just waited for her to continue.

She sighed dramatically. "I need some money. I have a contact who can get me the board exam question paper before the exam. If you help me, I will share it with you too. It'll be easy for both of us."

Shaunak was shocked. For a moment, he could not believe what he was hearing. Buying question papers? Cheating? He had never thought about it, not even once.

A few months ago, he might have been blinded by his feelings for her and agreed to anything she asked. But not today. Not anymore.

Without hesitation, he said, "No."

She frowned. "Why? You do not want to pass with good marks?"

"I'll pass with whatever marks I deserve," he said firmly. "And I don't have money anyway."

Her expression changed from surprise to irritation. "You've changed," she snapped. "Fine. Forget it."

She stormed off without another word.

Shaunak watched her leave, but he felt nothing—no regret, no guilt, no sadness. For the first time, he truly did not care. He had let her go long ago. Now, she was just another person in his past.

And for the first time, he felt proud of himself.

CHAPTER XIII

The Result That Changed Nothing and Everything

Shaunak studied harder than ever, putting his full effort into every subject. He wasn't aiming to be the topper, but he wanted to score well enough to make his family proud—or at least not disappoint them.

As each exam passed, he felt a mix of relief and nervousness. Some papers went well, some were tricky, but he had given his best. Now, all he could do was wait for the results.

In the meantime, he started preparing for the reactions he would face at home. His elder brother had always been an exceptional student, and comparisons were inevitable. He mentally rehearsed all the excuses he would give if his marks weren't as good as his brother's—

"The questions were tough this year."
"I focused more on sports, that's why."
"I wasn't feeling well during the exams."

But deep down, he knew none of these excuses would matter. He just wished his family would see his effort rather than just his marks.

Days passed, and soon, the results were just around the corner. The tension in the house grew, with relatives calling and asking, *"Result kab aa raha hai?"* (*When is the result coming?*)

Shaunak tried to stay calm, but the anxiety was creeping in. This was a moment that could shape his next steps—his career, his future, and most importantly, how his family would see him.

The result day was just a sunrise away.

As the result day arrived, the tension in the air was heavy. Shaunak wasn't alone in this moment—his three old friends had gathered at the house of their fourth friend, the one who had been paralyzed. They all wanted to be together when the results were announced.

The official announcement time had passed, but they struggled to check the result from home. The website wasn't opening properly, and Shaunak's anxiety grew with each failed attempt. After a few more minutes of frustration, they decided to go to a cyber café.

For the first time since his paralysis, their fourth friend made an effort to leave the house, determined to be there for Shaunak. His presence alone meant a lot. No matter what the result would be, Shaunak knew one thing—he wasn't alone.

They reached the cyber café, which was filled with other students and their families, all waiting to check their results. The atmosphere was thick with nervous whispers, excitement, and occasional sighs of disappointment.

As they found a vacant computer, Shaunak hesitated for a moment. His hands trembled slightly as he typed his roll number. His friends stood close, watching the screen with the same anticipation as him.

The page loaded.

His heart pounded.

And there it was—his result.

He had passed with good grades, even better than his elder brother.

For a moment, Shaunak couldn't believe his eyes. He double-checked the numbers, making sure there wasn't a mistake. His friends erupted in joy, patting his back and congratulating him. His paralyzed friend, who had struggled to reach the café, smiled with pure happiness.

"Dekha? Tu soch raha tha ki fail ho jayega!" one of them teased. (*See? You thought you would fail!*)

"Tu toh topper nikla re!" another laughed. (*You turned out to be a topper!*)

Shaunak smiled, his eyes slightly moist. Not because of the marks, but because of the people around him who truly cared. He had spent years thinking about being left out, being unloved, but in this moment, he realized—he had always been surrounded by love. He just needed to see it.

After a while, he took out his phone and hesitated before dialing his home number. His mother picked up.

"Maa... result aa gaya," he said softly.

"Aur?" she asked, her voice tense.

"Achha aaya hai," he replied.

There was a pause, and then his mother let out a deep breath. He could hear the happiness in her voice, even if she didn't say much.

"Achha kiya beta, ghar jaldi aaja," she simply said. (*You did well, son, come home soon.*)

He cut the call and turned to his friends.

"Chal, ab party toh banti hai!" one of them shouted. (*Come on, this calls for a party!*)

They all laughed and decided to celebrate, not just for Shaunak's result but for the fact that they had each other.

That same evening, they decided to throw a party—not just to celebrate Shaunak's result, but also to acknowledge everything they had been through. Life had been full of ups and downs, and now, with one member missing from their group forever, things felt different. They had been meaning to drink together for a while, but something or the other always came up. Tonight, they wanted to relive old memories, even if just for a few hours.

They found a quiet spot near the outskirts of their town, a place they often visited when they wanted to escape from daily struggles. The night was calm, the sky clear with a full moon watching over them. They sat in a circle, bottles in hand, reminiscing about their past—how they met, the fights they had, the countless teas they drank at the stall, and how life had changed so much in just a few years.

Shaunak was quieter than usual. He knew this might be one of the last times they would sit together like this. He had to leave soon, not just this town but this phase of his life. He had to plan his future, focus on his studies, and compete in his respective field. His heart was torn between the comfort of old friendships and the uncertainty of the path ahead.

One of the friends raised a toast.

"To the one who left us," he said, referring to their late friend.

They all took a sip in his memory.

"To Shaunak, for proving himself!" another added, making them all cheer.

Shaunak smiled, but deep inside, he felt the weight of everything changing. He had once been unsure about his career, but now, he knew he had to make a decision soon. This place, these people—they had shaped him, but they couldn't decide his future for him. That was something he had to figure out on his own.

As the night went on, they laughed, talked, and shared their hopes for the future. Some wanted to stay in town, some wanted to leave and explore new opportunities, but no matter where they ended up, one thing was certain—this friendship, these moments, would always stay with them.

As the night went on, one of Shaunak's friends casually asked, "So, what have you decided about your career? What stream are you going to choose?"

Shaunak hesitated for a moment before replying, "I don't know."

His friends were surprised. "But you scored well! You have good grades. Why are you still unsure?"

Shaunak sighed and decided to be completely honest with them. "Yes, I got good grades, but that doesn't mean I actually understand everything. If I take science, I know I won't be able to handle physics and chemistry. They've always been tough for me. I can't choose biology either because becoming a doctor is too expensive, and my family can't afford that kind of education."

His friends listened carefully as he continued, "Arts and commerce aren't an option either. I've seen how tough it is to find a good job in those fields. And on top of that, my family has already decided my career path for me. They expect me to become an engineer. How do I tell them that I don't want that? That I don't see a future for myself in engineering?"

One of his friends asked, "Then what do you actually want to do?"

Shaunak fell silent for a moment before finally admitting, "I do not know... I just want to play sports. That is the only thing that makes me happy. But let us be honest—I'm not good at studies. The only reason I scored well is that my school teachers were kind enough to give me good marks in practicals and projects. I memorized equations, and by luck, the same questions appeared in the exams. That doesn't make me intelligent. It just means I got lucky this time."

His friends exchanged glances, understanding the weight of his words. Shaunak was not just struggling with career choices—he was struggling with the expectations placed upon him, with the reality of his capabilities, and with the fear of disappointing his family. And yet, deep inside, all he truly wanted was to chase the one thing that made him feel alive—sports.

Shaunak, though hesitant, decided to take a step forward. He applied to a few coaching institutes that prepared students for the JEE exam. To his surprise, he got selected in one of them with a full scholarship. It felt like an unexpected opportunity knocking at his door.

Excited yet unsure, he went straight to his friends and shared the news. "I got a full scholarship at a coaching institute for JEE preparation. But I don't know if I should join. Engineering was never my plan, but I also don't have many options. What should I do?"

His friends, who had seen him struggle with self-doubt for years, gave him an honest answer. "You should join," one of them said. "This is a golden opportunity. You've been saying that you're not good at studies, but every time, you end up scoring well. Maybe you're not giving yourself enough credit. Sometimes, we fail to see our own potential."

Another friend added, "Think about it. You always underestimate yourself, but results prove otherwise. This scholarship means that someone out there sees talent in you. Maybe it's time you see it too. And who says you have to leave your passion for sports? You can balance both. Many great athletes have pursued education alongside their passion. You can do it too."

Shaunak listened carefully. Deep down, he knew they had a point. Maybe he had been too harsh on himself.

Maybe he had more potential than he thought. He had spent so much time believing he wasn't good enough that he never stopped to consider that he was capable.

After a long pause, he finally nodded. "Alright, I'll do it. I'll join the coaching. But I won't leave sports either. I'll find a way to balance both."

His friends smiled, knowing that this was a turning point for him. They had always believed in him—now, it was time for Shaunak to believe in himself.

Shaunak continued his routine, attending coaching classes and trying his best to keep up. But physics and chemistry felt like a never-ending puzzle he couldn't solve. No matter how much he studied, the concepts didn't make sense to him. The only subject where he found solace was mathematics—it was the only thing that made him feel confident.

As the eleventh-grade exams approached, he knew that these marks wouldn't count for his final board results, yet he couldn't shake off the pressure. When the results came out, he had almost failed in all subjects except mathematics. It was the first time he had performed so poorly.

Ashamed and disappointed, he didn't have the courage to share this failure with his family. Instead, he told them he had done well. Only his closest friends knew the truth. They tried to console him, saying, "It's just one set of exams. You'll improve next time." But deep inside, Shaunak wasn't sure. This failure affected him more than he admitted.

His confidence took a huge hit. He had never thought of himself as a genius, but he had also never failed like this before. The belief that he wasn't good at academics only grew stronger. Now, he stopped studying with the goal of understanding. He studied just to pass.

The pressure increased as the board exams came closer. Every day felt like a struggle, filled with stress and self-doubt. He barely found time for sports anymore. His mind was constantly occupied with thoughts of failure. What if he failed in the final exams too? What if he disappointed his family? What if all his efforts went to waste?

When the day of the board exams finally arrived, he went in with mixed feelings. He gave his best, but in some papers, he was sure he had done terribly. He walked out of the exam hall feeling defeated, convinced that failure was inevitable.

Shaunak's board exam results finally arrived, and as he had feared, he barely managed to pass. His marks were just enough to cross the line—nothing exceptional, nothing to be proud of. Along with that, his engineering entrance exam rank was far below his expectations.

While his school classmates were celebrating their admissions into prestigious colleges, sharing their success stories on social media, Shaunak silently enrolled in an average engineering college—one that nobody would boast about. There were no celebrations at home, just a quiet acknowledgment that he had cleared the exams.

With every passing day, self-doubt grew heavier on his shoulders. He couldn't stop comparing himself with others. He imagined how his old classmates would be discussing their new colleges, making new friends, and preparing for a bright future.

"What if I fail in engineering too?" he kept asking himself.

He began to fear that his life was heading towards one mistake after another. The thought of disappointing his family haunted him constantly. The burden of being the one who always fell behind weighed heavily on his heart.

The day before leaving for college, he sat with his old friends at the tea stall. They sensed his restlessness without him even saying a word.

"You think going to an average college will decide your future?" one of them asked.

Shaunak kept silent, staring into his half-empty tea glass.

Another friend added, "It's not about where you study, it's about what you learn. No college, no exam can decide what you're going to be."

The third one, the oldest of the group, leaned in and said, *"A place can only give you a roof, but what you become beneath that roof is entirely up to you."*

Their words stuck with him.

That night, as he packed his bags, Shaunak promised himself something—no matter how average the college was, no matter how many doubts clouded his mind, he would give his best.

Maybe he wasn't the smartest. Maybe he wasn't the luckiest. But one thing he still had left was **hope**.

CHAPTER XIV

The One Who Didn't Belong

The day had finally arrived. Shaunak was leaving for college. His bags were packed, his tickets were in hand, but his heart was heavy. He had spent his entire life in the same town, surrounded by the same faces, sipping tea at the same stall. And now, everything was about to change.

All his friends came to drop him off at the railway station. They had seen him grow, struggle, and dream. They were the ones who had stood by him during his lowest moments, and now, they were the ones sending him off into the unknown.

As they waited for the train, there was an awkward silence—everyone knew this was a final goodbye. No one wanted to say it out loud, but they all felt it.

To break the tension, one of his friends nudged him and teased, "Now you can finally make a girlfriend."

The group burst into laughter, trying to lighten the mood. Shaunak smiled, shaking his head. Deep down, he knew this was not just a joke—it was a symbol of how much things were about to change.

The train arrived, its loud horn breaking the moment. Shaunak picked up his bags, hesitated for a second, and then turned to his friends.

"Take care of yourselves," he said, his voice lower than usual.

"You too, idiot," one of them replied, playfully punching his shoulder.

His friends, the ones who had been his family outside home, gathered at the railway station to see him off. The tea stall owner, who had watched him grow from a boy to a young man, handed him a cup of tea for the last time before he left.

"**College ka ladka ban ke wapas mat aana, jo Shaunak ja raha hai, wahi Shaunak wapas aana,**" one of his friends joked, trying to lighten the mood.

He smiled faintly, but deep inside, he was not sure what kind of Shaunak would return. Would he come back as a failure, or would he finally find his path?

The train whistled, signalling its departure. One by one, his friends hugged him tightly, each goodbye heavier than the last.

"Take care, idiot," one of them said, punching his shoulder lightly.

"Don't forget us," another added, though they all knew that was impossible.

As the train started moving, Shaunak leaned out of the window, waving at them until they disappeared into the distance. A strange emptiness settled inside him. For the first time in years, he was completely on his own.

He turned back, resting his head against the window, watching the blurry landscapes rush past him. His heart was full of memories, but his future was a blank slate.

Full of confusion, full of fear—yet somewhere deep inside, a small part of him was ready. Ready to face whatever was waiting for him.

As Shaunak stepped onto the college campus, he took a deep breath. This was his fresh start—a chance to leave behind all the doubts, failures, and heartbreaks. He had already decided that he would focus entirely on his studies. No distractions, no unnecessary friendships, and no emotional attachments.

His first instinct was to check the college's placement records. He wanted to know what his future could look like after four years of hard work. He searched online, asked a few seniors, and went through various forums. While doing so, he stumbled upon something else—stories about ragging.

Apparently, his college had a reputation for it. Some seniors took it lightly, treating it as a way to "bond" with juniors, while others used it to assert dominance. Some incidents were harmless pranks, but others seemed borderline terrifying.

For a moment, Shaunak felt a tinge of fear, but he quickly brushed it off. *I just need to survive the first year. After that, I'll be a senior too, and none of this will matter.*

He decided to stay low-key, avoid unnecessary attention, and just focus on studies. He had already seen what happened when he got too involved with people—he had been betrayed, manipulated, and emotionally drained.

As Shaunak stepped onto the college campus, he was determined to make a fresh start. His past experiences had instilled in him a resolve to focus solely on his studies, avoiding distractions and immersing himself in academic pursuits. He envisioned a disciplined routine: attending lectures, spending hours in the library, and dedicating himself to achieving academic excellence.

However, as he navigated the bustling corridors and expansive grounds of the college, he couldn't help but notice the vibrant social interactions around him. Groups of students—both boys and girls—congregated outside classrooms, animatedly discussing lectures, sharing notes, or simply enjoying each other's company. The canteen buzzed with laughter and conversations, and the library, though a place of study, was also a hub where students collaborated and formed study groups.

Initially, Shaunak viewed these interactions through a critical lens. He believed that such socializing was a diversion, a misuse of the opportunities their parents had worked hard to provide. To him, college was a place for serious study, and he was determined not to squander his time on what he perceived as frivolous activities.

Yet, as days turned into weeks, an unexpected feeling began to creep into his consciousness. Despite his self-imposed isolation, he felt a growing void—a yearning for companionship, someone with whom he could share his daily experiences, challenges, and small victories. The laughter and camaraderie he observed among his peers began to evoke a sense of longing.

It was during one of his routine classes that Shaunak's world shifted. As he settled into his seat, his attention was drawn to a girl who entered the room. She possessed a natural grace, her presence illuminating the space around her. Her eyes sparkled with intelligence and warmth, and her smile seemed to carry an unspoken kindness. For the first time in his life, Shaunak felt an unexplainable connection to someone he hadn't even spoken to. It was as if, in that fleeting moment, his heart whispered, "She is the one."

Fate, it seemed, had a hand in intertwining their paths. When the professor began calling out roll numbers for lab partners, Shaunak's heart raced as he realized that his roll number was immediately after hers. This meant not only would they be seated near each other during lectures, but they would also collaborate closely in the lab sessions. The realization filled him with a mix of excitement and nervousness.

On the first day of their lab partnership, Shaunak found himself at a loss for words. Despite his usual confidence, he couldn't muster the courage to initiate a conversation. Instead, he stole glances, observing her as she meticulously approached each experiment. One particular instance caught his attention: during a simple mathematical calculation, she opted to work it out methodically with pen and paper, eschewing the calculator that most others hastily reached for. This deliberate and thoughtful approach intrigued Shaunak; he found it uniquely admirable.

As days passed, Shaunak's internal conflict grew. His initial resolve to remain detached was being challenged by his burgeoning feelings. He grappled with questions: Should he remain steadfast in his commitment to focus solely on academics? Or should he embrace the possibility of forming a meaningful connection that could enrich his college experience? The answers weren't clear, but one thing was certain—his heart was beginning to chart a course that his mind hadn't anticipated.

Shaunak believed that universe is giving him a sign. On his very first day in college, the universe had already granted him something unexpected. He silently thanked God for this small miracle.

But he didn't speak to her that day. He had too many questions swirling in his mind. *What should I say? Should I introduce myself casually or wait for the right moment? What if she finds me boring?*

For the first time in a long while, he felt nervous—nervous in a way that wasn't tied to exams or career choices but to something far more unpredictable.

As the days passed, Shaunak found himself battling a growing sense of insecurity.

In this new city, everything felt different. The students here were not just academically competitive; they were confident, well-dressed, and carried themselves with an ease that he lacked. No matter how poorly some of them performed in studies, their communication skills were remarkable. They spoke with such conviction, even when they were lying about their entrance exam scores, fabricating elaborate excuses to justify their failures.

Shaunak, on the other hand, had never thought much about appearances. As a sports enthusiast and a self-proclaimed nerd, he had always prioritized skills, knowledge, and physical fitness over fashion and socializing. But here, he realized that many students had invested heavily in their personalities—stylish clothes, trendy haircuts, expensive shoes. They moved through college like they belonged, while he felt like an outsider, struggling to fit in.

For the first time, he became conscious of his own looks. His simple wardrobe, his lack of a well-groomed appearance—it all made him feel inadequate. He started wondering if people judged him for it.

More than anything, he worried about her—the girl who had unknowingly captured his attention from day one. *Would she even notice someone like me?* he thought.

The day had barely begun when a group of seniors barged into the classroom, their expressions a mix of authority and mischief. The moment they entered, the atmosphere shifted—casual chatter ceased, and an uneasy silence filled the room.

One of the seniors clapped his hands loudly and smirked. "Alright, freshers, it's time to introduce yourselves, but there's a format," he announced.

He then recited a long and exaggerated introduction that included name, school percentage, JEE rank, hobbies, and even an embarrassing confession. "You all have to memorize this and say it exactly like this. If anyone messes up, be ready for punishment."

Shaunak and his classmates exchanged nervous glances. Some of them hesitated, but no one dared to resist. One by one, students stood up and tried to repeat the introduction word for word. Every minor mistake was met with laughter and absurd punishments—push-ups in the middle of the class, singing nursery rhymes loudly, or even dancing awkwardly in front of everyone.

Then came the set of strict instructions that followed the introduction ritual.

"All boys must get their hair cut to size one—no exceptions," a senior declared. "And yeah, no belts, no watches. You have to walk around looking as pathetic as possible."

Shaunak clenched his jaw. He had always kept his hair slightly longer, but now he had no choice.

"And whenever a senior crosses your path, you must look down. We don't want to see your ugly faces," another one sneered.

The worst part was the playground restriction. "No fresher is allowed on the ground unless we allow it. You can stare at it from a distance, but don't you dare step on it."

Shaunak felt his stomach churn. His one escape, the only place where he truly felt alive—the playground—was now off-limits.

Shaunak felt trapped between his passion and the harsh reality of college life. He knew he couldn't stay away from sports, but he also didn't want to be a constant target for ragging. Seeking a way out, he approached the warden, hoping for a solution.

"Sir, I want to play sports, but I also don't want to get ragged. Can't something be done?" he asked, trying to sound hopeful.

The warden, an old man with years of experience dealing with freshers, sighed and leaned back in his chair. "That's impossible, son. If you want to play, you have to follow their rules. That's how it works here."

Disappointed but not discouraged, Shaunak returned to his hostel and tried memorizing the introduction format seniors had given them. But no matter how hard he tried, he could never get it right. His mind kept wandering back to the ground, to the game he loved.

One evening, unable to resist any longer, he walked straight into the sports ground, ignoring all the warnings. The moment he stepped onto the field, a group of seniors spotted him.

"Look who's here," one of them smirked.

Another stepped forward. "Didn't we tell you freshers aren't allowed?"

Shaunak stood firm, meeting their eyes with quiet confidence. "I just want to play," he said simply.

The seniors weren't pleased. They made him do push-ups, made him recite the introduction again and again until he fumbled, and finally, they repeated their demand—"Cut your hair, or next time, it'll be worse."

Shaunak nodded, but in his heart, he knew he wouldn't listen. He had heard their threats, but he had also decided to forget them.

Over the next few days, he continued to go to the ground, bracing himself for whatever came next. At first, the seniors ragged him every time they saw him, but soon, they started noticing something else—his game. He was genuinely good, better than most of them.

Slowly, their attitude changed.

"You're decent," one of them admitted after watching him play.

Another nodded. "Not bad for a fresher."

The ragging didn't stop completely, but it softened. His skills earned him an unexpected kind of respect. He was still a fresher, still had to follow the rules, but now, he had something that made him stand out.

CHAPTER XV

She Watched, He Ran

Shaunak's routine slowly started revolving around two things—cricket and the girl. The cricket ground was close to the girls' hostel, and from their windows, the girls often watched the boys play. He strategically positioned himself near the hostel side, hoping to catch her attention.

From his classmates, he managed to find out her room number. It was on the second floor, right next to the ground, with a perfect view of where he played. Every evening, she would sit by the window, reading or simply gazing outside. Shaunak saw this as an opportunity.

Whenever he played, he made sure he was in her line of sight. He dived for catches, played his best shots, and even celebrated louder, just in case she was watching. He wanted her to notice him, to acknowledge his presence.

But no matter how much effort he put in, she never reacted.

She never called out his name. She never cheered for him. She never even gave him a single glance of appreciation.

At first, he thought she might not have noticed him. But soon, he realized—it wasn't that she didn't see him. She simply didn't care.

This frustrated him. He had always believed that effort leads to results, but here, despite all his silent gestures, she remained indifferent.

Still, he didn't stop.

Every evening, he returned to the ground, playing his heart out, hoping that maybe, just maybe, one day, she would say something—anything.

Shaunak had tried everything—being cheerful, cracking jokes, even pretending to be the most fun-loving person in the class—but nothing seemed to get her attention. She never asked about him, never showed even the slightest curiosity, despite being his lab partner. Yet, he often caught her observing other guys in the class, smiling at their jokes, engaging in casual conversations.

"Why not me?" The thought started bothering him.

One day, as he was heading to the sports ground, a group of seniors stopped him. They handed him a red rose and ordered him to give it to a senior girl and confess his love to her. Shaunak hesitated. He knew this was a trap—part of the ragging ritual. But refusing meant harsher punishments, so with no choice left, he took the rose and walked toward the senior girl.

His steps felt heavy. The moment felt ridiculous, yet humiliating. As soon as he reached her, he extended the rose and, in a barely audible voice, muttered, *"I love you."*

For a second, there was silence. Then came the sharp, unexpected slap.

A few gasps were heard from the crowd of juniors watching from a distance. Laughter followed from the seniors. The senior girl looked at him with disgust, then stormed off.

Unbeknownst to Shaunak, his lab partner had witnessed the entire incident from a distance. She stood frozen, unable to intervene, knowing she was powerless in the matter.

Things escalated when the senior girl, furious beyond reason, called her boyfriend—another senior—complaining about Shaunak's so-called misbehavior. Within minutes, the boyfriend arrived, towering over Shaunak with an intimidating glare.

"How dare you?" the senior guy growled, grabbing Shaunak's collar.

Shaunak didn't resist. He knew arguing would only make things worse.

The other seniors chuckled, enjoying the spectacle. One of them turned to the lab partner girl and ordered, *"You, go back to your hostel. No need to stand here."*

She hesitated but obeyed, retreating to her room. Yet, once inside, she couldn't help but walk to her window. She opened it and looked down at the ground, her gaze searching for Shaunak.

Below, the senior guy cracked his knuckles and smirked. "You love giving roses, right? Let's see how much love you have."

Then came the punishment—50 rounds of the sports ground.

Without a word, Shaunak started running.

His legs ached, his chest burned, but he didn't stop. He completed one lap, then another, and another. The seniors laughed, some counting out loud, others making jokes.

From her window, his lab partner watched everything unfold. She didn't move, didn't speak—just watched.

For the first time, she saw Shaunak in a way she never had before.

Shaunak's legs burned with exhaustion, his breath came in ragged gasps, but the moment he saw her watching from the window, something inside him reignited.

His body was screaming for rest, his mind begged him to stop, but his heart? His heart felt lighter than ever. She was watching him. *She saw him.*

He blinked away the tears that threatened to fall. He couldn't let them see him weak—not now. Not when *she* was looking.

"Maybe she'll feel bad for me. Maybe she'll come and talk to me after this. Maybe this is the moment she finally notices me."

These thoughts filled his mind, numbing the pain in his muscles. He ran with more determination, chest puffed out slightly, trying to look as athletic and strong as possible. He was no longer running as punishment—he was running to impress her.

His steps became steadier, his posture more confident, as if this was just another workout session for him. The seniors, expecting to see him struggle, started losing interest. Some turned away, laughing among themselves. Others shrugged and walked off.

But she was still there.

Still watching.

Still looking at *him*.

That was enough.

With each lap, a part of him wished she'd call out his name, tell him to stop, show concern—but she didn't. She simply rested her chin on her hand, her expression unreadable.

After what felt like an eternity, he finally completed the 50 rounds. His legs wobbled, his chest rose and fell rapidly, but he stood tall, refusing to bend over or gasp for breath in front of her.

He looked up at her window one last time.

She was still watching.

Then, as if realizing she'd been staring too long, she casually turned away and closed the window.

Shaunak stood there, drenched in sweat, a strange mix of exhaustion and elation filling him.

She saw me.

That was all he needed for now.

The warden's stern voice cut through the air, breaking the silence of the dimly lit corridor.

"Shaunak, go back to your room," he ordered.

Too exhausted to argue, Shaunak turned around and dragged himself toward his hostel room. His body ached with fatigue, and all he wanted was to collapse onto his bed and drift into a deep, undisturbed sleep.

As he pushed open the door, he was met with an unexpected sight. A boy, seemingly full of energy, was unpacking his belongings. The room was meant for two occupants, and from the looks of it, Shaunak now had a new roommate.

The boy radiated enthusiasm, his face beaming with excitement. He appeared healthy, well-groomed, and carried himself with a confidence that hinted at wealth. His neatly pressed clothes, expensive wristwatch, and the ease with which he moved made it clear—he came from a different world than Shaunak.

"Hey! I'm Aryan," the boy greeted cheerfully, his voice filled with eagerness.

Shaunak barely glanced at him. He wasn't in the mood for introductions, let alone conversations. His head felt heavy, his body sluggish. Without a word, he walked straight to his bed, sank onto the mattress, and shut his eyes.

But Aryan wasn't one to be ignored.

"So, where are you from?" he asked, his tone friendly. "Which branch are you in? Have you been here long?"

Shaunak heard every question, but exhaustion wrapped around him like a heavy blanket. He didn't respond. He didn't want to.

Shaunak barely had the energy to respond. His entire body ached from the 50 rounds, and his mind was still stuck on the image of his lab partner watching him.

He mumbled a tired *"hmm"* in response to his new roommate's questions, but the guy didn't seem to take the hint.

"Bro, you look dead tired! What happened? Some crazy workout?" the roommate asked with enthusiasm.

Shaunak didn't reply. He just turned to his side, hoping that the guy would understand and let him rest.

But no.

"I'm Aryan, by the way! Aryan Khanna." His voice was full of confidence, the kind that came naturally to people who had always lived comfortably.

Shaunak gave a weak nod, eyes half-closed.

Aryan continued unpacking, pulling out expensive-looking sneakers, neatly folded branded clothes, and even a gaming laptop. Shaunak, who had barely carried a few sets of clothes and some books, didn't fail to notice the stark difference between them.

"Dude, I swear, this hostel is kinda depressing," Aryan said, stuffing his wardrobe with his things. "But whatever. College is gonna be fun! What's your story? Where are you from?"

Shaunak exhaled deeply, trying to ignore him. But Aryan wasn't the type to get ignored easily.

"You don't talk much, do you?" Aryan laughed.

Silence.

"Okay, okay. No problem, bro. You rest. We have a whole year to get to know each other."

Finally, Shaunak heard him stop talking. The sound of his things being unpacked faded as he drifted into sleep.

But even in sleep, his mind kept replaying the scene—her watching him run, the closed window, the unanswered questions.

113

CHAPTER XVI

Missed Calls & Mixed Signals

Saunak's phone buzzed. He glanced at the screen—his parents. He let it ring and turned his gaze away. A few seconds later, it rang again. Then again. And again. He clenched his jaw and ignored it each time. After the third attempt, they finally stopped calling.

An hour later, he picked up his phone, scrolling mindlessly, when he noticed a missed call from an unknown number. His heart skipped a beat. Could it be her? His lab partner? He had been waiting for a chance to talk to her outside of class.

His mind raced ahead, forming the perfect conversation. He would tell her about his work, his ideas—everything that made him proud. With a deep breath, he called back.

"Hello?" A female voice answered.

Saunak straightened. "Uh... I missed a call from this number."

"Oh, yes. I called," she said, her voice slightly unsure.

Saunak's excitement faded as confusion took over. It wasn't his lab partner. "Who is this?" he asked.

"I'm a senior from your college," she replied. "I—uh—heard about what happened. I didn't know you were being ragged." Her tone shifted, laced with guilt. "I feel terrible about it now."

Saunak let out a small chuckle. "No problem at all," he said, brushing it off.

They continued talking. From college life to favourite books, their conversation flowed effortlessly. The initial awkwardness melted, replaced by curiosity and familiarity.

They shared common interests, their words weaving an unexpected connection.

Then, she hesitated before asking, "Hey... do you think we can be friends?" Shaunak was caught off guard. A senior girl—someone who had slapped him just a few hours ago—was now asking to be his friend? He hesitated for a moment. His mind was still lingering on his lab partner, but the thrill of an unexpected friendship was tempting.

"Uh... yeah, sure," he replied, trying to sound casual.

She sighed on the other end. "I really feel bad, you know. I thought you were another random junior trying to act smart. I had no idea you were forced into it."

"It's fine," Shaunak said, rubbing his sore legs. "I've been through worse."

She chuckled. "Worse? Oh, so you're a tough guy?"

Shaunak smirked slightly. "You could say that."

There was a brief silence before she spoke again. "So, tell me about yourself. What do you do apart from getting into trouble with seniors?"

He hesitated again. He wasn't used to girls asking about him. Usually, he was the one trying to impress them.

"I play cricket," he finally said. "Used to play at the district level."

"Seriously? That's cool! No wonder you finished 50 rounds without collapsing!"

Shaunak felt a tiny swell of pride but didn't say anything.

"Listen," she continued, "I know I slapped you, but since we're friends now, let me make it up to you. Let's meet tomorrow after classes. I'll treat you to something."

Shaunak's mind raced. Should he go? What if his lab partner saw him with this senior girl? Would she finally notice him?

"Alright," he said before he could overthink.

"Great! See you tomorrow then, junior."

The call ended.

Aryan laughed. "Man, you didn't even want to talk to me, but now you're all excited just because a girl called you?"

Shaunak smirked and threw a pillow at him. "Shut up, it's not like that!"

"Oh, really?" Aryan raised an eyebrow. "You literally ignored my 'tell me about yourself' question, but the moment she asked, you spilled your whole life story."

Shaunak chuckled. "Well, maybe I just don't like talking to guys."

Aryan shook his head, still amused. "Okay, okay, I won't take it personally. But tell me, who was on the call? A love interest?"

Shaunak leaned back, staring at the ceiling. "Nah, nothing like that. It was that senior girl—the one who slapped me today."

Aryan sat up straight. "Wait, what? The same one?"

"Yeah. She called to apologize. Turns out she didn't know I was being ragged. We talked for a bit, and now we're... friends, I guess?"

Aryan grinned. "Oh, so this is how it starts. First, the apology, then the 'let's be friends,' and before you know it, you're the junior who stole a senior's heart."

Shaunak rolled his eyes but laughed. "It's not like that! She just felt bad and wanted to make up for it."

Aryan wasn't convinced. "So, when are you meeting her?"

"Tomorrow after classes."

Aryan smirked. "That's it. You're done for. The college romance bug has bitten you."

Shaunak shook his head, still smiling. "Shut up, man. It's nothing."

Shaunak's heart raced as he received the call. She wanted to meet him in the college canteen. His mind instantly wandered—was this just a casual apology, or was there something more? He didn't think too much. Without wasting time, he freshened up and made his way to the canteen.

As he stepped inside, his eyes instinctively scanned the area, and then he saw her—the senior girl sitting at a corner table, waiting for him. But just a few tables away, he noticed someone else. His lab partner. The girl he had secretly admired from day one. She had just finished her coffee, gathering her books, seemingly lost in her own world. His gaze lingered on her for a moment before he shook himself back to reality.

He approached the senior girl's table, and she smiled as he sat down. "What will you have?" she asked. "Tea, coffee, or maybe something to eat?"

Shaunak hesitated. He wasn't sure if he was even hungry; his mind was still occupied by the presence of his lab partner nearby.

Before he could answer, she continued, "You know, I just realized something crazy yesterday. We studied in the same school."

Shaunak's eyebrows raised in surprise. "Wait, what?"

She nodded. "Yeah. That's why your name sounded so familiar. At first, I didn't recognize you, but then it hit me—I've heard your name so many times in school. You won the cricket championships, right?"

Shaunak smiled, remembering his school days. "Yeah... that was a long time ago."

"I feel terrible," she admitted. "I should have recognized you sooner. I even saw you multiple times at tea shops back then." She sighed, looking genuinely guilty. "And then, after everything that happened yesterday, I feel even worse."

Shaunak shook his head. "It's okay. You didn't know."

But she wasn't convinced. "No, still... I shouldn't have reacted like that."

She looked at him, trying to gauge his thoughts. But Shaunak's focus kept drifting. He couldn't help it—his eyes found their way back to his lab partner again and again. He wasn't even subtle about it. The senior girl noticed.

A small smirk appeared on her face. "You seem distracted," she said, leaning forward.

Shaunak quickly looked back at her, trying to act normal. "What? No, I was just—"

She followed his gaze and found the answer herself. "Ah," she said knowingly, glancing at his lab partner. "I see."

Shaunak felt caught, but he stayed silent.

The senior girl chuckled. "You're really bad at hiding things, you know that?"

Shaunak exhaled, rubbing the back of his head. "It's nothing."

"Sure," she teased. "It's 'nothing,' and yet you've looked at her at least five times in the last two minutes."

He had no defense.

The senior girl smirked, clearly enjoying Shaunak's nervous energy. She casually waved at the waiter and ordered another coffee. Before Shaunak could ask, she turned towards his lab partner, Shraddha, and called out, "Hey, why don't you join us?"

Shaunak's eyes widened. His heart started racing. He shook his head quickly. "No, no, don't do that," he muttered under his breath, his face heating up.

But deep inside, he wanted nothing more than to sit across from Shraddha, to share a conversation, to see her up close without pretending not to notice her.

The senior girl grinned. "Relax, it's just coffee."

Shaunak felt helpless. "Still..."

She ignored him completely. When Shraddha didn't react immediately, the senior girl raised her voice playfully, "Shraddha! Come join us."

Shraddha, who was about to leave, stopped in her tracks. She looked at them, a little confused.

Shaunak gulped. His hands fidgeted under the table.

Shraddha hesitated but then walked towards them. "Uh... okay," she said softly, pulling out a chair.

The senior girl smiled, standing up as she grabbed her bag. "Oh, by the way, I just remembered—I have a practical class right now. Gotta go!"

Shaunak's mouth fell open. "What? But—"

Before he could say anything else, she winked at him and walked away, leaving him alone with Shraddha.

Now it was just the two of them.

Shaunak felt like his entire world had slowed down. He had imagined this moment so many times, but now that it was happening, he didn't know what to say.

Shraddha took a sip of her coffee and looked at him. "So...?" she said, raising an eyebrow.

Shaunak's brain scrambled for words. He could face the fastest bowlers on the pitch, but this? This was an entirely different kind of challenge.

Shaunak sat there, his heart hammering in his chest. He had imagined talking to Shraddha a thousand times, but now that she was right in front of him, words seemed to escape him. He fidgeted with his fingers, looking down at his coffee cup, unsure of how to begin.

Shraddha, sensing his hesitation, broke the silence. "So... what's going on? How's your studies? You seem really good at calculations."

Shaunak's eyes lit up at the topic. Numbers were something he could talk about without overthinking. "Oh, I just like maths. It's the only subject that makes sense to me," he said, finally finding his voice.

Shraddha smiled. "And what about physics? I was struggling with a few problems. You seemed to get them so quickly in class."

Shaunak hesitated. Physics wasn't exactly his strong suit, but he did enjoy solving problems logically. He quickly explained a few concepts, and Shraddha listened intently, nodding along.

As the conversation flowed, she casually asked, "Where did you study? I heard from that senior girl that you both were from the same school."

Shaunak nodded. "Yeah, I studied in a small school, nothing fancy. Just regular school life."

Shraddha tilted her head, curious. "Are you really good at sports? I heard your name mentioned a few times in class."

Shaunak shrugged, trying to act nonchalant. "I played cricket a lot, mostly for the school team. That's all."

She smiled. "That's all? You say it like it's nothing, but I saw you running so many rounds of the ground the other day."

Shaunak's hands stiffened around his coffee cup. He had assumed she saw him, but hearing her acknowledge it made his heart race. "Oh, that... umm... just some practice."

Shraddha laughed lightly. "Practice or punishment?"

Shaunak looked down, grinning slightly. "A bit of both."

For the first time, the conversation felt easy. He wasn't overthinking, wasn't planning every response. He was just talking to her, and she was listening. It was a small moment, but for him, it felt like something special.

As Shaunak entered his hostel room, he found Aryan sitting cross-legged on the bed, casually munching on some snacks. The room was filled with the faint aroma of something spicy and fried. Aryan's face lit up as soon as he saw him.

"There you are! I was waiting for you. Come on, let's eat!" he said, patting the space next to him.

Shaunak, still lost in thoughts about his conversation with Shraddha, shook his head slightly to clear his mind and sat down. Aryan pulled out a packet of snacks from his bag. "Brought these from my last ride. You should try them," he said, pushing the packet toward Shaunak.

Shaunak hesitated before taking one. The crispy texture and burst of flavors made him realize how hungry he actually was. "Where did you go this time?" he asked between bites.

Aryan grinned. "Bihar. Before that, Rajasthan. Before that, Uttarakhand. I just love traveling, man. The roads, the freedom—it's like nothing else."

Shaunak had always assumed Aryan was just another rich kid wasting his father's money, buying expensive bikes and roaming around without responsibilities. But the more he observed him, the more he realized that Aryan wasn't just aimlessly spending money—he was genuinely passionate about traveling. He wasn't in a hurry for anything, never seemed worried, and took life as it came.

"You always travel alone?" Shaunak asked, curious.

"Yeah," Aryan nodded. "My cousin is a solo traveller too. Guess it runs in the family." He leaned back against the wall, stretching his legs. "Solo traveling teaches you a lot. You meet strangers, you learn to manage on your own, and most importantly, you get to know yourself."

Shaunak stared at him for a moment. He had never met someone like Aryan before—someone who wasn't constantly stressed about the future, who didn't let worries weigh him down. Shaunak was always overthinking, always carrying the pressure of expectations. But Aryan? He was like a free bird, living life on his own terms.

As Shaunak settled into his bed, Aryan, who had been casually scrolling through his phone, suddenly turned to him with a smirk.

"So? How did the big meeting go?" Aryan asked, raising an eyebrow.

Shaunak, who had been lost in his thoughts, blinked and looked at him. "Huh? What meeting?"

Aryan chuckled. "Don't play dumb. You had a meeting with that senior girl, remember?"

"Oh... yeah," Shaunak muttered, running a hand through his hair.

Aryan sat up, crossing his arms. "Wait, wait. You're acting weird. That means something interesting happened. Spill it."

Shaunak sighed and leaned against the wall. "Well... yeah, I met the senior girl in the canteen. But that's not even the highlight of the day."

Aryan's curiosity piqued. "Oh? Then what is?"

Shaunak hesitated for a moment, but then, with a small smile, said, "I finally talked to Shraddha today."

Aryan's mouth fell open dramatically. "No way! The same Shraddha you've been staring at all this time? The one whose window you played cricket near?"

Shaunak nodded, a bit embarrassed. "Yeah, that Shraddha."

Aryan whistled. "Wow. This is history being made. But hold on—weren't you supposed to meet the senior girl? How did you end up talking to Shraddha?"

Shaunak grinned and started explaining the events of the day—the canteen meeting, the moment when the senior girl noticed him constantly glancing at Shraddha, and how she called her over, forcing them to sit together.

Aryan burst out laughing. "Oh man, she totally set you up! That senior girl is a legend."

Shaunak rolled his eyes but couldn't help smiling. "Yeah, she excused herself and left us alone. So Shraddha and I ended up having coffee together."

Aryan sat up straight. "And? What did you talk about?"

"She asked about my studies, how I'm good at calculations, and—"

Aryan waved his hand. "Boring. Did she ask anything personal?"

Shaunak thought for a moment. "Well, she asked about my school, if I was really good at sports, and... she mentioned seeing me running around the ground last night."

Aryan gasped dramatically. "Dude! She noticed you! That's huge!"

Shaunak, unable to hide his happiness, just nodded.

Aryan smirked. "Alright, alright. You've officially moved from 'random classmate' to 'guy she's aware of.' Now, listen carefully—I'll give you some love tips."

Shaunak groaned. "Oh no, here we go."

Aryan ignored him and continued, "First rule—don't look too desperate. Girls don't like guys who seem too eager."

Shaunak frowned. "But I'm not—"

Aryan held up a hand. "Shh. Second rule—give her a reason to notice you more. That means you have to keep being good at sports, keep excelling in something she respects."

Shaunak listened, half-amused, half-annoyed.

"And third," Aryan continued, leaning in as if revealing a great secret, "make her laugh. A girl remembers the guy who makes her smile."

Shaunak raised an eyebrow. "You sound like you have a Ph.D. in love."

Aryan grinned. "Of course. I've watched tons of movies and given love advice to many... not that they always worked, but that's beside the point."

Shaunak shook his head, laughing. "You're unbelievable."

Aryan stretched his arms. "But admit it—you're feeling hopeful now, aren't you?"

Shaunak hesitated but then nodded. "Yeah... maybe."

Aryan patted his shoulder. "Good. Now, next mission—getting her to text you first."

Shaunak groaned. "One step at a time, Aryan."

Aryan chuckled. "Fine, fine. But remember—she already noticed you. That's the first win."

CHAPTER XVII

A Rose Before the Rain

As Shaunak lay in bed, staring at the ceiling, a small smile played on his lips. Deep inside, he was silently thanking the senior girl. If it were not for her, he might never have had the chance to talk to Shraddha. Today had been one of the best days of his life.

Just then, his phone buzzed. He glanced at the screen—it was the senior girl calling.

He sat up, feeling a mix of surprise and curiosity. Answering the call, he casually said, "Hello?"

"So, tell me everything," she demanded without any formalities.

Shaunak chuckled. "Everything?"

"Yes, everything! What did you two talk about?" she insisted.

Shaunak leaned back against the headboard, recalling every moment. He told her how Shraddha had asked about his studies, his skills in calculations, and even mentioned seeing him running on the ground. He shared every detail, word for word, without even realizing how openly he was speaking.

And then, without hesitation, he admitted something he hadn't said aloud before. "I think I have a crush on her."

There was a brief pause on the other end of the call. Then, the senior girl spoke, her tone filled with amusement. "Oh really? That's interesting."

Shaunak rubbed the back of his head, feeling a little embarrassed. "I don't know... it's just—there's something about her."

The senior girl chuckled. "Well, if you like her, then do something about it."

Shaunak frowned. "What do you mean?"

"I mean," she said, her voice playful yet serious, "you should let her know. Give her a rose. Tell her that you like her."

Shaunak's eyes widened. "What? That's crazy! What if she doesn't feel the same way?"

"So what?" the senior girl replied. "At least you won't have regrets. And trust me, girls like guys who have the courage to express their feelings."

Shaunak fell silent, his heart beating faster. The thought of confessing to Shraddha felt both thrilling and terrifying.

Sensing his hesitation, the senior girl added, "Listen, you've already come this far. You talked to her, she noticed you, and now you have a chance to stand out. Don't waste it."

Shaunak sighed, running a hand through his hair. "I don't know…"

The senior girl laughed. "Think about it. But don't take too long—someone else might give her a rose before you do."

That sentence hit Shaunak hard. The idea of losing this chance made him feel uneasy.

"Fine," he said, taking a deep breath. "I'll think about it."

"Good," she said. "Now go to sleep, Romeo. You have a big decision to make."

Shaunak chuckled. "Goodnight."

As he ended the call, he stared at his phone for a long moment. Was he really going to do it? Could he actually walk up to Shraddha and tell her how he felt?

He didn't have the answers yet, but one thing was clear—his heart had never beaten this fast before.

Later that night, as Shaunak lay awake in his dimly lit hostel room, his mind was a jumble of emotions. The call from the senior girl had left him both exhilarated and confused—now he had to decide whether to follow her advice and confess his feelings to Shraddha with a rose, or to wait until he knew her better. Unable to sort through the conflicting thoughts, he half-whispered his worries in the dark.

In his half-asleep state, he mumbled, "Aryan, what should I do? I... I'm not even sure what she really likes..."

Aryan, who had already been awake and quietly reading on his side of the room, looked over with a knowing smile. Recognizing the vulnerability in Shaunak's tone—even though he was barely awake—Aryan sat up and gently said, "Buddy, listen. You need to understand her fully before making any moves. It's not just about handing over a rose or blurting out 'I love you.' You need to know her likes, her dislikes—what makes her laugh, what makes her think. You don't want to rush into this without knowing who she really is."

Shaunak mumbled incoherently at first, his eyes still half-closed, but Aryan's tone was calm and steady. "I mean, think about it. If you confess too soon, without understanding her true self, you might end up hurting both of you. Get to know her better. Spend time talking with her, listening to her, and see if you connect on a deeper level. Don't just do it because you feel pressured by today's events."

As the words sank in, Shaunak's troubled expression slowly softened. Though he was still in a haze of sleep, Aryan's advice was like a gentle tap on the shoulder—a reminder to be patient and thoughtful when it came to matters of the heart.

By morning, as the early rays of sunlight filtered through the window, Shaunak awoke with Aryan's advice echoing in his mind. Though his emotions were still raw and his heart raced with uncertainty, he resolved to take things slowly, to learn more about Shraddha, and to build a genuine connection before making any bold moves.

While making his way toward the classroom, Shaunak noticed a small rose plant growing by the side of the pathway. It wasn't a fully bloomed rose, but its delicate petals and subtle fragrance caught his attention. In that quiet moment, he couldn't help but think of Shraddha—of how only someone as special as her deserved such a tender, beautiful bloom. "A beautiful rose for my rose," he thought to himself, a warm smile tugging at the corners of his mouth.

As he paused to admire the tiny flower, Shaunak felt as if the universe had whispered a secret directly to him. The rose, still in its early stages of growth, symbolized hope and the promise of something more—a sign urging him to take action. It was as if nature itself was encouraging him to be brave, to move beyond his uncertainties, and finally express the feelings that had long been confined within his heart.

In that brief encounter with the rose, every worry and hesitation seemed to melt away. Shaunak resolved that he wouldn't let this moment pass by unnoticed. With the soft glow of the morning sun illuminating the fragile rose, he silently vowed to let his heart lead him and to make the next move that could change everything.

After the physics lab that day, Shaunak's heart pounded with a mix of hope and dread. Earlier, he had plucked a single, perfect rose—a small, delicate flower he'd found on his walk to class—and made up his mind to confess his feelings. The plan was simple, yet nerve-wracking:

approach Shraddha, his lab partner, and tell her what he had long kept hidden in his heart.

After the lab session ended, Shaunak spotted Shraddha sitting alone near a window in the lab room, absorbed in her notes. With the rose clenched in his hand, he gathered every ounce of courage and walked over to her. His voice was barely above a whisper when he finally said, "I love you."

For a long, suspended moment, Shraddha looked at him, her eyes searching his face. Then, with a soft but teasing tone, she replied, "This time, I must ask—whom are you proposing to?" There was a gentle amusement in her voice, tempered by a note of caution. "It's okay," she continued, "I'm your friend, and I promise I won't slap you like that senior girl did."

At those words, Shaunak felt a sudden surge of terror mixed with relief. The senior girl's harsh treatment still echoed in his memory, and the idea of being hurt again made him flinch. Overwhelmed and unprepared for the vulnerability of the moment, he blurted out a lie, "You're right—I only said it because the senior girl asked me to do it."

Inside, however, his true intention was clear. He had wanted to know her feelings, to see if she might feel the same way he did. In a burst of desperate honesty, he asked, "But what if she hadn't asked me to? What would your response be if I truly meant it?"

Shraddha paused, her eyes softening as she regarded him. With calm sincerity, she replied, "Even if you had said it on your own, my answer would still be the same. I admire you for your intelligence, for your kindness, and for the person you are. But I only see you as a friend."

Her words fell like a quiet verdict. Shaunak's heart sank. He had hoped for something more, had pictured a future where she might return his love. Instead, he was met with the unyielding truth of their friendship. In that moment, he felt both exposed and strangely grateful. Even though her answer wasn't what he had secretly wished for, it was honest and clear.

Later, when he recounted the entire episode to Aryan—his roommate and confidant—Aryan couldn't help but tease him gently. "So, you had a little chat with Shraddha today, huh? And you admitted you've got a crush?" he said with a knowing grin. Then, in a lighter tone, he added, "Maybe next time, try giving her a rose without blaming the senior girl, okay?"

Though Shaunak felt a mix of embarrassment and disappointment, Aryan's teasing was meant to comfort him, to remind him that every experience—even a painful confession—was part of growing up. Deep inside, Shaunak knew that the rose he'd offered and the confession he had attempted would remain a cherished memory, a moment of courage in his journey of understanding both himself and the complexities of love.

In that quiet afternoon, as he sat back and processed everything, he resolved to learn from this moment. He would continue to nurture his friendship with Shraddha, and perhaps, one day, find a love that blossomed fully. For now, the rose—a symbol of his hopes and vulnerabilities—remained a reminder that sometimes, love is about honest beginnings, even if they don't lead to the romance we dream of.

Later that evening, as the hostel room settled into quiet after a long day, Shaunak turned to Aryan with a genuine, curious look. "Have you ever fallen in love?" he asked softly, as if the question carried the weight of the world.

Aryan paused, then smiled wryly. "Yes, actually—I'm in love." He leaned back, rubbing his chin thoughtfully. "There is a girl I care about deeply. She lives in another city—about 80 kilometres away. I do not know how it happened exactly; it was just one of those moments, a sudden spark. But lately, things have not been going smoothly between us."

Shaunak listened intently as Aryan continued. "You see, these days she has been fighting with me over the smallest things. I'm not very good with handling emotions—I often end up saying the wrong thing or freezing up. It's frustrating for both of us." Aryan's voice grew softer, laced with both regret and hope. "Tomorrow, I'm going to meet her in person to try and sort things out. She said she'll meet me at 6:00 p.m., and I'm nervous about it."

He paused, glancing at Shaunak as if seeking reassurance. "I was wondering, would it be okay if you come with me? It might help having a friend around, someone who can keep me grounded when I'm drowning in my own feelings."

Shaunak could see the vulnerability in Aryan's eyes—a vulnerability he understood all too well from his own trials in love and life. Aryan's confession was raw and honest, unfiltered by the bravado he sometimes put on in front of others. In that moment, Shaunak nodded firmly, his expression gentle. "Of course, Aryan. I'll be there," he said, feeling a sense of camaraderie and understanding deepen between them.

Aryan's face brightened a little at Shaunak's response. "Thanks, man. It means a lot to have someone by my side. I guess we all need a little help sometimes to navigate the crazy world of emotions."

As they both sat in the dim glow of the hostel room's single lamp, Aryan continued, "I really hope that tomorrow, when I see her, I can be honest about how I feel—and maybe, just maybe, she'll understand. I want things to work out, but I also know I have a lot to learn when it comes to dealing with feelings."

Shaunak listened and offered a quiet smile, silently reminding himself that every heart learns in its own time. In that moment, they both understood that love was a journey filled with uncertainties, missteps, and sometimes even pain. Yet, it was also a journey they wouldn't walk alone.

With a newfound resolve and the comforting presence of his friend beside him, Shaunak decided to support Aryan in his quest. Tomorrow's meeting, with its 6:00 p.m. promise, would be a test of both courage and vulnerability—a test that, no matter the outcome, would mark another step forward in their young lives.

Shaunak had been cooped up in the hostel for days—trapped by the constant ragging culture that made every step outside feel like a risk. He longed to break free, even if just for a short ride to feel the open air on his face. Today, the opportunity came when Aryan offered him a ride on his bike. Aryan, ever the free spirit, always seemed so lucky—untouched by the weight of college rules and expectations, able to simply ride and enjoy life. For Shaunak, who often felt caged by the campus restrictions, the promise of the bike was irresistible.

"Sure, I'll come with you," Shaunak said, excitement mingling with a hint of nervousness. With the bike, seniors wouldn't be able to stop him—he'd have his freedom for those precious hours outside. So, despite his hesitations about leaving the safety of the hostel, he agreed.

They left the hostel two hours before their planned arrival, cruising down the road with Aryan riding coolly, as if the world were his playground. The wind whipped past them, and for a brief moment, Shaunak forgot about the constant pressures of college life. They reached their destination by 5 p.m., still with an hour to spare before their next engagement.

Feeling a sudden craving for a small comfort, Shaunak suggested they stop at a tea stall. The stall, a familiar refuge from the monotony of hostel life, was bustling with activity as they waited for their tea. As he sipped his hot, spiced tea, Shaunak's heart ached with longing—he missed their old friends and the comforting banter of days gone by. The memories of laughter and shared struggles echoed around him, making him momentarily forget his worries.

At around 6:40 p.m., while the cool evening light bathed the street in a gentle glow, Aryan's phone began to ring persistently. He was calling his girlfriend, checking to see if she had arrived at their meeting point. At first, there was no answer. The calls kept coming, one after the other. Finally, after about 30 minutes, a message came through: she wasn't feeling well and wouldn't be able to meet him.

Aryan's voice was laced with a mixture of frustration and disappointment as he spoke, "I've traveled 80 kilometers and planned this whole week to see her, and now she's not coming!" His words carried a sense of betrayal—an ache of unmet expectations that contrasted sharply with the freedom and excitement Shaunak had felt earlier.

Shaunak listened quietly, feeling the weight of his own hopes and Aryan's dashed expectations. For Aryan, who had always been so self-assured, this was a bitter pill to swallow. And for Shaunak, already caught between longing for freedom and missing the warmth of friendship, this news only deepened the feeling of isolation that sometimes crept in.

Yet, even as the disappointment settled in the cool evening air, Shaunak couldn't help but reflect on how far he'd come—from a boy confined by constant ragging to someone who was daring enough to ride out and savor life's small, unplanned moments. And though Aryan's plans had been thwarted, for a brief time that day, the ride, the tea, and the open road had reminded him that every setback was just another part of the journey.

Aaryan felt a deep sting of embarrassment that day. His plan to meet his girlfriend had backfired miserably—she never showed up, leaving him humiliated in front of everyone. In that awkward moment, as he stood by the bike with disappointment etched on his face, Shaunak, sensing the tension and wanting to salvage some of the day's lost enthusiasm, suggested that they head back to the hostel. However, before turning around, Shaunak decided he still needed to feel the freedom of the open road. He asked Aaryan for the bike keys, a silent request that carried the promise of a brief escape from the oppressive college atmosphere.

Without a word, Aaryan handed over the keys, his eyes downcast, as if apologizing silently for the failed meeting. Gripping the keys tightly, Shaunak mounted the bike and revved the engine. Determined to lift their spirits and impress his friend, he pushed the bike to pick up speed. For a moment, the world blurred into streaks of color as he raced down the road, his heart pounding with adrenaline and a desperate need to feel alive and in control.

But fate had other plans. Just as they were cruising back, a sudden obstacle emerged—a speed breaker, more formidable than any Shaunak had encountered before. At the same time, from the opposite direction, a large truck came barreling down the road. In that split second, as Shaunak tried to navigate the unexpected speed breaker, the bike lost its balance. The collision with the truck was swift and brutal; the bike was forced under the massive vehicle before it could come to a stop.

In a flash of chaos and noise, both Shaunak and Aaryan were thrown from the bike. The impact sent them sprawling onto the rough pavement, their world spinning in a disorienting mix of pain and disbelief. In that harrowing moment, the thrill of speed and the hope of impressing a friend were abruptly replaced by the stark reality of the consequences of reckless ambition.

CHAPTER XVIII

When the Crash Wasn't the Worst Part

After five minutes, Shaunak's senses began to return. Slowly, his eyes fluttered open, and the first thing he saw was Aryan, leaning over him and gently rubbing a cool substance on his forehead and eyebrows. Shaunak noticed with relief that his helmet had protected him—he hadn't sustained any severe head injuries. However, his glasses had not fared so well; the frame was shattered, a broken piece now resting against his skin.

Still disoriented, Shaunak tried to piece together what had happened. His mind recalled the sudden swerve, the inevitable collision with the truck, and then darkness. Now, in the soft light of the afternoon, a small crowd had gathered around them. Concerned voices floated through the air as bystanders asked if they were okay.

Curious despite the throbbing in his head, Shaunak managed to ask, "Aryan, where did you get the ice?"

Aryan offered a tired smile as he continued to press the ice gently against Shaunak's injured area. "There was a fisherman nearby selling fish—and he had a cart full of ice. I grabbed a few blocks to help cool your head," Aryan explained, his tone a mix of practicality and genuine care.

Shaunak marvelled at the resourcefulness of his friend. Despite the chaos of the accident and the embarrassment of being caught in such a reckless moment, Aryan's quick thinking had provided him with a small comfort. The cool relief of the ice helped dull the pain, and the concerned murmurs of the onlookers faded into the background as Shaunak focused on the kindness before him.

In that quiet, surreal moment, Shaunak felt a renewed sense of gratitude. Even though the day had taken a drastic turn, it was moments like these—when a friend stepped up in a crisis—that reminded him he wasn't alone in his struggles. The incident, though painful and frightening, had forged a deeper bond between them. And as the crowd continued to ask if he was fine, Shaunak managed a weak smile and nodded, silently promising himself that he would take better care and perhaps learn to ride a little more carefully next time.

After the accident, when Shaunak finally began to regain consciousness, he noticed something that made his heart clench—blood was trickling down from Aryan's knees. Yet, despite his own pain and disorientation, Aryan was still bending over, doing his best to help him stand. The world around them was a blur of scattered metal and harsh shouts until, almost as if summoned by fate, the flashing lights of traffic police emerged and officers rushed toward the scene.

Within minutes, a couple of police officers arrived on the scene. Their stern voices and the sight of cameras pointed in their direction made it clear that this incident wouldn't go unnoticed. Both friends exchanged worried glances, aware that a formal police report might be filed and that they could be hit with fines for the accident. The tense atmosphere grew even thicker as one of the officers announced, "There's a government hospital just a kilometre away. I'm taking you both there."

For a fleeting moment, the thought of running away crossed their minds—a desperate attempt to escape the legal consequences. However, as they surveyed the situation, they realized that every moment had been captured on camera and that a concerned crowd had already gathered. With no realistic way to evade responsibility, they reluctantly followed the officers.

At the hospital, the clinical fluorescent lights and the calm, measured tone of the doctor offered a stark contrast to the chaos of the accident. After a quick examination, the doctor advised that the cuts required stitching and prescribed some medicines to prevent infection. Despite the lingering sting of the pain and the shock of the day's events, both Shaunak and Aryan felt a small measure of relief when the hospital staff completed their treatment. Later, to their astonishment, the police officers informed them that no fines would be imposed—perhaps the circumstances and the clear evidence of the accident had worked in their favor.

As they left the hospital and made their way back to the hostel, the weight of the day's ordeal slowly began to lift. The experience had been frightening and humbling, yet it also served as a potent reminder of life's unpredictability. The two friends shared a silent understanding, a bond forged in adversity, and together they resolved to be more cautious in the future. Despite the scare, they returned to the hostel with an odd sense of gratitude—grateful that they were safe, that the accident hadn't derailed their futures, and that sometimes, in the face of misfortune, compassion and leniency find their way through even the darkest moments.

After returning to the room, Aryan immediately began recounting every incident of the day to his girlfriend over the phone—the failed meeting, the accident, the rush to the hospital, and even the makeshift first aid with ice. As he narrated the events, his tone shifted from excitement to frustration, and soon, the conversation escalated into an argument.

His girlfriend's voice grew sharp as she said, "Because of you, all this happened! Because of you, I had to worry about your friend's safety!" The words cut through the air, echoing in the quiet of the room. Aryan listened, his heart sinking with each accusation. The familiar pattern of blame and endless quarrels had taken over once again. In that heated moment, something in him shifted—he realized that the constant fighting, the endless reasoning, and the stress of trying to please someone who never seemed satisfied were weighing him down.

For a fleeting second, he wondered if being single might not be so bad after all. There was a strange relief in the thought of no longer having to justify every misstep, no longer having someone to argue with over every little mistake. The idea of freedom—a life unburdened by conflict—seemed increasingly appealing.

As the argument continued in the background, Aryan leaned back, contemplating the possibility of a life without these recurring disputes. The chaos of the day, the accident, and the harsh words from his girlfriend all converged into one stark realization: sometimes, solitude could offer a sense of peace that a troubled relationship never did. In that moment, Aryan silently acknowledged that single life might bring its own kind of happiness—one where he wouldn't constantly be held accountable for every twist of fate, where he could finally breathe without having to offer endless explanations.

Though he cared for her deeply, the weight of the argument and her harsh words left him feeling isolated and misunderstood. As the phone call ended, Aryan stared at the dark ceiling of the room, the echoes of her voice still ringing in his ears. In that silence, he understood that while love could be beautiful, it could also be complicated and exhausting. And for now, the thought of being on his own—free from the constant barrage of reasons and recriminations—offered a small, bittersweet solace.

That night, Aryan made a quiet promise to himself: he would take some time to reflect on what he truly needed from life and from love. Whether that meant working through their issues or stepping back to reclaim his peace, he knew one thing for certain—sometimes, the absence of conflict was as valuable as the presence of love.

Deep inside, Shaunak often felt the sting of loneliness whenever he saw couples around campus. While he played cricket, the cheers from the girls were always for someone else—their boyfriends or even other boys who they fancied. Each time, he couldn't help but feel isolated, as if everyone had found a connection except him. He longed for someone to share his day with, to listen as he poured out his thoughts about every little moment, every triumph and every disappointment.

Unable to bear the silence that followed his own experiences, Shaunak began investing more time in texting Shraddha. At first, their conversation blossomed naturally. They exchanged messages about mundane things, but also deeper reflections on their day. He would ask her about her favorite color, her favorite animal, her favorite actor, even her favorite film—and in doing so, he hoped to understand her better, to find the spark of connection he so desperately sought.

In those early days, the text exchange was lively. Shraddha's replies would come quickly, each message a small thread weaving their connection closer. They would chat about the little quirks of life—a funny incident during a lab session, the taste of the tea from the canteen, or the way a certain song reminded them of simpler times. For Shaunak, these exchanges were a balm to his lonely heart, a space where he could be himself without judgment.

But as time went on, things began to change. Shraddha's responses grew delayed, and sometimes his messages were left unseen for hours. The immediacy they once had started to wane, leaving Shaunak in a limbo of anticipation. Every morning, he'd wake up with the hope that today, Shraddha would text back as promptly as before, and every evening he'd check his phone obsessively, waiting for her reply.

Despite the delays, Shaunak continued to text her—almost compulsively. He'd send silly questions in rapid succession: "What's your favourite ice cream flavour?" "Do you prefer cats or dogs?" "Which movie could you watch over and over again?" These trivial questions were his way of keeping the conversation alive, of feeling connected even if just for a moment. Each unanswered message filled him with a mix of hope and uncertainty, leaving him to wonder if she still cared, or if she was slowly drifting away.

He started scrutinizing each of her responses, reading between the lines for hints of warmth or indifference. Sometimes, her words would sparkle with a hint of playful banter, and his heart would soar with a fleeting sense of validation. Other times, the silence that followed was deafening, and he was left questioning whether he was over-investing his emotions.

In those moments, Shaunak would recall the times he'd seen couples around campus—laughing, sharing private jokes, and creating memories together. He couldn't help but compare their easy closeness with his own struggle to find a kindred spirit. It hurt to think that while others had found solace in each other, he was left to navigate his own thoughts in solitude.

Yet, even in his moments of doubt, he clung to the hope that one day, Shraddha would look at him differently—that she might see past the delays and the silence to the genuine person he was. Each text, each silly question, was a small step toward breaking through his isolation, a way for him to keep dreaming that someone would understand his heart.

And so, despite the unpredictable rhythm of her replies, Shaunak continued texting, investing his hopes in every word she sent, believing that one day, the conversation might turn into something more—a connection that could fill the void he felt whenever he was surrounded by happy couples. Until then, every unanswered message was both a reminder of his loneliness and a beacon of possibility, urging him to keep trying, to keep believing in the chance of finding true companionship.

CHAPTER XIX

Cool Enough to Bleed

Shaunak's heart burned with a familiar, unsettling jealousy. Every time he saw Shraddha's calm indifference toward him, the sting of rejection festered inside him until he reached a breaking point. Determined to gauge her true feelings—and perhaps to provoke a reaction—he decided on a bold, if reckless, experiment. If he could make her feel a fraction of the envy that consumed him, maybe he'd finally understand where he stood in her eyes.

Over the next few days, the quiet, unassuming boy that everyone had known began to change. In class, where he had once kept to himself, Shaunak started engaging with other girls—those he had previously only exchanged polite nods with. With a confident smile he'd never dared to wear before, he approached them with friendly banter and playful compliments. Even the girls who shared Shraddha's room were not spared; he found excuses to call out to them, laugh at their jokes, and weave himself into their conversations.

As the days passed, his transformation became more evident. Shaunak's usual reserved demeanour was replaced by an air of bold flirtation. He made a point of lingering near groups of girls, his eyes sparkling with a mixture of mischief and challenge. His words were light and teasing, carefully chosen to ignite interest and, above all, to send a subtle message to Shraddha—that he was desired by others.

In a particularly daring move, Shaunak even began flirting with the senior girl—the one who had once unwittingly set off the chain of events that had changed his life. Her presence had always commanded attention, and now his flirtatious remarks in her direction only intensified the buzz around him. Every smile exchanged and every laugh elicited served as his silent test: Would Shraddha notice? Would she feel the jealousy he now nurtured?

Deep down, however, Shaunak wasn't entirely sure if this was the right path. The exhilaration of being the centre of attention clashed with an underlying pain—the fear of losing Shraddha completely. Yet, for now, he pressed on, desperate to feel something, anything, that might finally break the silence between them.

One day, Shaunak heard the news that sent his heart soaring: the senior girl—whom he had long admired for her bold spirit—had broken up with her boyfriend. In that moment, a surge of hope and excitement rushed through him. He felt invigorated, as if the universe had finally granted him a chance. There was something irresistibly attractive about her guts, her unyielding character, that had always drawn him in, and now it seemed that fate might be aligning in his Favor.

Determined not to let this opportunity slip away, Shaunak began to shift his approach. He started calling her every day, but not without a carefully crafted excuse. One day it was the need for notes from a missed lecture, the next it was a question about a tricky concept he just couldn't grasp. Each call was a small pretext, a way to engage her in conversation and slowly bridge the gap between them.

Before long, these interactions led to meetings in the library—a quiet refuge from the chaos of college life. In the hushed corners between the stacks of books, they spent entire afternoons discussing everything from class material to their thoughts on life. The library, once a solitary sanctuary for Shaunak, had transformed into a space of unexpected connection, where every shared glance and thoughtful exchange brought him one step closer to what he secretly desired.

As days turned into weeks, the rhythm of their conversations grew more natural. With every call and every study session, Shaunak felt that elusive spark of possibility. He clung to the hope that these moments of academic camaraderie might one day blossom into something deeper—a bond built not only on shared notes and concepts but on mutual respect and affection.

And so, in that gentle, understated way of young hearts finding their way, Shaunak nurtured his feelings quietly. Each day in the library became a chance to rewrite his story—a story where persistence, hope, and the courage to seize every opportunity might eventually lead him to a love he had always dreamed of.

Rumours began circulating around campus—whispers that Shaunak and the senior girl were in a relationship. At first, these stories unsettled him, but over time, he found himself oddly proud of the rumour. Deep down, he longed for a connection, and the idea of being seen as a couple gave him a sense of validation he had rarely experienced before.

One afternoon, while the two friends were hanging out in their hostel corridor, Aryan nudged Shaunak and asked, "So, is it true? Are you and her together?"
Wanting to appear cool and confident, Shaunak grinned and lied, "Yeah, we're together." He wasn't ready to admit his insecurities, but that single word felt like Armor shielding him from the loneliness he often carried.

Emboldened by the rumour and his newfound image, Shaunak mustered up the courage to ask the senior girl for a bike ride—a gesture that, he hoped, would confirm the rumours for everyone. At first, she hesitated. "If we ride together, everyone will think we're a couple," she argued, unsure if the public display was something she was ready for.

But Shaunak persisted, asking day after day, until finally she relented with a quiet, "Alright."

Overwhelmed with excitement, Shaunak rushed to Aryan and asked for the bike keys. With a resigned yet supportive smile, Aryan handed over his bike without a word, knowing that this was one of those rare moments that could change Shaunak's world.

From that day on, Shaunak began riding with the senior girl every other day. Their rides became a cherished ritual—a blend of stolen smiles, shared laughter, and long stretches of open road that seemed to wash away the burdens of college life. The wind in his hair and the freedom of the ride filled him with a sense of joy he hadn't known before.

He started enjoying his life to the fullest, embracing the rumours that once made him feel exposed and transforming them into a badge of honour. The campus chatter, the knowing glances from classmates, even the teasing from Aryan—all of it bolstered his confidence.

Shaunak had started borrowing bikes, clothes, and shoes from Aryan—an act born out of a desperate need to transform himself into someone cool, someone who could finally stand out in the crowded, judgmental corridors of college life. Aryan never refused him; his generosity had become a silent support that Shaunak leaned on, even as he tried to reinvent his image.

One fateful day, as Shaunak wandered the campus alone in one of his borrowed outfits, fate took an unexpected turn. A notorious ex-boyfriend of one of the girls he admired spotted him. Without warning, the ex-boyfriend rallied several seniors, and in a matter of moments, a horde of them descended on Shaunak. Their ragging was relentless—taunts quickly turned into rough handling, and before long, Shaunak found himself bruised and bloodied. Though the injuries were minor, the humiliation and pain cut deep.

As he limped back to the hostel, a surge of anger mixed with loneliness welled up inside him. In that moment, he bitterly lamented that if he truly had real friends by his side, he wouldn't have to endure days like this. The sting of isolation was almost as unbearable as the physical pain.

Later that evening, his phone buzzed with a call from the girl he cared about. In a bid to salvage whatever sliver of sympathy he could, Shaunak hesitantly answered. When she asked how he had gotten hurt by his ex, he found himself weaving a tale far more dramatic than the reality. With his heart pounding, he lied, exaggerating the extent of his injuries. "I'm not even able to walk," he claimed, his voice trembling as he added unnecessary details to make his plight sound more dire.

Determined to solidify the impression and garner her compassion, Shaunak then took a daring step. He visited a private medical shop and purchased fake bandages and even some simulated stitches—a makeshift remedy to prove his suffering. With these contrived wounds, he hoped to evoke the sympathy he craved, to finally be seen as someone in need of care and understanding.

In that single day—ranging from his efforts to look cool with borrowed accessories, to the cruel ragging by seniors, to the desperate lies meant to capture a shred of her attention—Shaunak's world had shifted. The scars on his body were real, but those on his heart were deepened by loneliness and the bitter taste of betrayal. Each moment was a reminder that the quest for acceptance often came with a heavy price, and that sometimes, in trying to impress others, one risks losing oneself entirely.

Shaunak sat alone in his dimly lit room, staring at the half-finished text on his phone, and wondered if he was losing himself. Every action he'd taken lately, every borrowed bike ride and every flirtatious conversation, seemed to come from a singular, desperate impulse—to make Shraddha feel the sting of jealousy. It was the same sharp pang he felt whenever he saw her with her boyfriend—a feeling he had come to both despise and long for.

In that quiet moment of reflection, he realized he wasn't even sure what he was doing anymore. Was he trying to prove that he could be desired, or was he merely trying to recapture a feeling he once thought would define his worth? The line between love and envy had blurred, leaving him in a haze of uncertainty. His actions—flirting with others, pushing boundaries he'd never considered before—were no longer about genuine connection, but rather a calculated attempt to provoke a reaction from her.

Yet, as the digital clock on his bedside table ticked slowly, Shaunak's heart ached with the realization that each step he took in that direction only deepened his own isolation. He craved the attention he once saw in her eyes, but in doing so, he felt as if he were chasing a phantom, a mirage born from jealousy and loneliness. And so, with a heavy heart and a mind clouded by self-doubt, he resolved to continue down this uncertain path—hoping, perhaps foolishly, that one day she might look his way with the same intensity that once made him feel alive.

Life in the college hostel had always felt confining to Shaunak. Every day, the strict rules and constant supervision made him feel like he was trapped in a small, unyielding cage. His longing for freedom grew even stronger as he listened to Aryan on the phone, chatting animatedly with his girlfriend—a conversation that starkly highlighted what Shaunak felt he was missing in his own life.

One evening, while staring out of his hostel window at the darkening sky, Shaunak's mind began to wander. What if he could break free from this suffocating routine? A daring idea took root: he would move out of the hostel and claim a slice of independence for himself. To achieve that, he decided that a second-hand bike would be the perfect symbol of his newfound freedom—a way to escape the restrictions of hostel life and explore the world on his own terms.

Fortunately, Shaunak had a small emergency fund that his parents had deposited into his account, a quiet reminder of their support even though they remained unaware of his inner turmoil. With that money, he knew he could afford a bike without having to alert them.

The next day, he confided his plan to Aryan. His eyes sparkled with a mix of excitement and nervous determination as he explained, "I'm thinking of moving out of the hostel and getting a second-hand bike. I just need to break free for a while, you know?"

Aryan's reaction was immediate and enthusiastic. "That's brilliant, man! You deserve some freedom. Go for it!" he said, his tone warm with genuine support.

In that moment, the decision felt less like a reckless escape and more like the first step toward a new beginning—a chance to shape his life on his own terms. The idea of riding down winding roads, without the constant restrictions of hostel life, filled him with anticipation. He imagined the wind on his face, the thrill of discovery, and the sense of liberation that only true independence could bring.

As Shaunak planned his departure in quiet confidence, he also recognized the bittersweet truth: the very freedom he craved might come at the cost of distancing himself further from the familiar. Yet, the prospect of building a life where he could be himself was far too enticing to ignore.

And so, with Aryan's enthusiastic approval echoing in his mind, Shaunak resolved to take that bold step—a leap toward a future where he could finally ride free and perhaps, in the process, discover who he truly was.

The next day, Shaunak approached Aryan with a determined glint in his eye. "Let's take leave today," he said, his voice low but resolute. Without a second thought, they bunked school, deciding that freedom was worth one more day of risk. Aryan, ever the expert when it came to bikes, agreed to join him. Together, they rode out to a second-hand bike store—a modest shop tucked away on a quiet side street.

Inside the shop, rows of pre-loved bikes lined the walls. Shaunak's eyes roamed over them, his heart fluttering with the possibility of finally owning his own ride. With Aryan's guidance and his own tight budget in mind, they eventually settled on one that seemed to promise both reliability and a chance for independence. They booked the bike, the transaction marking more than just a purchase—it was a step toward breaking free from the confines of his current life.

Yet as Shaunak handed over the cash he had withdrawn from the ATM, doubts began to creep in. A familiar question whispered in his mind: Was he simply waiting for his father's money? He recalled how he had once scoffed at rich kids wasting their parents' money on trivial things like flashy bikes. But now, facing this tangible symbol of freedom, his perspective had shifted. This wasn't about frivolous spending—it was about proving to himself that he could make decisions on his own, that he could be truly independent.

Before finalizing the deal, he turned to Aryan, his voice betraying both uncertainty and resolve. "Do you think I'm doing the right thing?" he asked quietly.

Aryan, ever the supportive friend, paused for a moment and then met his gaze. "What does your heart say?" he asked, his tone gentle yet firm.

Shaunak closed his eyes for a heartbeat, letting his feelings settle. When he opened them again, the answer was clear. "It says to buy the bike—and to be independent," he replied.

That same day, Shaunak rode his newly purchased second-hand bike back toward the hostel, feeling a rush of freedom mingled with cautious optimism. The wind brushed past him, carrying away remnants of the day's earlier adventures. Yet as he neared the campus grounds, his heart sank when he saw her—his senior girl, the one he had long assumed would be his, who he believed had turned a new leaf with him. Instead, she was sitting with someone else—a familiar figure from her past. It became painfully clear that she had reconciled with her ex.

For a fleeting moment, he slowed his pace as conflicting emotions swirled inside him—hope, jealousy, and a deep, aching disappointment. He parked his bike under a large tree, and with a heavy sigh, watched as the senior girl sat quietly, the weight of old decisions written on her face.

Before he could process the bitterness that crept in, a senior boy approached him. The man, whose earlier ragging had haunted Shaunak, offered a hesitant apology. "I'm sorry for what happened earlier," he said, his tone both contrite and casual.

Wanting to sound unruffled, Shaunak forced a smile. "No worries at all," he replied, striving for a cool detachment that belied the storm inside him.

The senior's eyes then shifted to the bike. "Whose bike is that you're riding?" he asked, clearly impressed—or perhaps merely curious.

Swallowing his doubts, Shaunak puffed out his chest and replied, "It's mine." He relished the sound of his own words, as if claiming ownership over a new, promising future.

But fate, as it often did, had one more twist in store. The senior then casually asked, "Mind if I borrow the keys for a quick ride?"

Before Shaunak could hesitate, the senior girl, now smiling faintly as if sharing an inside joke with him, climbed onto the bike with him. In that instant, they set off together, riding off into the fading light of the evening.

Shaunak watched them disappear down the lane, a sudden, overwhelming sense of loss and self-reproach flooding him. His heart felt as if it had been left behind with every mile they rode away. He cursed his luck and the cruel turns of fate—each act, each stolen moment of freedom, now a bitter reminder that nothing was as he had hoped.

In the quiet that followed, Shaunak sat by his bike, feeling small and insignificant, as if the promise of independence and the allure of change had slipped through his fingers. The day had brought him a fleeting taste of liberation, yet it ended with him standing alone, questioning if his heart had been led astray all along.

The next day, burdened by the weight of his recent experiences and desperate for a respite, Shaunak made a bold decision. He took leave from college and set out to find a place of his own—a sanctuary away from the suffocating environment of the hostel and campus. His heart was heavy with conflicting emotions, and all he craved was mental peace.

Everywhere he searched, however, doors seemed to remain firmly closed. Most landlords were unwilling to rent out a single room to a bachelor, and every potential space seemed to be reserved for couples or families. After what felt like an endless day of wandering through crowded streets and barren apartment blocks, fate intervened—a small flat sat empty in a modest building not far from campus. With little hesitation, Shaunak decided that this would be his refuge. He took the whole flat, knowing that it was his ticket to solitude and, hopefully, a fresh start.

The flat's windows overlooked the college playground, where he had once witnessed the carefree laughter of couples and friends—a painful reminder of the bonds he'd lost and the loneliness that now gnawed at him. As he began packing his meager belongings and preparing to shift out of the hostel, a sense of resolve mingled with sorrow. He wasn't entirely sure what feelings he was grappling with anymore; his heart was a tangled mess of regret, longing, and a desperate need for silence.

The move was swift, and by the time he had left the hostel behind, Shaunak was immersed in his new, solitary world. It was in this vulnerable state that he noticed his phone lighting up repeatedly with missed calls. The caller was none other than the senior girl—the same one whose presence had once stirred both hope and despair in him.

She had called him multiple times, perhaps out of concern or a desire to reconnect, but Shaunak, with his mind set on reclaiming his mental peace, deliberately ignored every call.

In that quiet, lonely flat, Shaunak was left alone with his thoughts—a world away from the chaos of campus life, where every call, every reminder of the past, seemed to echo his inner turmoil. And so, with each unanswered ring and every silent minute that passed, he clung to the hope that, in time, solitude would heal the wounds of a heart that had long known both passion and pain.

CHAPTER XX

Freedom, Interrupted

The memories of hostel life weighed on Shaunak like an old, familiar song. Even after leaving the cramped confines of his hostel in search of independence, he couldn't shake the comforting pull of those days. The food in the hostel, rich with flavour and warmth, stood in stark contrast to the bland, hurried meals he managed in his new flat. Every bite reminded him of shared laughter, bustling mess halls, and the simple pleasure of a home-cooked meal made for many.

At night, the emptiness of his flat grew all the more apparent. The silence was oppressive, and the vacant rooms seemed to whisper of loneliness. The once-anticipated freedom now felt like an isolating expanse—a vast, cold space where he was left entirely alone. Fear and melancholy crept in as darkness fell, and the memories of his hostel days, with all its chaotic comfort, became a bittersweet refuge in his mind.

Desperate to recapture even a fragment of that lost connection, Shaunak began making secret trips back to the hostel. Under the cover of night, he'd wander the familiar corridors, drawn by the irresistible aroma of the mess hall and the promise of a hot meal. These visits were a small rebellion against his solitude—a temporary escape where he could indulge in the lively chatter and warm camaraderie he so dearly missed.

And sometimes, when the memories of shared laughter were too much to bear, he would venture out to the college cricket ground. There, amidst the echo of bat meeting ball and the raucous cheers of fellow students, he found a fleeting sense of belonging. Even though his new life promised independence, the impromptu games on the field were a reminder that he still had a place among people—an affirmation that, even in isolation, connection was possible.

In these moments, as he savoured a bowl of hostel food or laced up his boots for a game of cricket, Shaunak grappled with the truth that freedom sometimes came at the steep price of solitude. Yet, with each return to the lively chaos of his past, he clung to the hope that he could someday weave together the best of both worlds—a future where independence and the warmth of genuine companionship could coexist.

On the occasion of Mahashivratri, the campus buzzed with excitement and anticipation. It was an annual celebration steeped in tradition—a time when the college allocated funds to the head of the institution for elaborate decorations, vibrant rituals, and cultural events. This year, as fate would have it, the responsibility fell on him. As the head of the college, he took his role seriously, meticulously arranging every detail for the celebration.

Beyond the official festivities, an undercurrent of mischief ran through the hostel corridors. There was an unspoken tradition among the hostellers to indulge in bhang—a potent, traditional concoction that, though unknown to the college administration, was celebrated quietly and cheerfully by the students. They would spend their allotted funds on modest decorations, and with the remaining money, they would purchase ingredients for bhang lassi and even hire a DJ for an impromptu dance party deep into the night.

This year, determined to experience every facet of the festival fully, he decided to take part in the hostel celebration. It was a stark contrast to his usual reserved demeanor. Never one to partake in bhang himself, he resolved that on this Mahashivratri, he would break his own rule. With the official funds in hand, he arranged for the finest dry fruits and a generous supply of milk to prepare the perfect bhang lassi—an offering to the spirit of the festival, and a small rebellion against his customary restraint.

As the day wore on and the campus transformed into a dazzling tableau of lights and decorations, he found himself swept up in the infectious energy. When the time came, he joined the hostellers in their secluded celebration. The aroma of the lassi mixed with the scent of marigolds and incense, and the soft beats of the DJ set the stage for an evening of unexpected freedom. That night, as he sipped the bhang lassi, he felt a surge of exhilaration—an unaccustomed lightness that promised to carry him away from the burdens of authority and into the realm of pure, unbridled joy.

For the first time, he allowed himself to revel in the festivities, to laugh and dance with the students, and to momentarily forget the constraints of his position. It was a transformative experience—a blending of duty and delight, of tradition and rebellion—that he knew he would remember long after the lights of Mahashivratri had faded away.

Shaunak had never touched bhang before, and he was blissfully unaware of the aftereffects that might follow. Despite Aaryan's repeated warnings, he kept downing the bhang lassi, confident in his tolerance and the thrill of the moment. As the evening progressed, Aaryan, noticing the subtle signs of a coming hangover—dizziness and blurred edges—suggested a change of scenery. "Come on, let's take a walk near the sports ground," he urged, hoping the fresh air would help Shaunak clear his head.

Reluctantly, Shaunak agreed, and together they strolled along the quiet paths of the campus. It was then that Shaunak's gaze fell upon Shraddha, who was walking alone, her expression calm and reflective in the soft glow of the evening. Without overthinking, he approached her.

"Hey, Shraddha," he said, trying to mask the unsteady tremor in his voice, "how are you? How's life treating you these days?"

Her smile was warm and genuine as she replied, "I'm doing well, Shaunak. Everything's good—just the usual ups and downs." For a few precious minutes, they shared a light conversation, the kind that left him feeling a spark of hope and connection he hadn't felt in a long time.

But as their exchange continued, a sudden wave of the hangover hit Shaunak like a tidal wave. The once-clear conversation blurred, and the cheerful energy in the air was replaced by a throbbing headache and nausea. Realizing he couldn't stay any longer in that moment of fragile clarity, he abruptly excused himself.

"Come on, Aryan," he called out, his voice strained as he waved his friend over. "I need to get out of here."

With Aaryan's steady support, Shaunak turned away from the lingering conversation and the open path, determined to find solace in the safety of their hostel. In that hurried exit, every step felt like a mix of disappointment and resignation—a stark reminder that even the briefest moments of connection could be shattered by the consequences of his impulsive choices.

As Shaunak made his way through the dimly lit campus corridor, still reeling from the hangover's fog, he suddenly heard a sharp, accusing call. Glancing around, he saw the senior girl's boyfriend standing a few paces away, his face etched with anger as he beckoned Shaunak over. Despite his muddled state of mind, something in the tone of that call triggered a surge of defiance in him, and he trudged toward the confrontation.

Before long, harsh words were exchanged. The boyfriend's voice was firm and unyielding, while Shaunak, fueled partly by the alcohol-induced haze and partly by a wounded pride, found himself rising to the challenge. In a moment of heated impulse, he reached out and grabbed the collar of the man before him—a gesture that seemed to freeze time, as the entire corridor grew suddenly tense.

The senior girl, who had been nearby, rushed forward in an attempt to de-escalate the situation. "Stop it, both of you!" she cried, her voice a mixture of anger and genuine concern. She reached out, trying to pull Shaunak's hand away, pleading with him to let go before things spiraled further.

At that critical moment, Aryan, who had been following at a cautious distance, stepped in. His tone was gentle yet earnest as he looked directly at Shaunak. "It's not really you," he said quietly, "it's just the hangover messing with your head." Aryan's words were like a soft anchor, urging Shaunak to regain his composure amidst the chaos.

Reluctantly, Shaunak released his grip. The senior girl's boyfriend shot him a final glare before storming off, and the senior girl continued to try to calm the situation, her eyes reflecting both relief and lingering frustration. As the echoes of the confrontation faded, Shaunak was left standing there, heart pounding and mind swirling with regret and confusion. The brief lapse into aggression felt foreign to him—a stark reminder of how easily his emotions could be hijacked by circumstances beyond his control.

In the quiet that followed, as Aryan's words resonated in his ears, Shaunak wondered how different his life might be if he could reclaim that sense of clarity and control. For now, however, all he could do was let the incident fade into another painful memory—a lesson in the dangerous interplay of pride, desire for attention, and the disorienting influence of a hangover.

As Shaunak made his way back toward the hostel, his mind still clouded by the effects of bhang, he noticed the director of the college standing near the DJ setup. The booming music still echoed across the campus, but the sight of the director sent a jolt of panic through him.

The director's sharp gaze scanned the area, and then, locking onto Shaunak, he called out his name. Shaunak immediately knew why—he was supposed to be the one managing the event, and by now, it was well past time to shut down the DJ. But there was a bigger problem. If he walked up to the director now, in his intoxicated state, there was no way he could hide the fact that he was under the influence. One misstep, one slurred word, and it would all be over.

Without hesitation, he turned on his heel and hurriedly made his way toward the hostel bathroom, pretending not to have heard the director's call. His heart pounded in his chest as he reached the bathroom, locked the door behind him, and immediately turned on the shower. He needed to sober up—fast.

The icy water crashed against his skin, shocking his senses, but instead of clearing his mind, it made things worse. As the minutes passed, the world around him started to shift unnaturally. The walls of the bathroom curved and bent as if they were moving, the water droplets glowed like tiny floating orbs, and everything took on a surreal 3D effect. He tried to focus, to look straight ahead, but his vision refused to stabilize.

Panic gripped him. He wasn't just high—he was completely lost in the hangover. He reached for the wall to steady himself, but even that felt distant, as if he were trying to touch something in a dream. The director was outside, waiting for him. He had to go, he had to talk—but how could he even walk in a straight line when the entire world around him was spinning and shifting like an illusion?

Taking a deep breath, Shaunak clenched his fists, trying to force himself back to reality. But no matter how much he willed it, his body refused to cooperate. Now, trapped between the fear of getting caught and his inability to function properly, he realized he had made a huge mistake.

As the night deepened and the festival's celebrations continued unabated, the director stood near the DJ booth, his patience wearing thin. The music blared across the campus, defying the late hour, and he was determined to bring the festivities to a close. Spotting Shaunak's absence, the director dispatched a student to summon him. However, Shaunak, ensconced in his hostel room and battling the effects of bhang, chose to remain hidden.

Undeterred, the director sent another student, and then another, each returning without Shaunak. Frustration mounting, Shaunak's emotions spiralled into inexplicable anger. Bursting out of his room, he marched toward the gathering, his vision still wavering from the intoxicant.

"The DJ will not stop!" he shouted, his voice cutting through the music. "Why do you insist on caging our spirits? This is a festival—a time to break free from the mundane, not to be shackled by routine. Sometimes, we need to truly live, to embrace joy without restraint."

The director stood silent, absorbing Shaunak's impassioned plea. Without uttering a word, he turned and walked away, leaving the music to play on and the celebration to continue.

CHAPTER XXI

From Campus to Conscience

The morning sun cast a gentle glow over the campus, but for Shaunak, the brightness only intensified the throbbing in his head—a relentless reminder of the previous night's indulgence. As he groggily prepared to face the day, a sharp knock echoed through his hostel room. A fellow student stood at the door, delivering a terse message: "The director wants to see you in his office."

Panic surged through Shaunak. His immediate instinct was to take a cold shower, hoping it would clear the lingering haze from his mind. However, Aaryan, ever the voice of reason, intervened. "Shaunak, don't," he cautioned. "A cold shower might make the hangover worse. Just dress neatly and face him as you are."

Heeding his friend's advice, Shaunak washed his face, donned a clean set of clothes, and made his way to the director's office. Each step felt heavy, burdened with apprehension. Upon arrival, he hesitated briefly before knocking, then entered, finding the director seated behind a formidable desk, his expression unreadable.

Before the director could utter a word, Shaunak launched into an earnest apology. "Sir, I deeply regret my actions last night," he began, his voice tinged with genuine remorse. "I allowed the festivities to cloud my judgment and behaved inappropriately."

The director's initial demeanour was stern, his eyes narrowing as he listened. "Shaunak," he began, his tone measured, "your conduct was unbecoming of a student leader. Such behaviour reflects poorly on both you and the institution."

Shaunak nodded, absorbing the reprimand, his gaze fixed on the floor. After a tense pause, the director's tone softened, a faint smile tugging at the corners of his mouth. "However," he continued, "I recall my own college days. Festivals were times of exuberance, and I too had my share of youthful indiscretions."

Surprised, Shaunak looked up, meeting the director's now empathetic gaze. "Consider this a learning experience," the director advised. "Enjoy these moments, but always remember to uphold the values of our institution. Let this be the last instance. Any repetition, and you'll face a fine or more severe consequences."

Relief washed over Shaunak. He expressed his gratitude, promising to be more mindful in the future. As he exited the office, the weight of anxiety lifted, replaced by a renewed commitment to balance youthful exuberance with responsibility.

In the days following his confrontation with the director, Shaunak found himself ensnared in a web of shame and regret. The memory of his altercation with the senior girl's boyfriend replayed incessantly in his mind, each iteration amplifying his embarrassment. The thought of facing her now was unbearable; he couldn't fathom meeting her gaze without recalling his own reckless behavior.

Despite his reluctance to see her, a part of him yearned for her outreach—a call, a message—anything that might bridge the chasm his actions had created. He wondered if she was concerned about him, if she pondered over his well-being, or if she sought answers to the chaos that had unfolded. Yet, as days passed in silence, Shaunak's hope waned, replaced by a gnawing uncertainty.

He questioned his own motives: Why had he confronted her boyfriend? Was it the intoxicating grip of bhang clouding his judgment, or did deeper, unacknowledged feelings drive him to such folly? The incident had not only strained his relationship with her but had also cast a shadow over his own self-perception.

In this period of introspection, Shaunak grappled with the repercussions of his actions, understanding that the path to redemption was fraught with challenges, especially when the silence between them spoke louder than words.

In the ensuing weeks, Shaunak's isolation deepened. He confined himself to his room, neglecting classes and distancing himself from peers. The silence from his college mates, especially from Shraddha and the senior girl, amplified his loneliness. Each day without contact felt like an affirmation of his fears—that he had alienated those he once held dear.

One evening, as the weight of his solitude pressed heavily upon him, his phone rang. A flicker of hope ignited within him, anticipating a call from Shraddha or perhaps the senior girl seeking reconciliation. However, the voice on the other end belonged to an old friend, someone from a chapter of his life that seemed distant now.

Hearing the familiar tone broke the dam of his emotions. Words tumbled out as he recounted his recent turmoil—the impulsive decisions, the ensuing shame, and the profound sense of isolation. His friend listened patiently, offering a compassionate ear without judgment.

After Shaunak had poured out his heart, his friend spoke with gentle firmness. "Shaunak, it's evident you're going through a rough patch. But dwelling in isolation won't mend your spirit. You need to rediscover what brings you joy and purpose."

He suggested several avenues:

"Remember the thrill you felt on the open road? Let the wind clear your mind and reignite your passion for adventure."

"Literature has always been your refuge. Dive into stories that transport you beyond your current confines."

"Reflect on what truly makes you happy. Whether it's music, art, or another hobby, immerse yourself in it."

His friend also emphasized the importance of setting goals and seeking support when needed. "Remember, it's okay to ask for help. Surround yourself with those who uplift you and challenge you to grow."

This conversation acted as a catalyst for Shaunak. He realized that while he couldn't change the past, he held the power to shape his future. Inspired by his friend's words, he resolved to step out of his self-imposed exile and seek the distractions and passions that once brought him joy.

Determined to break free from his cycle of isolation and despair, Shaunak resolved to embrace life anew. Drawing inspiration from his former roommate, Aaryan, and memories of his late cousin, both avid motorcyclists, he decided to embark on a journey of self-discovery through biking.

With a sense of purpose, Shaunak began taking his motorcycle on rides, initially exploring the outskirts of the city. The sensation of the wind against his face and the rhythmic hum of the engine beneath him provided an exhilarating sense of freedom. Each ride became a therapeutic escape, allowing him to momentarily set aside his worries and immerse himself in the present moment.

Embarking on his newfound passion for motorcycling, Shaunak often found solace and exhilaration on the open roads. However, one fateful day, his journey took an unexpected turn.

While navigating a secluded stretch of countryside, his second-hand motorcycle abruptly sputtered and came to a halt. Alone and without immediate assistance, Shaunak faced a daunting predicament. With no mobile signal and miles away from the nearest town, he was left with limited options.

Undeterred, he began pushing his motorcycle along the desolate road, the sun casting long shadows as hours passed. His determination was tested with each step, but the ordeal also ignited a resolve within him to become more self-reliant.

After what felt like an eternity, he stumbled upon a small village with a modest mechanic's workshop. The mechanic, noticing Shaunak's exhaustion and predicament, offered assistance. Observing the repairs, Shaunak realized the importance of understanding his vehicle's mechanics.

This experience became a turning point. Determined not to be caught unprepared again, Shaunak delved into the world of motorcycle maintenance. He invested in reputable repair manuals, such as those from Haynes and Clymer, renowned for their comprehensive guides on motorcycle upkeep. He also sought advice from online communities and forums, where seasoned riders shared invaluable insights on DIY repairs and maintenance tips.

Shaunak had always been different from the rest of his classmates. Unlike the carefree boys who spent their college days loitering in the canteen or making last-minute notes before exams, he followed a disciplined routine. But that didn't mean he was a nerd who only lived for books. His world was a blend of dedication and quiet rebellion.

For the entire year, his routine was simple yet unwavering—attend classes with utmost seriousness, make detailed notes, and revise regularly. But there were days when certain lectures felt unbearable. The monotonous voice of a professor or the endless theories that seemed more like a lullaby than a lesson often tested his patience. On those days, Shaunak did something unconventional—he bunked classes. However, unlike his classmates, who vanished to nearby cafés or went on long drives, he had only one destination in mind: the college library.

The library was his sanctuary. Rows upon rows of books, the faint smell of old paper, and the hushed silence gave him a strange sense of comfort. It was here that he found purpose beyond just excelling in his own studies. He started noticing a pattern—many of his classmates struggled with concepts that seemed basic to him. Some never asked questions out of fear of being mocked, while others had simply given up on understanding subjects they found too difficult.

It was then that Shaunak made a decision—he would teach them. And among them, he found himself especially drawn toward helping the girls in his class. It wasn't because he wanted their attention or admiration, but because he had always had a soft corner for them. He had seen how, in a society that often discouraged girls from excelling in fields like engineering and mathematics, many of them lacked confidence despite their potential.

What started as casual guidance soon turned into proper study sessions. Whenever he found a girl struggling with equations or theories, he would patiently explain, breaking down complex topics into simpler ideas. He wasn't just teaching; he was empowering. And when exam time approached, his role became even more crucial.

While most students panicked, hurriedly flipping through pages they hadn't touched all semester, Shaunak remained calm. He knew his preparation was solid, but more than that, he knew he had a responsibility. His classmates, especially the ones he had been tutoring, looked up to him. He would sit with them for hours, clearing their doubts, giving them last-minute tips, and sometimes even lending his notes.

There were days when he found himself sitting with a group of girls, solving mathematical problems while they nervously chewed their pens. Some teased him, calling him 'Professor Shaunak,' but their eyes held gratitude. He never asked for anything in return—just a silent acknowledgment that they understood what he had taught them.

As the year passed, something changed in the classroom. Those who had once felt lost now raised their hands to answer questions. The girls who used to hesitate before speaking had gained confidence. And Shaunak, who had begun this journey out of an innate kindness, realized that teaching had given him a purpose far greater than just acing his own exams.

The semester had finally come to an end, and Shaunak packed his bags to return home. College had been a whirlwind—classes, books, late-night study sessions, and those quiet moments in the library where he had unknowingly shaped the future of many of his classmates. But now, as he boarded the train, leaving behind the bustling campus, his mind drifted toward something much deeper—his home, his parents, and the life he had left behind.

As soon as he stepped into his house, the warmth of familiarity embraced him. The faint aroma of home-cooked food, the worn-out furniture that had stood witness to years of struggle, and the quiet hum of the ceiling fan brought a sense of peace. But within minutes, that peace was overshadowed by a realization that hit him like a storm.

His father, a man who had always stood strong like a pillar, was still working tirelessly in their small business. From dawn till dusk, he was out, ensuring the family had enough to sustain. The creases on his forehead, the slight bend in his back, and the way he sighed at the end of the day—Shaunak had never noticed these details before. Or maybe he had, but he had never let them sink in.

Inside the house, his mother moved like clockwork. From the moment she woke up, she was on her feet—cooking, cleaning, arranging things, making sure everything was in place. There was no pause, no rest, no moment where she simply sat and did nothing. He watched her quietly, guilt creeping into his heart.

All these years, he had never truly acknowledged their sacrifices. His parents had never asked him for anything. They never complained, never showed exhaustion in front of him. They simply worked, believing that this was their duty as parents—to provide, to nurture, to ensure he had the best life possible.

That night, Shaunak lay awake on his bed, staring at the ceiling. A strange restlessness gripped him. He had spent years in college, helping his friends, teaching his classmates, solving their problems—but what had he done for the two people who had given him everything?

His father's tired face, his mother's aching hands—these images wouldn't leave his mind. He had never helped them, never given them the comfort they deserved. He had been a good student, a responsible son in terms of academics, but he had never been the kind of son who lightened their burdens.

A thought settled deep within him—he couldn't let this continue. He couldn't watch them struggle while he merely sat back, waiting for his future to unfold. He had to change things.

The next morning, as he saw his father getting ready for work, Shaunak made a silent promise. One day, he would not allow him to work anymore. He would take charge, build a career, and ensure his father never had to leave the house in exhaustion again. His mother, too, deserved rest—she had spent her entire life managing the home, and soon, he would make sure she had all the help she needed. A servant, a comfortable life, and most importantly, the love and care she had always given without asking for anything in return.

CHAPTER XXII

From Fear to Foundation

Shaunak's days at home were filled with a newfound awareness of his parents' relentless dedication. Their unwavering support had always been a backdrop to his life, but now, each act of theirs resonated deeply within him.

One evening, as the sun dipped below the horizon, casting a warm glow through the windows, Shaunak sat at his study table, immersed in his books. The soft creak of the door announced his father's presence.

"Shaunak," his father began gently, "I was checking your bank account today. Do you have enough funds? If not, I can add some more."

A pang of guilt tightened Shaunak's chest. He had recently spent a significant portion of his savings on a second-hand motorcycle and had rented a room outside the hostel to create a peaceful study environment. These expenses, though justifiable in his mind, had depleted the emergency funds his father had diligently provided.

His father continued, his voice steady and reassuring, "No need to worry. I'll transfer some money into your account. Just focus on your studies."

Shaunak's heart ached with a mix of gratitude and remorse. His father's unwavering trust was evident; there was no interrogation about the depleted funds, no hint of disappointment. Instead, his father offered support without hesitation, embodying the selfless nature that had always characterized his actions.

In that moment, Shaunak vowed silently to honour his father's trust. He resolved to be more prudent with his finances and to ensure that his future actions would reflect the depth of gratitude he felt for his parents' sacrifices.

After returning to college, Shaunak made a resolute decision: he would no longer rely on his parents for financial support. Determined to stand on his own, he sought ways to earn a living while continuing his studies. Leveraging his academic strengths, he began offering tuition to juniors. However, the modest income from tutoring barely covered his flat rent, leaving little for other expenses.

In an effort to economize, Shaunak temporarily halted his beloved bike rides. The absence of this passion left a void, leading him to a pivotal realization: he couldn't envision life without riding. This introspection sparked an innovative idea. Drawing from his mechanical aptitude and love for motorcycles, he conceived a plan to buy second-hand bikes, refurbish them, and sell them to fellow college students.

Embracing this venture, Shaunak immersed himself in the world of motorcycle restoration. His dedication paid off; as he honed his skills, his reputation grew, attracting a steady stream of customers. The enterprise flourished, providing him with a substantial income.

One day, Shaunak received a call from Aaryan, a peer renowned for his extensive knowledge of bikes. Aaryan reminisced about the time Shaunak had invited him to inspect a bike he intended to purchase. Now, witnessing Shaunak's thriving business, Aaryan expressed genuine admiration. For Shaunak, this acknowledgment from someone he respected deeply was a profound compliment, validating his hard work and entrepreneurial spirit.

Buoyed by his financial success, Shaunak began embarking on trips, fulfilling dreams that once seemed distant. Each journey symbolized not just a physical adventure, but also his personal growth—from a student grappling with financial constraints to a self-reliant entrepreneur.

As the final year dawned upon Shaunak, the air around him felt different. The once unfamiliar corridors now seemed like an extension of his own world. He had seen it all—friendships that bloomed, dreams that shattered, and the ruthless cycle of ragging that every newcomer was subjected to. He remembered his own days as a junior, the way fear gripped him in those first few weeks, the helplessness in his eyes when seniors dictated absurd orders. But time had changed him. Experience had made him stronger. And unlike many of his batchmates, he refused to let tradition blind his morals.

The new batch had arrived, and with them, the same old cycle began again. Groups of seniors roamed around, searching for freshers to humiliate, to remind them of their "place." Shaunak watched from a distance as his classmates laughed, cheered, and imposed ridiculous tasks on the frightened juniors. It disgusted him. He knew that the justification behind ragging was always the same—"It helps them bond," "We all went through it," "It's a part of college life." But for him, nothing about it seemed right.

Instead of standing with his batchmates, Shaunak chose a different path. He approached the juniors not as a tormentor but as a guide, as someone they could turn to without fear.

"Hey, you don't have to do this," he told a hesitant first-year student who was being forced to dance in front of a group of laughing seniors.

"But... they will trouble me even more if I refuse," the junior whispered, fear evident in his voice.

Shaunak smiled reassuringly. "No, they won't. Not if you have someone standing up for you."

And so, he did. Whenever he found a junior being harassed, he stepped in—not with aggression, but with quiet defiance. His presence alone was enough to make his batchmates back off. At first, they dismissed his behaviour, thinking he was just being difficult. But soon, the murmurs started.

"Why is Shaunak acting like this?"
"Does he think he's better than us?"
"He's ruining the tradition."

Many of his classmates started disliking him. They distanced themselves, called him names, even tried to isolate him. But none of it bothered him. He wasn't here to please them.

As days passed, the juniors began noticing the difference. In Shaunak, they found a mentor rather than a tormentor. They started turning to him for guidance, not out of fear but respect. Whenever they were confused about studies, they sought his advice. When they faced trouble—academic or personal—they reached out to him.

"Shaunak bhaiya, what subjects should we focus on for placements?"
"Sir, how do we prepare for technical interviews?"
"Can you help me with this coding problem?"

Shaunak was always there. Patiently guiding them, ensuring they never felt lost the way he once did. Slowly, he became more than just a senior—he became their anchor. The juniors started admiring him, trusting him more than anyone else in college.

His bond with them grew so strong that even the professors took notice. "It's rare to see a senior so deeply invested in helping his juniors," one of them remarked during a class. "If only more students were like him."

The respect Shaunak earned wasn't forced—it was real. Unlike his classmates, who demanded obedience through fear, he gained loyalty through kindness.

His actions didn't change the entire system overnight, but they ignited a spark. Some of his batchmates, the ones who had once ridiculed him, started questioning their own actions. A few even chose to stand by him, abandoning the toxic culture they had once embraced.

Shaunak proved that respect wasn't something to be taken—it was something to be earned. And as he walked through the same corridors that had once intimidated him as a junior, he knew that his journey wasn't just about surviving college.

It was about changing it.

The placement season had finally arrived, bringing with it an air of nervous excitement. The campus was buzzing with energy—hopes, dreams, and silent prayers filled every corner. Shaunak had worked hard for this moment, but as the first company arrived for recruitment, his confidence wavered.

The selection list was announced. A few names from his class made it. His wasn't one of them.

His heart sank.

"It's just the first one," he told himself, trying to shake off the disappointment. But the sting of rejection lingered.

The second company arrived. Another round of tests, interviews, and hopeful waiting.

Again, his name was not on the list.

The pressure started building. Doubts crept into his mind. Was he not good enough? Had he not studied hard enough? Every rejection felt like a punch to his self-esteem. His classmates, the ones who had secured jobs, were celebrating, sharing their excitement, discussing plans. Shaunak, on the other hand, felt lost.

But he refused to give up.

He doubled down on his efforts, pushing himself harder. Late-night study sessions, practicing mock interviews, revising everything he had learned over the years—he did it all.

And then, the next opportunity came. Another IT company was hiring. Shaunak walked into the interview room, determined but calm. He answered every question with clarity, every challenge with confidence. This time, he wasn't just a student seeking a job—he was a fighter who had learned from his failures.

Days later, the results were announced.

Shaunak's name was on the list.

He had done it.

For a moment, he just stared at the screen, letting the reality sink in. And then, the overwhelming joy hit him. He had secured a job. All the stress, the sleepless nights, the self-doubt—it had all been worth it.

His first thought was of his parents. He grabbed his phone and dialed home.

"Ma... Papa... I got the job!"

There was silence for a second, and then came the laughter, the excitement, the tears of joy from the other end.

"We knew you could do it, beta!" his mother said, her voice full of pride.

His father, who rarely showed emotions, simply said, "I'm proud of you, son."

Shaunak felt a lump in his throat. This moment, this happiness—this was what he had worked for. And now, with the internship money he would earn, he knew exactly what he wanted to do first—buy a special gift for his parents.

As the final days of college approached, Shaunak found himself reflecting on everything he had heard over the years.

"Once you start working, you won't have time for yourself."
"Job life is nothing like college life."
"Enjoy these days, because you'll never get them back."

These words echoed in his mind, and he realized how true they were. He had seen his seniors, once carefree and full of life, now buried under responsibilities, lost in the monotony of corporate life. He didn't want to regret not making the most of his time here.

So, Shaunak decided—he would live his remaining college days to the fullest.

He started cherishing every little moment.

Late-night chai sessions with friends turned into deep conversations about life, dreams, and memories they had built together. Every evening, he would sit on the campus rooftop, watching the sun dip below the horizon, imprinting the sight in his mind as if he could carry it with him into the future.

He laughed louder, played harder, and spent more time with the people who mattered. The canteen food, once a daily complaint, now tasted like nostalgia in every bite. Even the long, boring lectures did not bother him anymore—he knew he would miss them someday.

He helped juniors, played pranks, took endless pictures, and made sure no day was wasted in stress or worry. College was not just a place for education anymore—it was a treasure chest of moments he wanted to fill to the brim.

One night, as he lay on the hostel terrace with his friends, staring at the endless sky, someone asked, "Shaunak, what will you miss the most?"

He smiled, looking at them.

"Everything."

CHAPTER XXIII

Bar Lessons

As Shaunak's final year unfolded, his routine found a new rhythm. The campus was buzzing with excitement—placements, farewell preparations, last-minute adventures—but for him, a small tea stall near the college gate had become his favourite spot.

It was not just about the tea. It was about the quiet moments, the smell of freshly brewed chai mixed with the scent of old newspapers, and the sight of students gathered around, lost in their own worlds.

And then, there was **her**.

Every evening, she came to the stall, a cigarette lazily resting between her fingers, her gaze lost in thought as she sipped her tea. She wasn't like the other students who came in groups, laughing and gossiping. She preferred solitude. A book sometimes accompanied her, sometimes just her thoughts.

Shaunak didn't know when it started, but he found himself looking forward to seeing her. She was a mystery he didn't want to solve—just observe, just admire from a distance.

Days turned into weeks, and the routine remained the same. She came, ordered tea, smoked, and left. Shaunak, sitting at his usual spot, pretended not to notice her, though he always did.

Then, one day, the silence between them finally broke.

She had just bought her cup of tea when a street dog, playful and full of energy, started circling around her. She smiled, trying to shoo it away, but the dog was persistent.

In the chaos, her cup slipped from her hands, and the warm tea splashed onto her shirt.

"Ahh!" she gasped, looking down at the mess.

Shaunak, without thinking, moved towards her. "Hey, wait..." He gently nudged the dog away and looked at her, concerned. "Are you okay?"

She glanced up at him, her surprised expression quickly shifting into a grateful smile. "Yeah, thanks for that. The little guy seems to love attention." She chuckled, shaking her head.

Shaunak smiled back. "Yeah, he's a regular troublemaker around here."

A brief silence followed before he hesitantly asked, "By the way, I see you here often. What's your name?"

She took a moment before replying, as if deciding whether she should answer. "Sanya."

"Sanya," he repeated, as if testing how the name sounded in his voice. "Nice to meet you. I'm Shaunak."

"Nice to meet you too, Shaunak," she said, wiping the tea stain from her shirt with a tissue.

"You want another tea?" he offered.

She looked at him, then at her now-empty hand, and shrugged. "Sure, why not?"

They ordered their tea and stood near the stall, the first real conversation between them unfolding.

"So, what do you do?" Shaunak asked, sipping his tea.

"I'm in my final year, psychology major. And you?"

"Engineering. Also, in my final year."

"Ah, the 'busy people' department," she teased.

He laughed. "Something like that."

Shaunak and Sanya had unknowingly slipped into a routine. Every evening, without needing to confirm, they would find each other at the tea stall. Their conversations had grown deeper—moving from casual talks about college to life, dreams, fears, and everything in between.

And then, one evening, as they stood sipping their tea, Shaunak casually said, "Wanna go for a ride?"

Sanya raised an eyebrow. "A ride?"

"Yeah. Just us, the bike, and the road. No destination, just the journey."

She smirked. "That sounds... interesting. Let's do it."

A few minutes later, she was seated behind him, her arms loosely resting at her sides as the bike roared to life. The cold wind brushed against their faces as they left behind the familiar streets of college and entered the open roads. Shaunak, who usually preferred riding alone, felt something different this time—her presence added a thrill he hadn't known before.

As they rode, Sanya leaned forward slightly and said near his ear, "Let's go somewhere new today. A bar maybe?"

Shaunak stiffened for a second. **A bar?**

He had never been to one before. But—he had lied once. Told her, in a passing conversation, that he drank sometimes. It was stupid, just a casual attempt to seem cooler in front of her. But now, that small lie had turned into a challenge.

"Sure," he said, trying to sound unfazed.

They parked the bike outside a dimly lit bar and restaurant. The neon lights glowed softly, the sound of music and laughter spilling out onto the streets. Shaunak followed Sanya inside, feeling slightly out of place.

The bartender greeted them, handing over the menu. Sanya scanned through it with ease, but Shaunak? He had no idea what to pick.

He glanced at the menu, eyes running over the fancy drink names. His mind raced—**what's cheap, what's**

strong, what's mild? He had no clue.

So, he did the only thing that made sense to him. **He randomly picked the third drink on the list.**

Trying to sound casual, he turned to Sanya. "Uh, this one. You think it's good?"

Sanya glanced at the menu, then at him, her expression unreadable. "Are you sure?"

"Yeah... I mean, I guess?" He tried to maintain his cool.

She smirked. "You have no idea what you just ordered, do you?"

Shaunak hesitated before sighing. "Not really."

She laughed, shaking her head. "Thought so. Here, let me pick for you." She turned to the bartender. "Two whiskey sours."

Shaunak quickly jumped in. "Actually... I'm changing my mind. I'll get the same."

Sanya gave him an amused look. "Good call, rookie."

As the drinks arrived, Shaunak took his first cautious sip. The warmth spread through his throat, unfamiliar yet oddly pleasant. Sanya watched his reaction and chuckled.

"So, your 'experience' with drinking was just talk, huh?"

Shaunak took another sip of the whiskey sour, but his face betrayed him. The taste was sharp, burning in a way he hadn't expected. He forced a smile, trying to act natural, but Sanya noticed.

"You don't like it, do you?" she asked, tilting her head.

"Uh... it's just that I'm not feeling well today," he said quickly, setting the glass down. "Otherwise, I would've been fine with it."

Sanya narrowed her eyes, her smirk returning. "Oh really?" She leaned forward, resting her chin on her hand. "Alright then, Mr. Drinker, name ten alcohol brands."

Shaunak froze. **Shit.**

He racked his brain, but nothing came to him except the most common names—Kingfisher? Old Monk? But what about the rest?

Before he could say anything, Sanya grinned. "I'll be back in a minute. Think about your answer." She got up and walked toward the restroom.

The moment she disappeared, Shaunak snatched his phone and called Aaryan.

"Bro, emergency!" he whispered.

"Emergency? What happened?"

"Just shut up and listen! I need ten alcohol brand names. Fast!"

Aaryan burst out laughing. "Wait... don't tell me. You lied about drinking, didn't you?"

"Yes, yes, now help me before she comes back!"

"Alright, alright. Here—Jack Daniel's, Johnnie Walker, Glenfiddich, Absolut, Bacardi, Jameson, Chivas Regal, Smirnoff, Budweiser, Heineken—"

"Enough! Wait—what's the difference between rum, whiskey, wine, gin, and beer?"

Aaryan sighed. "Okay, quick version. **Rum** is made from sugarcane, **whiskey** is from grains, **wine** is from fermented grapes, **gin** has a strong juniper flavor, and **beer** is the lightest of them all—brewed from barley."

Shaunak nodded furiously, committing everything to memory. "Got it. You're a lifesaver."

"Remember, bro—fake confidence sells."

As soon as he hung up, Sanya returned, wiping her hands. "Alright," she said, sitting back down. "Let's hear it. Ten alcohol brands."

Shaunak leaned back, suddenly relaxed. "Easy. Jack Daniel's, Johnnie Walker, Glenfiddich, Absolut, Bacardi, Jameson, Chivas Regal, Smirnoff, Budweiser, and

Heineken."

Sanya raised an eyebrow. "Hmm... not bad. And what's your go-to drink?"

He smirked. "Depends on the occasion. Whiskey for serious nights, rum when I want something smooth, wine for class, gin when I feel fancy, and beer for casual chilling."

Sanya stared at him for a moment, then laughed. "Well, well. Looks like you *do* know your drinks."

Shaunak simply shrugged, sipping his drink with new confidence. Inside, he was thanking Aaryan a thousand times.

Sanya leaned in, clearly impressed. "You're full of surprises, Shaunak."

He smirked. "You have no idea."

Shaunak and Sanya's meetings became a ritual. What started as casual tea stall encounters had evolved into something more—bike rides, late-night conversations, and bar visits where they explored different drinks together. With every sip, he felt like he was stepping into a world he had never known, a world she had opened for him.

Money never mattered to him in those moments. The stipend from his internship, the little savings he had—he spent it all on new experiences. New bars, new drinks, new adventures. Sanya always had a suggestion, and Shaunak never refused. It felt thrilling—being in her world, feeling like he belonged there.

But then, one evening, she didn't show up.

At first, he thought maybe she was busy. Maybe she had other plans. But as he walked past another café near campus, he saw her. She was sitting at a table, laughing, her fingers playfully twirling a cigarette. And across from her sat a guy—a stranger.

Shaunak stopped in his tracks.

His heart pounded. He wanted to look away, but he couldn't.

The next time they met, he couldn't hold back. "Who was that guy?" he asked, trying to sound casual, though his voice betrayed him.

Sanya raised an eyebrow, exhaling a cloud of smoke. "And who the hell are you to ask?"

Shaunak felt like someone had just punched him in the chest.

For a moment, he stood there, waiting—hoping she would say something else, something that would make it better. But she did not. She just looked at him, as if he were no one special.

That was the last time he saw her.

At first, he avoided the tea stall. Then, he stopped riding past the café where he had seen her. His phone remained silent—no messages, no missed calls.

But the bars?

They remained.

Now, instead of sitting across from Sanya, he sat alone. Instead of sharing drinks, he tasted them one by one, each night bringing a new experiment.

Whiskey. Rum. Vodka. Gin. Wine.

At first, he told himself it was just curiosity. He was just experiencing new things—**for himself this time**. But deep down, he knew the truth.

He was not drinking for the experience anymore.

He was drinking to forget.

CHAPTER XXIV

The Roads That Lead to Her

Shaunak had always believed that life was meant to be shared. The thrill of a late-night bike ride, the excitement of discovering a new place, the simple joy of watching the sun melt into the horizon—none of it felt complete without someone to talk to about it.

For a while, he thought Sanya was that person. But she wasn't.

Now, as he rode alone through the city streets, the wind whispering past him, he felt the absence of something—or someone. He no longer stopped by the tea stall, and the bars no longer held the same charm. He had tasted almost every drink on the menu, yet none could fill the emptiness that followed him home each night.

It wasn't about alcohol anymore. It was about conversations. About a voice at the other end of the day, asking, *"How was your ride?"* or *"What did you see today?"* He wanted someone to share in his adventures, someone who wouldn't disappear with the night.

Deep inside, he held on to a quiet hope.

Maybe she was out there.

His soulmate. The person who would listen when he spoke about the little things, who would hold onto his stories as if they were her own. The one who wouldn't leave him wondering where he stood.

And maybe—just maybe—he hadn't found her yet because she wasn't here.

A new chapter was waiting. His job offer meant moving to another state, another city. And while the thought of leaving behind his college life felt bittersweet, a part of him was ready.

Maybe the roads there would lead him to her.

The campus, once bustling with laughter and life, now carried a strange silence. Farewell day had arrived—a day everyone had been anticipating yet secretly dreading.

Shaunak walked through the decorated hall, watching his classmates embrace, click endless pictures, and scribble heartfelt messages on each other's shirts. Some were holding back tears, others were letting them flow freely.

He had thought he would feel nothing. After all, wasn't he already prepared to leave? He had his job lined up, a new city waiting for him, a new life to begin. But standing there, watching his friends share their last moments together, a lump formed in his throat.

Then, he saw her.

Shraddha.

She was making her way toward him, holding a marker in one hand and a smile on her lips. Shaunak had almost forgotten—she was the first person he had spoken to when he entered college. The first friend he made. And the first girl he had secretly liked.

"Hey," she said, handing him the marker. "Write something on my shirt?"

Shaunak took it, pausing for a second before writing:

"You were my first friend in college... and my first crush as well. All the best for your future."

He stepped back, handing the marker to her. She glanced at what he had written and smiled softly before writing something on his shirt too.

"No matter where life takes you, always stay the same crazy dreamer. Wishing you all the success in the world!"

They looked at each other, as if realizing how much time had slipped away between them. There was so much they had never said, so many moments they had left unspoken. But maybe, in this small exchange of words, everything was understood.

The night went on—tears, laughter, and endless goodbyes. Everyone knew the truth they didn't want to admit: they wouldn't meet as often anymore. Life would take them in different directions, and the memories they had created here would soon become stories to be reminisced about in phone calls and reunions.

As Shaunak walked out of the farewell hall, his heart felt heavier than he had expected.

This chapter was ending.

The morning of departure arrived, but Shaunak wasn't ready.

He stood in his almost-empty hostel room, staring at the walls that had witnessed his transformation—from a nervous first-year student to the man he was today. Everything he had lived through in the past four years came rushing back—his mistakes, his adventures, his heartbreaks, and his friendships.

He had walked into this college as a naive boy, and now he was leaving as someone entirely different.

The college itself never had the best reputation. People outside called it just another average institute, but to him, it had been so much more. It had been his battlefield, his playground, his home. It had broken him and rebuilt him in ways he never imagined.

As he picked up his bag, ready to step out, his juniors started arriving one by one. They had heard he was leaving today.

"Shaunak bhaiya, kaise rahenge aapke bina?" one of them asked.

Another one patted him on the back. "Aapne jo sikhaya hai, woh yaad rahega hamesha."

A small, proud smile formed on his face. He had entered this college as just another student, but he was leaving with a legacy. The respect of his juniors, the bond he had built with them—this was his real achievement.

Then, there was the bike. His second love after writing.

That old, rugged machine had been a part of his best memories—late-night rides, college trips, reckless races, and moments of solitude when only the road understood him. He ran his fingers over the handlebar, feeling a pang of attachment.

But he knew he couldn't take it home. If his parents found out he had secretly bought a bike during college, they'd be furious.

So, he made a decision.

He turned to one of his juniors, a guy who had always looked up to him. "Take it," Shaunak said, tossing him the keys.

The junior's eyes widened. "Bhaiya... paise toh—"

"Shut up," Shaunak chuckled. "This isn't a deal. It's a memory. Keep it, ride it well."

As he walked toward the college gate, pulling his suitcase along, he took one last glance at everything—the hostel, the classrooms, the canteen, the tea stall where so many of his stories had begun.

Even the memories of ragging, which once seemed so cruel, now felt like nothing more than harmless fun.

The place that had once scared him, that had challenged him, had now become a part of him.

He wiped his eyes quickly before anyone could notice.

Shaunak had always thought that getting a job would bring him relief. That once he secured an offer, his worries would disappear, and he would finally be at peace.

But now, sitting in his room with three or four offer letters in front of him, he felt anything but relieved.

He had worked hard for this, spent sleepless nights preparing for interviews, handled the stress of rejection, and now, when he had multiple options, he felt stuck.

Which one should he choose?

He knew he couldn't sit idle. His college days were over, and now, life wouldn't be as forgiving. **Without money, survival was impossible.** Rent, food, bills—everything needed cash. And as much as he hated the idea of working all day, every day, he had no other choice.

But something inside him felt restless. He knew himself too well. He wasn't built for a life where he sat in front of a screen for hours, doing the same thing every day. The thought of spending weeks, months, and years in a routine job felt suffocating.

Yet, reality didn't care about feelings.

He exhaled, rubbing his forehead. *This is just the beginning*, he told himself.

He had to start somewhere. Maybe, just maybe, this wasn't his destination—just a stepping stone.

With that thought, he picked up one of the offer letters.

Shaunak had made up his mind.

Among the multiple job offers, he deliberately chose the one farthest from his hometown. He knew this decision wouldn't sit well with his parents—they had wanted him to stay close, to pick a job nearby so that home was never too far. But Shaunak had different plans.

He wasn't just chasing a career; he was chasing experiences. He wanted to see different cities, meet new people, and **live** beyond the boundaries he had known all his life. This job was his ticket to exploring the rest of the country.

The first few days were overwhelming—new city, new office, new people. He was still adjusting when, one afternoon, his phone rang.

The number on the screen was unfamiliar.

"Hello?" he answered, his tone professional, assuming it was a work-related call.

"Hi, is this Shaunak?" a female voice asked.

"Yes, speaking."

"I'm calling regarding the new project that has been assigned to us...My name is Kavya"

Shaunak straightened up. *Must be someone from the HR team or maybe a teammate from another branch,* he thought. He replied with formality and respect, listening carefully.

But then, something unexpected happened.

The girl on the other end suddenly switched to her native language. The words flowed effortlessly from her, but to Shaunak, they meant nothing.

He hesitated, then smiled slightly. "Uhh... I'm sorry, but I don't understand. Could you please speak in English?"

There was silence for a moment, followed by a soft laugh. "Oh! I thought you might know my language," she said, switching back.

He chuckled. "Not yet. But maybe you can teach me?"

They talked for a few more minutes, discussing the project briefly before drifting into casual conversation. It was nothing too personal, just small talk—where she was from, how long she had been working, and the usual workplace pleasantries.

And then, the call ended.

Shaunak was still on his way home, walking down a busy street, when he realized something strange—he was smiling.

He had no idea why.

It was just a call, just another voice on the phone. But for some reason, hearing her speak, listening to her laughter—it had left a warmth inside him. It felt as though, for those few minutes, something inside him had healed without him even realizing it was broken.

As he put his phone back in his pocket, he shook his head, still smiling to himself.

CHAPTER XXV

Because Sometimes, You Just Know

Shaunak had never been the kind of person to buy gifts impulsively. But that day, something felt different.

It was a late evening, and he was out on one of his usual rides. The cool breeze hit his face as he navigated through the narrow lanes of the city, lost in his own thoughts. That's when he passed by a small roadside jewellery stall.

His eyes fell on a pair of silver **jhumkas**—delicate, intricate, with tiny bells that would probably make a soft, melodious sound when worn. He didn't know why, but he stopped his bike.

Without a second thought, he picked them up.

"Kisi ke liye le rahe ho?" the shopkeeper asked, smiling knowingly.

Shaunak hesitated for a second before nodding. He didn't explain that he hadn't even seen her yet. That he had only spoken to her once, through a phone call. That she was just a voice to him—yet, for some reason, that voice had lingered in his mind.

He paid for the earrings and, before leaving, did something even he found strange—he asked the shopkeeper to **gift wrap** them.

"Bhaiya, wrap kar do acche se. Aise hi dena ajeeb lagega."

As the shopkeeper carefully wrapped the tiny box in soft pink paper, Shaunak wondered—**what would she think when he gave it to her?**

Would she find it sweet? Or would she think it was too much, too soon?

Would she be surprised that someone who hadn't even seen her had thought of buying her something?

Or maybe... maybe she wouldn't take it at all.

For a moment, doubt crept in. *Am I being foolish?* he asked himself.

But as he took the neatly wrapped box in his hands, he smiled. It didn't matter.

He had bought the jhumka not out of expectation, but because, for the first time in a long while, something had felt right.

The day was finally here.

Shaunak had packed his bags, said his goodbyes, and was now seated by the window of a train heading toward his new life. The rhythmic clatter of the wheels against the tracks filled the silence around him, but his mind was far from quiet.

He stared outside, watching familiar landscapes fade into the distance. The trees, the small tea stalls, the stations with names he had known since childhood—all of them slowly disappearing behind him.

Ahead lay the unknown. A city he had never lived in, a workplace he had never seen, and people he had never met.

What will it be like? he wondered.

Would his colleagues be friendly? Would he be able to make new friends as easily as he did in college? Would he enjoy his work, or would he end up counting hours every day, waiting for the evening to arrive?

A part of him was excited—the thrill of a fresh start, of stepping into a world where no one knew him yet. A chance to reinvent himself.

But another part of him was anxious.

He had no idea about this city. He hadn't even visited once before deciding to move there. He didn't know its streets, its culture, or even where he would find the best tea stall to sit and think, like he used to in college.

Would he get lost in this crowd? Or would he find his place?

He let out a deep breath, shaking his head at his own thoughts. There was no point overthinking. Whatever awaited him, he would figure it out—just like he always had.

As the train raced forward, so did time. The familiar was now behind him, and the unknown was just a few hours away.

Shaunak stepped into the towering glass building of his new company, his heart pounding with a mix of excitement and nervousness. The lobby was filled with fresh faces—new joinees just like him, all dressed in crisp formals, carrying the same uncertainty in their eyes.

For a moment, he felt at ease. *I'm not alone in this*, he thought.

But that comfort didn't last long.

As the induction began, he was introduced to the **IT work culture**—something he had only heard about but never truly experienced. The long hours, the endless meetings, the deadlines that seemed to breathe down everyone's necks. The structured, mechanical nature of it all felt suffocating.

He saw employees glued to their screens, barely looking up. Some seemed stressed, some indifferent, and very few looked genuinely happy.

The realization hit him hard.

Is this what my life is going to be now?

A cold wave of panic rushed through him. His breath became shallow, his hands slightly sweaty. The walls of the office seemed to close in on him. **This wasn't him.** He wasn't made for a life where each day looked the same, where creativity took a backseat, and where people only spoke in the language of emails and reports.

He had spent his college days living freely, riding across cities, meeting people, experiencing life. But now, everything looked... robotic.

For the first time since accepting the offer, he **questioned his decision.**

Would he be able to survive in this environment? Or would this place slowly take away the parts of him that made him who he was?

He closed his eyes for a second, took a deep breath, and reminded himself—**this is just the beginning.** Maybe it would not be as bad as it seemed. Maybe he just needed time to adjust.

By the time Shaunak stepped out of the office on his first day, he felt like he had been drained of all energy. His back ached from sitting too long, his mind was numb from staring at screens, and his heart—well, his heart wasn't in it at all.

This wasn't what he had imagined.

The long hours, the constant pressure, the endless flow of emails—it all felt suffocating. He had always thought work would be about learning, exploring, and growing. But instead, it felt like being stuck in a loop, where every second stretched longer than the last.

There was, however, **one thing** that made it all a little bearable.

The **free tea and coffee.**

The first time he found out about it, he almost laughed. *At least they understand caffeine is necessary for survival,* he thought.

So, every time he completed even the smallest task—whether it was setting up his email or submitting a basic report—he rewarded himself with a trip to the **cafeteria.**

Tea breaks became his **escape.**

The warmth of the cup in his hands, the aroma of freshly brewed coffee, the sight of other employees just as tired as him—these little moments felt like stolen breaths in an otherwise suffocating day.

Soon, it became a habit. Finish a task? Tea. Feeling exhausted? Tea. Need a reason to leave the desk? Tea.

At one point, he wondered if the HR team kept track of how many cups an employee took in a day. If they did, his numbers would probably be **record-breaking.**

He smiled to himself as he sipped his fifth cup for the day.

Maybe work wasn't as exciting as he had hoped.

But at least, for now, there was **tea.**

The buzzing office, the flood of new faces, the monotony of work—Shaunak was slowly getting used to it. Or at least, he was trying to.

But then, one ordinary day turned into something unexpected.

As he lazily sipped his tea in the cafeteria, he noticed **her.**

A girl walking through the office corridor, her steps slightly unsteady, as if she had a limp. At first, he simply wondered—*Did she hurt herself?*

But then, his eyes lingered a little longer.

Kavya was beautiful. Not in the overly perfect way people imagined, but in a way that felt **real.** The kind of beauty that didn't need effort, that just existed effortlessly.

Something inside him shifted.

And in that very moment, as absurd as it sounded—**he knew.**

She was the one.

His soulmate.

The thought hit him so suddenly that he almost laughed at himself. He didn't even know her name. They had never spoken in person. The only connection between them was that one phone call—where she had spoken in a language he didn't understand, and he had asked her to switch to English.

But **logic had no place here.**

He had spent years wondering if he would ever find someone who truly belonged to him. Someone who would make his rides feel less lonely, someone he could talk to at the end of the day.

And now, just by looking at her, **he decided.**

He was not going to let her go.

Not without knowing her.

Not without trying.

Even if they hadn't exchanged a single glance yet—even if she didn't know he existed—**he had already made up his mind.**

Shaunak was sitting alone in the cafeteria, a cup of tea resting between his hands. He had been making this place his escape ever since joining, and today was no different.

Except today, something changed.

He was lost in thought, staring at the steam rising from his cup when he noticed someone approaching. He didn't need to look up to know who it was—**her.**

The same girl he had seen earlier. The girl whose presence had stirred something deep inside him.

And now, she was walking toward **him.**

Before he could even process what was happening, she sat down across from him, as if it was the most natural thing in the world.

"Why are you drinking tea alone?" she asked, her voice light and curious.

Shaunak blinked, caught off guard. For a moment, he forgot how to react.

Here she was, on **her first day**, surrounded by a group of friends, laughter and conversation filling the air around her. And yet, she had chosen to come and sit **with him.**

It felt... surreal.

The cafeteria noise seemed to fade as an unspoken energy filled the space between them.

The vibe was magical.

It wasn't just a simple question—it was an invitation, a moment that felt like the beginning of something **unexpected, yet inevitable.**

Shaunak, who had always struggled to put emotions into words, only smiled before answering.

"Because sometimes, tea tastes better in silence."

Kavya raised an eyebrow, intrigued, before taking a sip of her own.

Work had quickly become a cycle of exhaustion for Shaunak. Some days were manageable, but others felt like an endless battle—pressure, deadlines, mistakes, and the occasional harsh words from seniors.

On those days, when everything seemed **rubbish**, there was only one person who made it better.

Her.

She was always the first to call.

"What happened today?" she'd ask, her voice filled with concern.

At first, he found it strange. He wasn't used to people checking on him like this. But with her, it felt natural—like she just knew when he needed to talk.

"It's okay," she would say whenever he vented about the workplace pressure. *"Sometimes, you'll have to hear things you don't like. It's part of the job. Just learn from it and move on."*

She spoke as if she had mastered the art of handling criticism.

But soon, Shaunak realized—**she was just like him.**

Because when it was **her turn** to face those same harsh words at work, she wouldn't brush it off.

Instead, she would break down.

He had seen it—the way her strong front would crumble the moment things got too overwhelming. The way her voice would shake, and she'd struggle to hold back tears.

She was **different.**

Not like the others, who simply moved on without a second thought. She felt things deeply, just like he did.

And that's what made her **special.**

Not just special—**very, very special.**

At first, she was a mystery.

She never opened up easily, never shared too much about herself. Shaunak had noticed it early on—how she would listen more than she spoke, how she carefully chose her words, never revealing too much too soon.

But when she **did** start speaking, when she finally let her guard down—**she never stopped.**

She spoke in stories.

About her childhood, about the little moments that shaped her, about her dreams, her fears, the things that made her laugh, and the ones that made her cry.

And Shaunak?

He loved every word.

He loved the way she talked about her simple life with so much warmth, as if every ordinary moment had its own magic.

She wasn't the most intelligent person he had met, and she never pretended to be. But she was **confident.**

Fearless in her own way.

She never hesitated to speak her mind, never cared about what people thought. And that—more than anything—was what made her stand out.

She wasn't trying to impress anyone.

She was just **herself.**

And to Shaunak, that was **more than enough.**

CHAPTER XXVI

Half Conversations and Full Cups

He started grooming himself—trimming his beard, styling his hair, even choosing his outfits with more thought than before. He swapped his casual slang for more refined words, tried to sound more decent, more polished.

He didn't know when it had happened, but he knew **why.**

Her.

She wasn't someone who judged people for their habits, but still—he wanted to be the best version of himself around her. He wanted her to see him as **someone worth noticing.**

But habits were hard to break.

One evening, after a long and exhausting day at work, Shaunak stepped outside the office campus, cigarette in hand. The stress, the routine, the endless pressure—it all faded for a few minutes with every drag he took.

But then, as he exhaled a cloud of smoke, he saw **her.**

She had just arrived at the tea stall, casually looking around.

His heart skipped a beat.

Damn!

Panic rushed through him as he quickly tried to hide the cigarette behind his back, tossing it away when she wasn't looking.

He straightened himself, trying to act normal. He didn't want her to think he was **just another guy who smoked after work.**

But then, something unexpected happened.

She checked her pocket, pulled out a cigarette pack, and calmly lit one for **herself.**

And then, without hesitation, she lit **another one.**

For him.

Shaunak stood frozen, watching her take a slow drag before extending the second cigarette toward him.

He had no idea she smoked.

He had spent so much time trying to hide his habits, trying to change himself for her. And here she was—completely unbothered, **completely herself.**

He looked at the cigarette in her hand, then at her face.

And in that moment, he realized—maybe he didn't have to try so hard.

Maybe she would have liked him **just as he was.**

It had become a pattern—one he didn't notice at first.

Every time Shaunak asked her to join him for tea in the office canteen, her first answer was always a "**No.**"

But then, after a few minutes, she would change her mind.

"Fine, let's go. But not here. Let's go to the other canteen."

Shaunak never questioned it in the beginning. Maybe she just liked the other canteen better? Maybe the tea there was stronger? He didn't think much of it.

But as days passed, he started to notice—she **always** did this. She never agreed to sit in the main canteen where most employees gathered. She always dragged him somewhere quieter, somewhere **less crowded.**

It felt... strange.

One day, curiosity got the best of him.

"Why do you always do this?" he asked as they walked to the other canteen. *"Why can't we just sit there like everyone else?"*

She hesitated for a moment, then sighed.

"There are people from my village in that canteen," she admitted, keeping her voice low. *"If they see me sitting with you every day, they'll start gossiping. And then, those rumors will spread back home."*

Shaunak stopped walking.

He looked at her, trying to process what she had just said.

Rumors? About **what?** They were just having tea. Just two colleagues taking a break from work.

But in her world, it wasn't that simple.

For her, even **sharing tea with a guy** in a public space could turn into whispers, which would travel miles back to her village. People would twist the story, add their own versions, and suddenly, it wouldn't be just **tea** anymore.

Shaunak had never thought about things like that before.

For him, friendships were effortless. Simple. But for her, every interaction in public came with **consequences.**

He didn't say much after that. Just nodded, following her to the quieter canteen, understanding a little more about her world.

That evening, as they sipped tea in their usual quiet canteen, Shaunak noticed a strange look in her eyes—a hesitation, as if there was something more she wanted to say but wasn't sure if she should.

He waited, giving her space. And then, after a long pause, she finally spoke.

"There's something you should know."

Her voice was softer than usual, almost cautious.

"I'm not allowed to talk to someone on the phone at midnight."

Shaunak frowned. *"What do you mean?"*

She looked away, staring at her cup, as if searching for the right words. *"My family is... strict. They don't like the idea of me talking to anyone late at night. Sometimes, they even call me randomly—just to check if I'm on another call. Just to make sure I'm home."*

Shaunak blinked, trying to process it.

"Wait, they actually call to check on you?"

She nodded. *"Yes. If my phone is busy, they'll keep calling until I pick up. And if I don't answer, they start asking questions. Where was I? Who was I talking to? Why was my phone engaged?"*

There was no anger in her voice. No rebellion. Just... acceptance.

As if she had long ago stopped questioning it.

Shaunak felt something stir inside him—a quiet frustration.

He had always lived life on his own terms. He had made his own decisions, broken rules when he wanted, faced the consequences without answering to anyone.

But **her world was different.**

Her freedom had limits.

Her choices weren't just hers to make.

For a moment, he wanted to say something. Tell her it wasn't fair. Tell her that she had every right to live her life without being monitored like that. But he stopped himself.

She already knew that.

And yet, she had learned to live within those boundaries.

Shaunak looked at her, and for the first time, he truly saw her—not just the confident girl who spoke in stories but someone carrying an invisible weight on her shoulders.

He wanted to tell her that she deserved **more.**

But instead, he just sat there, sipping his tea, listening to her words, feeling an unfamiliar ache in his chest.

That evening, as they sat in their usual quiet spot, Shaunak noticed that she wasn't her usual self. She stirred her tea absentmindedly, her eyes lost in thought.

"What happened?" he asked gently.

She let out a deep sigh. *"There's something else I never told you."*

Shaunak leaned in, sensing the weight in her voice.

"I have a sister. She's strict too. Maybe even stricter than my parents."

He raised an eyebrow. *"Strict? In what way?"*

She hesitated for a moment, as if debating whether to say it out loud. And then, in a quiet voice, she continued, *"Once, she caught me chatting with a boy."*

Shaunak's hands froze around his cup.

"And?" he asked, already sensing that the rest of the story wasn't going to be pleasant.

She exhaled slowly. *"She beat me."*

The words were simple. But the way she said them—so matter-of-factly, as if it was just another incident, something normal—made Shaunak's stomach twist.

"She... hit you?"

"Yes." She nodded. *"And then she told my family."*

Shaunak clenched his jaw. He wanted to say something, to ask her **why** she let them treat her that way. But looking at her, he knew she had no choice.

This wasn't about **right or wrong.**

It was about **control.**

She had grown up in a world where every interaction was monitored, where even a simple conversation with a boy was seen as something *wrong.*

Where her own sister, instead of protecting her, became an enforcer of those rules.

Shaunak felt something tighten in his chest.

She was sitting in front of him, drinking tea as if nothing had happened. As if this was normal. As if this was **life.**

And maybe, for her, it was.

For the first time, he truly realized—she wasn't just fighting society. She was fighting her **own family.**

And yet, she still smiled. She still laughed. She still lived.

Shaunak looked at her with a strange sense of admiration and sadness.

She had been caged for so long, and yet she had learned to spread her wings in whatever little space she had.

After spending countless days in the new city, drowning in work, and adjusting to the corporate life, Shaunak finally decided—it was time to go home.

He had been away for too long. The walls of his room back home, the familiar streets, the old tea stalls where he had spent hours with friends—he missed all of it.

The moment he booked his tickets, the first person he thought of was **her.**

She was the only person in this city who made him feel like he belonged.

That evening, as they sat together with their usual cups of tea, he casually mentioned his plan.

"I'm going home for a few days."

She was mid-sip when she stopped. A slight frown appeared on her face. *"For how long?"*

"A week, maybe more."

There was silence. She kept stirring her tea, not looking up.

Then, in a voice that sounded lighter than she probably felt, she said, *"And what am I supposed to do without you?"*

Shaunak chuckled. *"What do you mean? You have so many friends."*

She rolled her eyes. *"Friends? Maybe. But none of them are as stupid as you when it comes to tea."*

He smirked, but before he could say anything, she continued, *"You know, I never used to drink so much tea before. But after meeting you, I don't even realize how many cups I have in a day."*

Shaunak smiled. *"Addicted, huh?"*

"Maybe." She took another sip and looked away. *"But now, I'll have to go alone."*

There was something in her voice—something that made Shaunak pause.

A kind of loneliness she rarely showed.

She wasn't just talking about **tea.**

She was talking about those stolen moments, the conversations, the comfort of having someone who just *gets* you.

"I'll be back soon," he said.

She nodded, but it didn't feel convincing.

As they finished their tea, she looked at him and said, *"Before you leave, meet me once. Just for a little while."*

The day before leaving, Shaunak felt an odd heaviness in his heart.

It was just a short trip home, but for some reason, he wanted to see **her** one last time before he left.

So, casually, he asked, *"Let's meet once before I go. Just a normal coffee, nothing fancy."*

She agreed.

That evening, as she walked toward him, he couldn't help but smile. She was dressed simply, but something about the way she carried herself made her stand out.

They went to a small café, the kind that smelled of freshly brewed coffee and soft conversations.

Sitting across from her, Shaunak found himself paying more attention to the way she spoke, the way she played with the coffee stirrer absentmindedly, the way her eyes sparkled when she talked about things that excited her.

They talked about everything—their childhood, the dreams they once had, the silly things that made them laugh.

Shaunak listened, completely absorbed.

He had always found her interesting, but today, **she felt different**.

Maybe it was because he knew he wouldn't see her for a while. Or maybe it was because, for the first time, he was truly seeing her—not just as a friend, but as someone who had unknowingly become a part of his daily life.

After coffee, neither of them wanted to leave just yet. So they started walking, letting the evening breeze guide them.

The streets were quiet, with only the occasional sound of distant traffic.

They walked side by side, their words flowing effortlessly.

Shaunak, usually hesitant to open up, found himself talking freely—about his fears, his doubts, his dreams. And she listened, really listened, in a way no one else ever had.

At one point, she laughed at something he said, and the sound of it made him feel warm inside.

For him, this wasn't just a conversation.

This was **something more**.

A moment he knew he would replay in his mind long after he left.

As the night grew darker, they finally stopped near her apartment.

She turned to him and smiled. *"So, when are you coming back?"*

"Soon," Shaunak said, though he wasn't sure if it was soon enough.

She nodded, not saying much.

But before walking away, she looked at him once more and said, *"Safe travels, tea addict."*

Shaunak chuckled.

As he watched her disappear into the building, he realized something—

This was the first time in his life he wished he wasn't going home.

Shaunak had been waiting for this trip home for so long. The familiar streets, the scent of his mother's cooking, the comfort of his old bed—everything was exactly the same.

And yet, something was different.

Something was *missing.*

He couldn't explain it, but no matter how much he tried to enjoy his time at home, there was a strange emptiness lingering inside him.

At first, he thought it was just the usual feeling of transition—from work life to home life. But as the days passed, he realized what was bothering him.

It wasn't about home.

It was about **her.**

He had unknowingly built a new routine, a new comfort, and she had become a part of it.

Back in his work city, seeing her, having tea together, sharing little moments—those things had made his days better. And now that she wasn't around, he felt the absence more than he had expected.

But Shaunak had always been the kind of person who didn't openly express his emotions. He had an image of being independent, someone who didn't *need* anyone. So, even though he thought about her often, he didn't call her too much.

He didn't want to seem *too attached.*

However, she surprised him.

She called.

The first time, it was just a casual check-in. *"Hey, how's home treating you?"*

They talked, not for too long, but just enough for him to hear her voice.

And that small conversation changed everything.

For the rest of the day, he found himself *waiting*—waiting for the next call, waiting for the next message, waiting for some sign from her.

And she did text.

Not all the time, not constantly, but just enough to keep the connection alive.

And when she did, Shaunak replied almost instantly, even though he tried to play it cool.

He told himself it was nothing. Just a habit. Just something to pass the time.

But deep down, he knew.

He wasn't just missing his work city.

He was missing **her.**

CHAPTER XXVII

You Were Never Just a Colleague

The next morning, as Shaunak was lazily scrolling through his phone, it rang.

Her name flashed on the screen.

He felt an unexpected rush of excitement but picked up the call in his usual calm tone.

"Hello?"

"When are you coming back?" she asked, cutting straight to the point.

Shaunak smirked, leaning back on his chair. *"What will I do there alone? There's no one for me in that city anyway."* His voice carried a hint of sarcasm, but he wanted to see what she would say.

She went silent for a second. Then, in the same sarcastic tone, she replied, *"You're right. There is no one there for you. So don't come back."*

Shaunak expected a playful comeback, maybe a teasing remark, but her words hit differently.

He chuckled, pretending not to care, but as soon as the call ended, he sat there, staring at the blank screen.

Her words echoed in his mind.

"There's no one there for you."

Was she testing him? Did she mean it?

And why did it bother him so much?

The thought of staying home suddenly felt unbearable.

He didn't want to overthink it. He didn't want to sit there for days wondering what she truly meant.

So, without hesitation, he picked up his phone again—this time to book a flight back.

No calls, no messages.

This time, he would surprise her.

Shaunak had imagined the moment a hundred times in his head—her reaction, her smile, the way her eyes would light up with surprise. He had it all planned.

As soon as he landed, he didn't waste a second. He went straight to their usual tea shop, the place where they had shared countless cups of tea and endless conversations.

And there she was.

Sitting in her usual spot, her fingers wrapped around a steaming cup, lost in thought.

He took a deep breath and walked straight up to her.

"Missed me?" he said casually, as if he had never left.

She looked up, startled. For a split second, her expression was unreadable—shock, confusion, maybe even a hint of happiness.

"You—" she started but stopped, trying to process his sudden presence.

Shaunak grinned. He wasn't done with his surprises yet.

Just as she was about to say something, the tea shop owner pressed *play* on the speaker.

Her favorite song began playing softly in the background.

She turned to look at the shop owner, then back at Shaunak, narrowing her eyes. *"Did you...?"*

He just smirked.

Before she could respond, he pulled out a small box from his pocket and handed it to her.

"Here. I made these for you," he said, his voice filled with mischief.

She raised an eyebrow as she opened the box, revealing neatly packed homemade chocolates.

"You made these?" she asked skeptically.

"Of course," he lied smoothly, watching her expression.

She picked up a piece and took a small bite. The moment the flavor melted in her mouth, she smiled. *"This tastes like..."*

Shaunak held his breath.

"...something a mother would make."

His smirk faltered for a second.

She looked at him, amused. *"Did you really make this?"*

He cleared his throat, trying to keep up the act. *"Obviously. Why would I lie?"*

She laughed, shaking her head. *"Your mom made these, didn't she?"*

Shaunak sighed, defeated. *"Fine, you caught me. But the intention was mine."*

She smiled, looking down at the chocolates, then back at him.

"You're ridiculous."

"I know."

For a moment, neither of them spoke. The music played softly in the background, the tea shop buzzed with life, but in that moment, it felt like they were in their own little world.

After returning, life slipped back into its familiar rhythm. The tea shop became their regular escape after exhausting workdays.

Shaunak began to notice a pattern—every time they sat together, their conversations naturally drifted toward their teammates. Complaints, frustrations, little office dramas. She had a way of expressing her annoyance that made even workplace struggles sound amusing.

"You won't believe what happened today," she would start, and he would lean in, pretending to be shocked, even though he already knew that some teammate must have

done something idiotic again.

Shaunak enjoyed these conversations. But deep down, he didn't want to be just another person nodding along. He didn't want to seem dumb in her eyes.

So, he started learning.

Not for himself, not to get ahead in his career, but for *her*.

He studied everything he could about their work—new tools, problem-solving techniques, even things that weren't part of his job role. Every time she seemed frustrated, he would jump in with a solution.

"Try doing this, it might help."

"If that's the issue, maybe tweak this setting?"

At first, she was surprised. Then, she started relying on him. Whenever she got stuck, she instinctively turned to Shaunak.

And he loved it.

But in between all this, something else grew inside him—a quiet resentment toward his job.

Every single minute at work felt like a weight on his chest. The never-ending tasks, the suffocating deadlines, the robotic routine. He often caught himself staring at the clock, counting hours, thinking— *Is this it? Is this how I'm going to spend my life?*

"I swear, I can't do this anymore," he would say at least once a day.

Yet, at the end of the month, the salary notification would pop up on his phone.

Every evening, as the office lights dimmed and exhaustion settled in, Shaunak and she found themselves at the same old tea shop. With cups of steaming chai in hand, they would lean back, letting the cool breeze wash over them, and talk about everything—work, dreams, and the meaning of life.

"One day, we'll quit this job and start our own thing," she would say, stirring her tea absentmindedly.

"Of course," Shaunak would nod. *"A startup where we won't have bosses breathing down our necks. Where we work because we want to, not because we have to."*

It became their ritual. Each day, they would fuel their conversations with new ideas.

"What should we start?" one of them would ask.

"Something meaningful," the other would reply.

But neither of them had a concrete plan. It wasn't about that, really. It was about hope. The mere idea that *one day* they could break free from this monotonous corporate life was enough to keep them going.

Between sips of tea, their conversations often drifted into philosophy.

"You ever wonder why people chase money so much?" she once asked.

"Because life is expensive," Shaunak smirked.

She rolled her eyes. *"No, but seriously. Does it really matter? Will we ever be happy even if we have enough?"*

"Maybe happiness isn't about having, but about doing something that doesn't feel like a burden."

"Then let's find that thing," she smiled.

Every day, new thoughts, new perspectives, and new plans emerged. They knew their startup dreams were just words for now, but those words gave them a reason to wake up and work, a reason to believe that something better awaited them.

One evening, as Shaunak walked into the office, he noticed something unusual—her seat was empty. She was never late. A strange uneasiness crept in. He hesitated for a moment before picking up his phone and calling her.

Her voice on the other end was weak. *"I'm not feeling well. Just a little fever,"* she said.

"Have you eaten?" he asked.

"Not hungry," she replied lazily.

That was enough for Shaunak to worry. He knew she was alone in this city, away from her family. If she didn't take care of herself, who would?

That night, after work, he showed up at her doorstep with a bag of food.

"You didn't have to—" she started, but he interrupted.

"Shut up and eat," he said, handing her a spoon.

Over the next few days, this became his routine. Every morning, he would check if she had taken her medicines. During lunch breaks, instead of eating with colleagues, he would pick up something she liked and bring it to her. After work, he would drop by to make sure she wasn't feeling lonely.

She was stubborn at first, refusing help. But slowly, she started accepting it.

"You're acting like my mom," she teased one evening.

"Then listen to me like a good daughter and take your medicines," he smirked.

Despite the exhaustion from work, Shaunak didn't mind. He wanted to be there for her. Not because he had to, but because he *wanted* to.

By the end of the week, when she finally felt better, she looked at him with tired but grateful eyes.

"Nobody has ever taken care of me like this before," she admitted softly.

It had been a few days since she had gone home. Shaunak had dropped her off at the station, watching as she disappeared into the crowd. He knew she needed this break, but he also felt a strange emptiness after she left.

The tea shop didn't feel the same, the office breaks felt longer, and even work, which he already disliked, felt more unbearable without her sarcastic comments and rants.

One evening, as he sat on his bed scrolling through random posts, his phone rang. It was her. A rush of happiness filled him—he had been waiting for her call. But the moment he picked up, all he heard was her soft sobbing.

"Hello?" he said, sitting up straight, suddenly alert.

She didn't say a word. She just kept crying. Then, before he could say anything else, she hung up.

His heart dropped.

What had happened? Was she okay? Why was she crying? Did someone hurt her? A thousand questions raced through his mind, but there were no answers.

He called her back immediately. No response. He tried again. Nothing. His fingers hovered over the keyboard, unsure what to text.

"Hey, what happened? Are you okay? Please talk to me."

No reply.

Shaunak couldn't sit still. He paced around his room, his mind filled with worst-case scenarios. Was she in trouble? Was her family okay? Did she have an argument with someone?

Minutes felt like hours. He kept checking his phone every few seconds, hoping for a message, a missed call—anything. But the screen remained blank.

For the first time, he felt powerless. He had always been able to help her in some way—whether by bringing her food when she was sick or listening to her work frustrations. But now, when she needed him the most, he didn't even know what was wrong.

And that feeling was killing him.

CHAPTER XXVIII

Halfway to Her, Fully into Love

The moment she hung up, Shaunak couldn't sit still. He had never heard her cry like that before, and the silence after the call was unbearable. He knew something was wrong. He didn't know what, but he wasn't going to wait for an explanation over the phone.

Without thinking twice, he packed a small bag, grabbed his wallet, and left home. He didn't even know her exact address—just the name of her town from the employee records at work. It wasn't much, but it was enough to start.

The journey was long, stretching across the entire day. He switched between trains, buses, and autos, constantly checking his phone for any sign of a message or call from her. But there was nothing. The more time passed, the more restless he became. His mind was filled with scenarios, each one worse than the last. Was she in danger? Was she forced into something against her will? Was she—

He shook his head, refusing to let his thoughts go in that direction. He had to focus on finding her first.

By the time he reached her town, the sun had already set. It was a small place, quieter than the bustling city they worked in. He couldn't just walk up to her house—he knew her family was strict, and if they found out he had come all the way for her, it could create more trouble for her.

So, he did the only thing he could. He stayed in the shadows, observing from a distance, hoping for a glimpse of her. He asked around carefully, pretending to be an old friend visiting the town. Slowly, he gathered bits and pieces of information—enough to get close but not enough to walk straight to her door.

Shaunak's fingers trembled slightly as he dialed her number. His heart was still racing from the exhausting journey, but all of that would be worth it if she was okay.

She picked up.

"I'm here," he said, his voice filled with concern. "Tell me where you are, I just need to see you."

Silence. Then, her voice, colder than he had ever heard before.

"Go back, Shaunak. Why are you even here? Who asked you to come?"

His breath hitched. He had expected relief, maybe even a little gratitude. But this? This felt like a slap.

"You were crying... I thought—"

"I was just not feeling well. That's all." Her tone was dismissive, as if the past twenty-four hours of his desperation meant nothing. "You shouldn't have come."

Something inside him snapped.

His mind flashed back to his college days—Aaryan's girlfriend. The girl for whom they had travelled miles, riding endlessly, only for her to ignore Aaryan completely, not even bothering to meet him. He remembered how Aaryan had stood outside, waiting for hours, hoping for a moment that never came. Shaunak had laughed at him back then, telling him he was being foolish.

And now, here he was. Living the same story.

But he wasn't ready to leave. Not yet.

He stood outside her home, looking up at the dark windows, hoping—just like in those Bollywood movies—she would peek out, see him standing there, and realize his efforts. Maybe she'd feel guilty, maybe she'd understand how much she mattered to him. Maybe...

But nothing happened.

The street was quiet. The windows stayed shut.

Hours passed. The night grew colder. The romanticism of waiting under the moonlight slowly turned into exhaustion. His legs ached, his eyes burned from lack of sleep, and reality started to sink in.

Bollywood lied.

In the movies, love was grand gestures, unexpected reunions, and tearful embraces. In reality, love was just another gamble, where effort didn't always equal reciprocation.

By morning, he wasn't sure what hurt more—his body or his heart.

Shaunak boarded the train back to his job town, his heart heavy with disappointment and resentment. The rhythmic clatter of the tracks matched the storm in his mind. He had traveled miles for her, stood outside her house all night like a fool, only to be dismissed like he was nothing.

She didn't even come to the window.

That thought gnawed at him, fueling his anger.

By the time he reached his apartment, he had made a decision—he wouldn't speak to her. Not because he didn't want to, but because he wanted her to feel what he had felt. The helplessness, the longing, the frustration.

The next morning, his phone rang. Her name flashed on the screen.

He let it ring.

Then, his office laptop buzzed with an incoming call. It was her again.

He smirked, ignoring it. She was desperate now.

For the first time, Shaunak felt in control. He had spent so much time thinking about her, chasing after her, waiting for her. Now, it was her turn. He wanted her to wonder why he wasn't answering. He wanted her to feel restless, to go through the same agony he had faced while standing outside her house, waiting for something that never came.

The calls kept coming throughout the day.

And each time, he ignored them.

A part of him was still angry. But another part? That part was enjoying this. Because now, he was in her mind. Now, she would think of him, worry about him, miss him.

For now, that was his win.

Days had passed since Shaunak had last spoken to her. He had ignored her calls, her texts, everything. And yet, he couldn't deny the way his heart skipped a beat when he heard she was coming back.

She hadn't told him. Maybe she wanted to surprise him, to show up unannounced and see his reaction. But he knew. Somehow, he always knew when it came to her.

So, he called her.

"Hey," he said casually, as if nothing had happened.

"Hey," she replied, her voice soft.

They talked like everything was normal, as if they hadn't been avoiding each other for days. But he didn't let her know that he was aware of her arrival. He wanted to play along, let her believe she had the upper hand.

The next day, she arrived.

She walked into their usual spot—the tea shop where they had shared countless conversations, where their story had unfolded one sip at a time. She looked around, expecting to see him, but he was nowhere to be found.

A flicker of disappointment crossed her face. Had he found out and decided not to come?

And then, out of nowhere, warm hands gently covered her eyes from behind.

She froze for a second, then smiled.

She didn't need to guess. She knew it was him.

Shaunak leaned closer and whispered, "Surprise."

She let out a small laugh, shaking her head. "You knew, didn't you?"

He grinned, removing his hands as she turned to face him. "Maybe."

She rolled her eyes. "You ruined my surprise."

He chuckled. "You ruined mine first."

For a moment, they just stood there, looking at each other. The tension, the silence, the unanswered calls—all of it faded into the background. Because in that moment, nothing else mattered.

She was here. And that was enough.

Shaunak's heart raced as he approached her apartment that evening. She had invited him over for dinner—a gesture that felt both intimate and nerve-wracking. He had once boasted about his culinary skills, a claim far from the truth. Tonight, however, she had taken the reins, offering to cook for them both.

The aroma of spices greeted him as she opened the door, her smile warm yet tinged with a hint of nervousness. They exchanged pleasantries, the usual comfort of their conversations now laced with an unspoken tension. The table was set modestly, two plates facing each other, symbolizing the closeness they shared.

Dinner was a blend of flavours and laughter, each bite accompanied by stories of their past, dreams, and fleeting glances that spoke volumes. Shaunak found himself wishing the night would stretch on, that he wouldn't have to leave the cocoon of warmth they had created.

"I truly love you, Kavya," he whispered, his voice trembling with the weight of his emotions. "And no matter what, I will marry you."

Kavya looked at him — not surprised, but sad. There was a softness in her eyes, the kind that carried pain deeper than words could explain. She didn't respond immediately. Instead, she looked away, as if trying to gather strength from the silence between them.

"I know, Shaunak," she finally said. "I know you love me... maybe more than anyone ever has. But love isn't always enough."

Shaunak frowned. "What do you mean?"

She took a deep breath. "Even if you're ready to fight the world, my family won't accept me. I've seen this before. My previous relationship ended the same way. He wanted to marry me too... and he loved me, deeply. But when my family disapproved, everything started to fall apart. I could never go against my family either — I never have. So, day by day, we drifted. We stopped talking the way we used to, started hiding feelings instead of sharing them. And just like that... four years of love faded into nothing."

Shaunak listened, his heart heavy, but he still wanted to understand her completely. "But why, Kavya? Why did it end? There must've been more."

She hesitated. For a long moment, her eyes searched the ground as if the truth lay buried there.

"There was one mistake," she said softly, barely above a whisper. "Something I regret... not because I did it, but because of what it cost me."

He looked at her, urging her to continue.

"In the past... before that breakup," she said slowly, "I slept with one of my school friends. It was a mistake, a moment I didn't think through. My boyfriend found out. And even though we had been together for four years, even though I loved him... he couldn't forgive me. He walked away."

Shaunak's heart sank.

Kavya looked into his eyes now, tears brimming but not falling. "If he truly loved me, why did one night, one mistake, matter more than everything we had shared? Why did it become the reason to end it all?"

Shaunak had no answer. He wasn't expecting this part of her story. He had imagined everything — disapproving parents, fading connections — but not this. A part of him wanted to say that love should come with forgiveness. But another part, the quieter one, didn't know what to feel.

And in that moment, between two people trying to build something on the ruins of past pain, silence grew — not of judgment, but of reflection.

Shaunak realized love isn't just about the promise of forever. It's also about accepting the shadows that come with the light.

Whether he would accept hers or not... he still hadn't decided.

But he knew this — he still loved her.

As the evening drew to a close, he hesitated, searching for an excuse to prolong his stay. "It's quite late, and the roads back aren't the safest at this hour," he murmured, avoiding her gaze.

She looked at him, understanding dawning in her eyes. "You can stay here tonight," she offered softly.

Relief washed over him, but with it came an unexpected turn. She disappeared briefly into another room, returning with a box filled with memories. Among them was a meticulously crafted birthday card, vibrant and detailed.

"I made this for my ex-boyfriend," she confessed, her voice tinged with sadness. "He returned it after we broke up, claiming I never truly loved him."

Shaunak examined the card, admiring the intricate designs and the effort poured into it. He felt a pang of envy, realizing someone else had once held her heart so deeply. But more than that, he felt admiration for her artistic spirit, a trait he deeply respected.

Tears welled up in her eyes as she continued, "I miss him sometimes."

Shaunak's heart ached at her vulnerability. He wanted to comfort her, to bridge the gap between them, but words eluded him. Instead, he reached out, gently holding her hand, offering silent support.

The room was filled with unspoken emotions, a testament to the complexities of human connections. They sat together, surrounded by memories of the past, both yearning for a future that remained uncertain.

The evening had already been a tapestry of emotions, woven with shared stories and unspoken sentiments. As they settled into the cozy ambiance of her apartment, she rose quietly and retrieved a small, ornate box from a nearby shelf. With a gentle smile, she opened it to reveal an assortment of keepsakes: dried flowers, trinkets, and even a chocolate wrapper, each meticulously preserved.

"These are from my past," she began, her fingers lightly brushing over the items. "Each one holds a memory, a moment I wanted to keep alive."

Shaunak observed silently, understanding that these mementos were fragments of her journey, tokens of experiences that had shaped her. He admired her ability to cherish these pieces of her history, recognizing the courage it took to confront and preserve memories, both joyous and painful.

"What about you?" she asked, her eyes meeting his. "Tell me more about your story."

Taking a deep breath, Shaunak delved into his past. "As a child, I spent years away from my parents due to their work commitments."

"That must have been hard," she interjected softly.

He nodded, a distant look in his eyes. "It was. I remember nights when I'd cry myself to sleep, the silence of the room amplifying my loneliness. There was no one to hold me, to tell me it would be okay."

She reached out, placing a comforting hand on his. "I'm sorry you had to go through that."

He offered a faint smile. "Those experiences shaped me, made me resilient. But they also left scars, a lingering fear of abandonment."

The room grew quiet, the weight of their shared vulnerabilities hanging in the air. In that moment, they found solace in each other's presence, a mutual understanding that transcended words.

As the night deepened, they continued to share fragments of their lives, each story a step towards healing, each revelation a brick in the foundation of their burgeoning bond.

As the clock's hands inched past 3 a.m., the weight of the evening's revelations hung in the air. The dim glow of the room cast gentle shadows, creating an intimate cocoon around them. Seeking to ease the lingering tension, Shaunak retrieved a beer bottle, its cold surface a stark contrast to the warmth of the moment.

They shared the drink, each sip a silent acknowledgment of their shared vulnerabilities. The alcohol, though minimal, acted as a catalyst, amplifying the unspoken emotions that simmered beneath the surface. Shaunak's heart began to race, each beat echoing louder in his chest. A surge of courage intertwined with apprehension washed over him.

He had never kissed anyone before, and the weight of that inexperience pressed heavily upon him. Yet, the magnetic pull between them was undeniable. Summoning his resolve, he inched closer, the world narrowing to the space between them.

Their lips met softly, a tentative exploration that quickly blossomed into something profound. The kiss felt magical, a culmination of shared stories, mutual respect, and burgeoning affection. It was as if time had momentarily paused, allowing them to exist solely in that fleeting, intimate connection.

The kiss deepened, a silent conversation of desires and emotions. One thing led to another, and they found themselves entwined, sharing a night of passion that neither had anticipated. For Shaunak, it was a profound experience, a melding of souls that transcended the physical act.

As they lay together afterward, the room bathed in the soft hues of impending dawn, a comfortable silence enveloped them. The night's events had shifted the dynamics of their relationship, adding layers of complexity and depth. In the quiet moments before sleep claimed them, they both understood that their bond had evolved, setting them on a path neither had foreseen but both were eager to explore.

CHAPTER XXIX

A Rose, A Lie

The first light of dawn filtered through the curtains, casting a soft glow over the room. Shaunak stirred, a contented smile playing on his lips as memories of the night before danced in his mind. He turned to her, expecting to see a reflection of his own happiness, but was met with a distant gaze and furrowed brow.

"We need to talk," she murmured, her voice tinged with hesitation.

A knot tightened in Shaunak's stomach. "What's wrong?" he asked, concern etching his features.

She took a deep breath, avoiding his eyes. "Last night... it shouldn't have happened."

Confusion clouded his thoughts. "What do you mean?"

"There's someone else in my life," she confessed, her voice barely above a whisper. "I didn't mean for things to go this far."

The weight of her words crashed over Shaunak, leaving him reeling. Just moments ago, he had been silently thanking the universe for bringing them together, believing he had found his soulmate. Now, that dream was unravelling before his eyes.

"Someone else?" he echoed, struggling to process the revelation.

She nodded, tears brimming in her eyes. "I'm so sorry, Shaunak. I never meant to hurt you."

His mind raced, replaying their countless conversations, the shared dreams, the intimate moments. "What about everything we talked about?" he asked, his voice tinged with disbelief. "Was any of it real?"

She reached out, her hand trembling as it touched his. "It was real, but... complicated."

Shaunak pulled away, the sting of betrayal cutting deep. He had waited so long to open his heart, to share his first kiss with someone he genuinely cared for. And now, he felt like just another chapter in her story, a fleeting moment in her complicated life.

Silence enveloped them, the chasm between them widening with each passing second. Shaunak's heart ached, the pain of unrequited love settling in. He had envisioned a future with her, but now that vision lay shattered at his feet.

As he dressed and prepared to leave, she whispered, "I hope one day you can forgive me."

He paused at the door, not trusting himself to speak. With a heavy heart, he stepped out into the morning light, each step echoing the hollow emptiness he felt inside.

In the days that followed, Shaunak grappled with his emotions, seeking solace in friends and family. He immersed himself in work, trying to distract his mind from the lingering pain. But in the quiet moments, her words would resurface, a painful reminder of a love that could never be.

Through time and reflection, Shaunak began to heal, understanding that some chapters in life are meant to teach lessons, not define destinies. He learned to cherish the memories without letting them anchor him to the past, opening his heart to the possibilities that the future held.

Upon returning to his room, Shaunak felt an overwhelming surge of emotions. The weight of the morning's revelation bore down on him, and he succumbed to his sorrow, tears streaming down his face for hours. Each sob echoed the shattering of his dreams, the profound connection he believed they shared now tainted by the knowledge of another in her life.

As the intensity of his grief began to wane, a resolute determination took its place. Wiping away the remnants of his tears, Shaunak's thoughts shifted from despair to resolve. He couldn't fathom a life without her and became steadfast in his belief that their bond was unique, transcending any existing relationships she might have.

He recalled their deep conversations, shared dreams, and the undeniable chemistry that had drawn them together. In his heart, he was convinced that she was his soulmate, destined to be with him despite the current circumstances. This conviction fueled his determination to win her love, to show her that he was the one who truly understood and cherished her.

Shaunak embarked on a journey of self-improvement, aiming to become the best version of himself—not just for her, but to ensure he was worthy of the love he sought. He delved into understanding what makes someone fall in love, realizing the importance of being genuine, attentive, and supportive. He learned that maintaining eye contact, being a good listener, and sharing genuine laughter could foster deeper connections.

He also understood the significance of patience and respect. Recognizing that she was currently involved with someone else, Shaunak chose to be a supportive friend, offering a shoulder to lean on without imposing his feelings. He believed that by being present and understanding, he could demonstrate the depth of his affection and the stability he could bring into her life. Shaunak's resolve to win her love intensified, especially given that her current boyfriend resided in another town and seldom visited. This physical distance between them presented Shaunak with opportunities to be more present in her life, nurturing the bond they shared.

As their relationship deepened, moments of intimacy became more frequent. However, during these encounters, she often voiced concerns, questioning whether their actions were right. Each time, Shaunak reassured her, affirming that what they were doing felt right to him.

Over time, Shaunak's moral compass wavered, overshadowed by his desire to be with her. He became increasingly consumed by his emotions, willing to compromise his principles to maintain their connection. This internal conflict began to take a toll on his well-being, as he grappled with the ethical implications of their relationship.

Despite the joy he found in their closeness, an undercurrent of guilt and uncertainty persisted. Shaunak's unwavering determination to win her love led him down a path where he struggled to reconcile his actions with his beliefs, highlighting the complexities and emotional turmoil inherent in such situations.

The day arrived when her boyfriend was scheduled to visit. She informed Shaunak that they wouldn't be able to see each other for a few days during this visit. Outwardly, Shaunak accepted this news with composure, not expressing any objections or concerns. However, beneath this calm exterior, he was engulfed in a storm of emotions.

Alone in his room, Shaunak's mind was consumed by thoughts of her with someone else. Each moment felt like an eternity, his imagination conjuring scenarios that intensified his anguish. He struggled to maintain his composure, the weight of his emotions pressing heavily upon him.

To the outside world, Shaunak appeared unaffected, maintaining his daily routines without a hint of the turmoil within. But in solitude, he grappled with his feelings, yearning for the days to pass swiftly so he could be with her once more. His longing was a testament to the depth of his affection, a silent struggle endured in the shadows of his own heart.

As the days stretched on, Shaunak clung to the hope that her boyfriend's visit would be brief. He envisioned the moment they would reunite, cherishing the thought of her presence and the solace it would bring. In the meantime, he bore his suffering in silence, a solitary journey through the complexities of love and longing.

As days turned into weeks, her boyfriend's visit extended beyond the anticipated duration. Each morning, he accompanied her to the office, often lingering outside after dropping her off. Shaunak observed these interactions from a distance, his heart heavy with a mix of jealousy and determination.

He meticulously noted every detail about her boyfriend—the way he dressed, his mannerisms, and how he spoke. Shaunak's intent was clear: by emulating these traits, he hoped to align himself more closely with the qualities she seemed to appreciate. This behaviour aligns with findings that jealousy can drive individuals to perceive themselves more like their rivals, potentially as a subconscious strategy to compete more effectively.

After ten days, her boyfriend finally departed, and almost immediately, she reached out to Shaunak, inquiring about his well-being and suggesting they meet. During her boyfriend's visit, she hadn't contacted Shaunak, leaving him feeling isolated and questioning his significance in her life. Her sudden eagerness to reconnect after her boyfriend's departure led Shaunak to wonder if she valued him only when it was convenient. Despite these doubts, he chose to focus on her positive qualities, convincing himself that her intentions were genuine.

One afternoon, as the sun cast a warm glow over the city, she approached Shaunak with a shy smile and handed him a single red rose. The gesture caught him off guard; never before had anyone given him a rose. He accepted it with a mixture of surprise and gratitude, feeling a warmth spread through him.

Understanding the significance of a red rose—a universal symbol of love and deep affection—Shaunak was deeply moved by her gesture. Traditionally, giving a red rose is a way to say "I love you" without words.

Back in his room, Shaunak carefully placed the rose in a vase, ensuring it had water to keep it fresh. Each day, he would gaze at its vibrant petals, bringing it close to inhale its delicate fragrance. The rose became more than just a flower; it was a tangible reminder of her affection and the bond they shared.

This simple yet profound gesture resonated deeply with Shaunak, reinforcing his feelings and the belief that their connection was special.

After days of contemplation, Shaunak mustered the courage to express his feelings to her. Attempting to do so in person, he found himself unable to articulate his emotions, so he resorted to texting her instead. After a few minutes, she responded, stating that she didn't envision a future with him. She acknowledged his belief in love but emphasized her practical outlook, suggesting that he deserved someone better suited for him.

Upon reading her message, Shaunak felt a mix of emotions. While her words might have deterred others, he remained undeterred, interpreting her continued presence in his life as a sign of hope. He rationalized her response, convincing himself that, in time, he could change her perspective. This unwavering determination reinforced his commitment to his plan, nurturing the belief that their future together was still within reach.

As the days unfolded, a familiar and painful pattern emerged in Shaunak's life. Her boyfriend would arrive, and Shaunak would find himself relegated to the shadows, unable to bear witnessing their togetherness. The emotional turmoil became unbearable, prompting Shaunak to make the difficult decision to return to his hometown during these periods. This cycle repeated itself with disheartening regularity, each instance deepening the chasm of despair within him.

During these times apart, Shaunak's existence felt like an unending torment. The distance from her, coupled with the knowledge of her being with someone else, gnawed at his soul. Every moment was consumed by thoughts of her—memories replaying in his mind, her laughter echoing in his ears, and the phantom sensation of her touch haunting him. The solitude of his hometown, once a place of comfort, now served as a stark reminder of his isolation and longing.

Nights were the most punishing. Sleep eluded him as he lay awake, staring at the ceiling, his mind a whirlwind of emotions. He grappled with feelings of inadequacy, jealousy, and an overwhelming sense of loss. The walls of his room seemed to close in, mirroring the constriction in his chest. The pain was so profound that it manifested physically—a heavy weight pressing down on him, making each breath a laborious task.

Despite the agony, Shaunak clung to the hope that this separation was temporary. He envisioned a future where circumstances would change, where he wouldn't have to retreat, and where their relationship could flourish without clandestine meetings and stolen moments. This hope, however faint, was the thread that kept him from unravelling completely.

Shaunak often found himself secretly hoping for discord between her and her boyfriend, yearning for a rift that might draw her closer to him. This silent wish for their separation became a recurring undercurrent in his thoughts, a testament to his deep-seated longing for her affection.?

In an attempt to distance himself from the emotional turmoil, Shaunak decided to return to his hometown. He believed that physical separation might provide clarity and respite from the constant ache of unreciprocated love. However, the universe had other plans.?

During a family trip, tragedy struck. Their vehicle met with a severe accident, leaving his parents in critical condition and Shaunak himself badly injured. Amidst the chaos and pain, as he lay in a hospital bed surrounded by the sterile scent of antiseptics and the distant beeping of monitors, a singular thought dominated his mind: her.?

Desperate for solace, he reached for his phone with trembling fingers and dialed her number. Her voice, calm and reassuring, flowed through the receiver, offering him a glimmer of hope amidst the darkness. She assured him that his parents would recover, that he would heal, and that brighter days lay ahead. Her words were a balm to his wounded spirit, momentarily alleviating the weight of his despair.?

Yet, as their conversation unfolded, an unsettling realization began to take root within Shaunak. The physical distance, compounded by his current incapacitation, ignited a profound fear of losing her. He sensed an intangible drift, as if the universe was subtly signaling him to let go, to release the tenuous grasp he held on a love that remained just out of reach.?

This internal conflict was exacerbated by the emotional and psychological strain he was already under. Unrequited love, especially during times of personal crisis, can intensify feelings of isolation and despair. Studies have shown that such one-sided emotional investments can lead to heightened stress, anxiety, and a diminished sense of self-worth. The yearning for reciprocation, coupled with the stark reality of its absence, can create a chasm between hope and acceptance, making the process of healing all the more arduous.?

As days turned into nights in the hospital, Shaunak grappled with these revelations. The juxtaposition of his family's critical condition and his own emotional turmoil painted a poignant picture of a man at a crossroads. He began to question the path he had been treading, recognizing the toll it had taken on his well-being. The universe, in its enigmatic ways, seemed to be urging him toward introspection, to reevaluate his choices and the unyielding pursuit of a love that remained elusive.?

In the quiet moments between medical procedures and restless sleep, Shaunak confronted the depth of his attachment and the reality of his situation. He understood that his emotional investment in her had overshadowed other vital aspects of his life, including his own health and familial bonds. This epiphany marked the beginning of a transformative journey—a journey toward self-discovery, acceptance, and the realization that true healing begins with letting go of what was never truly his to hold.

Upon returning to his hometown to care for his injured parents, Shaunak initially maintained regular contact with her. Their daily conversations became a source of comfort amidst his familial responsibilities. However, as days turned into weeks, he noticed a gradual decline in her calls and messages. The once-frequent interactions dwindled, leaving him feeling increasingly isolated.

Concerned and yearning for connection, Shaunak reached out to mutual friends for updates. Through these conversations, he learned that she had begun dating someone new. This revelation was a heavy blow, stirring a whirlwind of emotions within him. Questions plagued his mind: What had become of her previous relationship? Had her feelings for him been merely casual? The uncertainty gnawed at him, amplifying his sense of loss.

Each day, Shaunak found himself anxiously awaiting her calls or texts, clinging to the hope of rekindling their connection. Instead, he resorted to seeking information about her through their shared acquaintances. This indirect form of contact only deepened his longing and confusion, as he grappled with the reality of her moving on.

In the wake of his parents' devastating accident, Shaunak's life took a harrowing turn. The once vibrant household was now shrouded in a somber silence, punctuated only by the hum of medical equipment and the occasional murmur of caregivers. The weight of responsibility bore down on him, transforming his demeanor and straining his relationships.

Days blurred into nights as Shaunak assumed the role of primary caregiver. The relentless routine of administering medications, attending to his parents' needs, and managing household affairs left him physically exhausted and emotionally drained. The mounting pressure manifested in unexpected outbursts; he found himself snapping at friends and family over trivial matters. The frustration even extended to his ailing parents, as he irrationally blamed them for the accident that had upended their lives.

The doctors' prognosis was grim: his parents might never walk or speak again. This bleak outlook plunged Shaunak into a chasm of despair. Nights were spent in tearful solitude, questioning the cruel twist of fate. Guilt gnawed at him; he tormented himself with "what if" scenarios, wondering if his presence could have averted the tragedy. The aspirations he held—to achieve greatness for his parents' pride—now seemed like a cruel joke played by destiny.

Shaunak's relationship with her had become a tumultuous cycle of hope and despair. Whenever he inquired about her interactions with another man, she would curtly dismiss his concerns, claiming she was busy with work and unwilling to discuss the matter. At times, she insisted that the other man was merely a friend, but during other conversations, her tone turned defensive and confrontational, questioning Shaunak's right to even ask. These inconsistent responses left Shaunak feeling broken and confused.

Determined to break free from this emotional turmoil, Shaunak resolved to distance himself from her. He managed to avoid contact for a month, ignoring her calls and messages, attempting to heal and regain his sense of self. However, the separation only intensified his longing. After weeks of silence, he found himself reaching out to her once more, slipping back into their familiar pattern as if nothing had happened.

This on-again, off-again dynamic took a significant toll on Shaunak's mental health. Studies have shown that individuals in such cyclical relationships often experience heightened psychological distress, including increased symptoms of anxiety and depression. The repetitive cycle of breaking up and reconciling can create a sense of instability, leading to emotional turbulence and decreased well-being.

CHAPTER XXX

The Day She Blocked the Sun

Shaunak had made up his mind—it was time to end everything once and for all. The weight of unspoken words, broken promises, and lingering emotions had been suffocating him for far too long. He knew she had moved on, knew she was with another boy now, but the ache in his heart refused to subside. He needed closure, and for that, he had to see her one last time.

With a deep breath, he dialled her number. The phone rang, echoing in the hollow silence of his room. No answer. He tried again, and again, but each time, the call went unanswered. Frustration crept into his veins, twisting into something darker—was she deliberately ignoring him? Just as he was about to give up, the call was finally answered. But it wasn't her voice that greeted him.

"Hello?" a male voice spoke on the other end.

Shaunak clenched his jaw. It was him—the boy she was with now. A strange mix of anger and pain surged through his body, but he kept his voice steady.

"I need to meet her. Just once."

There was a pause, a hesitation. Then, the boy responded, "Come to my place if you want to talk."

Shaunak knew this was it—the perfect moment to sever the last thread tying him to her. He wasn't sure what he expected from this meeting, but he knew one thing: he had to do this for himself.

The journey to the boy's house felt longer than it actually was. With every passing street, his memories of her played in his mind like a cruel film reel—her laughter, their conversations, the nights spent dreaming about a future that would never be. But those were all illusions now. A mirage he had chased for far too long.

When he reached the place, he saw them standing together. She looked at him, eyes filled with something unreadable—guilt, sadness, or perhaps, indifference. It didn't matter anymore.

"So, what do you want, Shaunak?" she asked, her voice carrying an unfamiliar distance.

He stared at her for a moment, his heart hammering against his ribcage. "I wanted to talk. To ask you if there was ever a moment when you thought of telling me the truth. About him. About everything."

She lowered her gaze, but before she could respond, the boy beside her smirked. "You should have taken the hint earlier, man. She's with me now."

That was it. That single sentence was enough to shatter the last bit of control he had. The bottled-up frustration, pain, and betrayal erupted within him like a storm. Without thinking, without restraint, Shaunak lunged at the boy, his fists landing with years of pent-up emotions.

The boy struggled, but Shaunak didn't stop. Every punch was a release of the agony he had endured silently. The girl screamed, tears streaming down her face as she tried to pull Shaunak away. "Stop! Please, Shaunak, stop!"

Her voice cut through his haze of rage. He stepped back, breathing heavily, staring at her as she sobbed. For a fleeting second, regret flickered in his chest. But then, reality hit him—this wasn't his battle anymore. She wasn't his to fight for.

His heart clenched at the sight before him. She was crying. Her face, which once lit up with laughter at his stupid jokes, was now buried in her hands. And beside her sat another man, his hand gently resting on her shoulder, whispering words of comfort. Shaunak didn't need to hear them to know what they were. He had spoken the same words to her countless times before, in her moments of sorrow, in her moments of doubt. He had been her pillar, her refuge. But today, she had found solace in someone else.

Something inside him cracked. A sharp, unbearable pain surged through his chest. He had spent months, maybe years, trying to be the one who mattered to her. He had convinced himself that if he stayed, if he loved her enough, one day she would look at him the same way he looked at her. But deep down, he had always known the truth—she had never truly loved him.

Yet, knowing it didn't make it any easier.

A storm raged within him. His fists clenched as memories flashed through his mind—how she had leaned on him during her worst days, how she had called him at odd hours just to talk, how she had laughed, cried, and shared fragments of her world with him. And in all of it, he had woven a dream—a dream where she was his.

But that dream shattered tonight.

Before he could stop himself, his feet carried him forward. The man beside her barely had time to react before Shaunak's fist collided with his jaw. The impact sent the man sprawling onto the pavement. She gasped, her tear-filled eyes widening in horror.

"What are you doing, Shaunak?" she cried, scrambling to her feet, shielding the man who was now groaning in pain.

Shaunak stood there, breathing heavily, his body shaking—not from the fight, but from the turmoil inside him. He looked at her, at the girl he had poured his soul into, and for the first time, he saw the truth in her eyes.

She wasn't his. She never was.

She had told him—again and again—that she didn't love him the way he loved her. He had refused to accept it, had let himself believe that one day she would. But love doesn't work that way. Love cannot be forced. And yet, he had held on, blindly, foolishly, until it brought him to this moment.

Tears blurred his vision, but he refused to let them fall.

"I was supposed to be the one comforting you," his voice broke, filled with anguish. "I was the one who stood by you when you had no one. And now... now I have to watch you lean on someone else?"

She looked at him, pain flickering in her eyes. But it wasn't the kind of pain he had hoped for. She wasn't heartbroken for *him*. She felt sorry for him.

And that hurt more than anything else.

"I never asked you to wait for me, Shaunak," she whispered. "I told you I didn't feel the same way. I never wanted to hurt you, but... I can't love you just because you love me."

The words cut through him like a blade, but they weren't new. He had heard them before. He had just never listened.

A bitter chuckle escaped his lips as he stepped back, his fists unclenching. He looked at the man still on the ground, holding his bruised jaw. He wasn't the villain. Neither was she.

The real villain was his own expectation—the belief that if he loved her enough, she would love him back.

He turned away, his footsteps echoing in the empty street. He wasn't sure where he was going, but he knew one thing—he had to find a way to let go. Not just of her, but of the dream he had built around her.

Because love isn't about holding on. Sometimes, it's about knowing when to walk away.

The next day, Shaunak woke up with a heavy heart, feeling a sense of emptiness he couldn't shake off. He opened his phone, hoping to catch a glimpse of her profile, even if it was just a small reminder of the moments they shared. But to his shock, he found that her profile was no longer visible. His heart sank as he tried to search for her again, only to discover that she had blocked him from everywhere—social media, messaging apps, everything.

A wave of sorrow engulfed him, and tears flowed freely. He cried for days, unable to make sense of what had happened. The weight of confusion and regret weighed down on him like a never-ending storm. He couldn't figure out what he had done wrong, or if he had done anything at all. He kept replaying the moment in his head when he had made the difficult decision to push her current boyfriend away, hoping it would bring them closer. But now, it felt like he had lost everything.

Shaunak spent countless nights wondering if it had been the right choice, if it was the mistake that had driven her to block him. The more he thought about it, the more he doubted his actions. Did she ever truly mean the words she had said to him? Were those promises and sweet gestures just part of a passing phase, or had they been sincere all along? The more he questioned, the more his mind spiralled into uncertainty.

Days turned into weeks, and with each passing moment, Shaunak felt the heaviness of the situation deepen. He realized that the chance to see her again, to apologize or at least make amends, was slipping away. The one thing he had hoped for, a simple moment of closure, now seemed impossible.

Shaunak had never been the kind of man to show his wounds. He laughed loudly in rooms full of people, cracked jokes that made even the saddest hearts smile, and carried the weight of his world quietly—without letting it tremble in his voice. But after *she* left, even silence in his life started echoing louder than his laughter ever could.

It began with a simple thought—an innocent question that soon consumed every inch of his sanity.

"Did I do the right thing?"

Shaunak asked himself this again and again, like a prayer whispered into the void, expecting no reply—only peace. But peace didn't come. Instead, it brought guilt.

He cursed his own luck. It wasn't the first time God had taken away something he loved. It felt like a pattern now—as if the universe had made a pact against him. He would find love, pure and unfiltered, and just when it began to bloom into something meaningful, it would be snatched away like a cruel joke. And this time, it was her.

He believed—no, he was *sure*—that if he had been with her, if he hadn't let distance or doubts or pride come between them, she wouldn't have fallen for someone else. Maybe she wouldn't even have looked in another direction. Maybe her heart would have stayed where it once belonged—with him.

But love is a fragile thing. Sometimes, it doesn't break with loud shouts or big betrayals. Sometimes, it shatters in silence—in the pauses between conversations, in the "good mornings" that no longer come, in the names that slowly stop appearing on your screen. That's how she left—quietly, without slamming any doors, yet somehow leaving every one of them open in his heart.

Shaunak hated himself. Not just for losing her, but for fighting with the person she started liking. His ego had lashed out like a wounded beast. And in trying to protect his pride, he had only bruised his soul more deeply. He became the villain of his own story—a character he never intended to write.

He thought of meeting her. Of clearing things. Of maybe turning the page together. But life, unlike books, doesn't always let you revisit the chapters you skipped or ruined. She had already moved on, and there were no options left for him to choose from—no roads leading back to her, no words left unspoken, no chances waiting in corners.

And then, something strange began to happen.

He started seeing her *everywhere*.

In coffee shops where a girl tied her hair just like she used to. On streets where someone wore the same shade of earrings she loved. At bus stops, in malls, in dreams—she appeared in different forms, as if the world itself was teasing him with her memory. Every time he blinked, he half-expected to open his eyes and see *her*.

But she never came.

Haunted by her shadow and the voice of his regrets, Shaunak withdrew from the world. He locked himself in his room, not metaphorically—but literally. Curtains drawn, phone switched off, lights dimmed like the flame of his spirit. He didn't step out for days. Those days turned into weeks. Weeks into months. The walls of his room bore witness to a man breaking silently. He cried like a child in the dead of night. Pillows soaked. Eyes swollen. Memories circling like vultures over his loneliness.

People outside thought he was just busy. That he was healing. That time, like always, would patch things up.

But inside that room, a storm was raging. Not one that destroyed, but one that left him numb—cold and hollow.

He didn't want the world to see him like that. The boy who once spoke about dreams and stars and love—was now afraid of mirrors, afraid of hope, and mostly... afraid of himself.

But perhaps, that's how real healing begins—not with strength, but with surrender. Not with denial, but with acceptance. Maybe, one day, he'd step out again—not to forget her, but to remember her without pain.

But until then, his story remains paused—somewhere between what was and what could've been.

CHAPTER XXXI

When the Silence Knocks

It was a quiet evening, and the world outside was slowly sinking into dusk. Shaunak was alone at home. The house, though familiar, felt oddly unfamiliar that day. He had returned early from college, hoping to enjoy some time by himself—just him, his thoughts, and a bowl of hot, comforting Maggi.

He headed to his room, which had become his little haven. Posters of old rock bands, a stack of unread books, and a soft dim light that barely reached the corners. The silence wasn't new, but today it felt... thick. Almost like it was carrying something within it.

He put a vessel on the induction stove and started boiling water. The comforting sound of the water heating up filled the room. He tore open the Maggi packet, pouring the noodles in with care and adding the tastemaker. A pinch of salt. A little more masala. His hands moved mechanically, but his mind wasn't entirely present.

A strange uneasiness was creeping in—slow, but steady. The kind you feel when you walk into a room and sense someone had just been there. Or worse, *still* is.

He tried to shake it off.

"It's nothing," he mumbled to himself, brushing his hair back and trying to focus on the bubbling vessel. But the air in the room had shifted. There was a strange chill that hadn't been there moments ago. He could feel it against the back of his neck like someone was breathing down on him... watching.

Reluctantly, his hands paused. He turned slowly.

And there it was.

A faint silhouette in the corner of the room near his study table. Not quite formed. Not quite visible. Just *there.* Flickering like a shadow that didn't belong to anything. It wasn't moving. And yet, it felt alive.

His breath caught in his throat. He didn't scream. He didn't run. He *froze.* His heart was pounding like a drum inside his chest. His mind scrambled through every horror story he had ever heard. The ones his grandmother whispered during power cuts. The ones told at night in hostel rooms. And in all of them, there was always one advice—

Take the name of God.

Shaunak closed his eyes tightly and began chanting the Hanuman Chalisa under his breath. His voice trembled, but the words came naturally.

"Bhoot pisach nikat nahi aave,
Mahavir jab naam sunave..."

He kept repeating it. Again. And again.

With every chant, he felt a little calmer. Like he was building a shield around himself. The presence in the corner didn't move, didn't come closer. But it felt less threatening. Less consuming. Still there... but powerless.

After a while, he stopped. Opened his eyes.

Nothing.

The corner was empty. Just his old study table, his worn-out diary, and a water bottle.

Had he imagined it?

Shaunak wasn't sure. But he knew one thing—fear lives in the mind, and the mind can play tricks.

He turned back to his half-cooked Maggi, stirring it slowly, quietly. He tried to focus on the smell, the warmth, the familiar comfort of a simple meal. He didn't look back again. Didn't entertain the whispering doubts that crept in through the silence.

He chose to ignore the battlefield of thoughts.

he day had drained him completely—meetings, code reviews, and a pile of unread emails that still waited like unfinished chores. With heavy eyes and a heavier mind, he walked into his dimly lit bedroom, switching on the lamp that cast a soft golden hue across the room.

But something felt...off.

As he turned to his bed, his heart nearly leaped out of his chest. There—right there—on his own bed, someone was already lying under his blanket. The shape was subtle yet unmistakable, like a person curled into sleep, breathing slowly.

Shaunak didn't wait to confirm it. He jumped back as if the ground beneath had turned to fire. Panic overtook his senses. His instincts overpowered logic, and before he knew it, he had sprinted out of his flat—barefoot, leaving his slippers behind, and forgetting to even close the door.

The corridor was silent, unusually so. The kind of silence that screams in your ears. Cold tiles kissed his bare feet, and the chill of midnight air crept under his shirt. He paced, heart pounding, brain racing with questions. *Who was that? Did I leave the door open earlier? Is someone playing a prank? Or... something worse?*

He stood outside for nearly an hour, debating, spiraling into every possible thought his fear could feed. His phone trembled in his hand, but no one answered his calls. The shadows around him began to grow darker in his mind, and even the smallest sounds felt magnified—distant footsteps, the creak of a pipe, the whistle of wind.

Finally, gathering every ounce of courage he could muster, Shaunak decided he had to go back.

Not to face whoever—or whatever—was in his room, but just to wear his slippers, grab his keys and phone, and lock the door. Just those three things. That's all. He repeated it like a mantra as he walked back toward the open flat, which stared back at him like the mouth of a sleeping beast.

His legs trembled as he stepped inside. The light was still on, and oddly, the bed was now... empty. The blanket was neatly folded as if no one had touched it. As if nothing had ever been there.

He didn't waste a second more. He wore his slippers, snatched his phone from the table, picked up his keys, and locked the door as fast as his shaking hands allowed. Then he went back to the corridor, breathless.

With trembling fingers, he dialed his friends again. No answer. He tried another number. This time, someone picked up.

It was Abhishek.

Shaunak stammered his words, his voice cracked with panic. He narrated everything—the figure on the bed, the forgotten slippers, the missing person, the empty room.

But all Abhishek did was laugh.

"Dude, you've officially lost it," he chuckled. "Maybe you saw your reflection in the mirror or your own blanket folded weirdly."

Shaunak didn't find it funny. His voice dropped. "I *know* what I saw."

There was silence for a moment on the other end. Then Abhishek sighed. "Alright, come to my place. You clearly can't stay alone tonight."

Shaunak didn't argue. He just walked away from the flat, his thoughts tangled like thorny vines. As he descended the stairs, one question kept gnawing at him:

If no one was really there... then why did the room feel colder than usual when he returned?

The night had already taken its toll on Shaunak—mentally, emotionally, and now physically. After that chilling encounter in his own flat, the only thing he craved was human presence, a comforting voice, or even the flicker of a TV screen in someone else's living room.

So, when his friend Abhishek finally answered the phone and agreed to take him in, it felt like salvation.

But fate wasn't done playing its cruel tricks.

When Shaunak reached Abhishek's building and knocked on the familiar wooden door, there was no response. He rang the bell. Waited. Knocked again. Nothing. After a few minutes, he called him—only to hear the dull ringing echoing from inside the apartment. No answer. Abhishek's phone now went straight to voicemail.

The realisation hit like a stone: **He was alone. Truly alone.**

The idea of returning to *that* flat twisted his stomach into knots. He needed a place—**any** place—where he wouldn't be surrounded by silence or shadows.

As he walked aimlessly through the empty lanes of this unfamiliar town, his eyes landed on a flickering red neon sign that read: **"Hotel Rajdeep."** The building stood awkwardly between a closed ration shop and a broken lamppost, its paint peeling, its gate half-open like an invitation and a warning rolled into one.

He entered hesitantly.

Inside, the lobby was deserted. No sound. No receptionist. Just a creaking ceiling fan and the faint smell of damp walls and old cigarette smoke. He waited for someone—anyone—to appear. Minutes passed.

Then, from a side corridor, a thin man in stained clothes, holding a mop, walked in. A hotel sweeper. His face was worn, eyes tired but oddly alert.

"You waiting for someone?" the sweeper asked, wiping his hands on a ragged cloth.

"Uh... yeah. I need a room. Just for one night," Shaunak replied.

The sweeper raised an eyebrow, his lips curling into a sly grin. "Staying with a girl?"

Shaunak gave an awkward laugh, more confused than amused. "No no, nothing like that. I just need a place to sleep. Alone."

The man took a step closer. "Purpose?"

Shaunak exhaled and tried to explain, "I'm new in town. Staying with friends. But they're not home tonight and... I didn't want to go back. I just need a bed till morning."

The sweeper tilted his head, scanning him top to bottom. "Room's a thousand rupees for the night."

Shaunak frowned. "I... I can pay 500."

They haggled like it was a fish market, not a hotel lobby. Eventually, they settled at 700. The sweeper nodded slowly, then said, "ID?"

Shaunak felt his heart skip again. "I didn't bring it. But... I have a photo of my Aadhaar on my phone."

For a second, the sweeper just stared at him. Then, with a shrug, he motioned toward a rusted keybox behind the desk. He fished out a key labeled *203* and handed it over.

"No noise. No drinking. Lock your door," the sweeper mumbled, almost like a warning, before walking away.

Shaunak stood there for a moment, holding the cold iron key in his hand, unsure if he had found shelter or stumbled into a new mystery.

But at this point, exhaustion had blurred every line between fear and desperation.

He walked toward the stairs, hoping that Room 203 would offer him something his own home couldn't anymore—**peace.**

Yet, somewhere in the back of his mind, a question lingered:

Why was a hotel with no receptionist still open at midnight... and why was a sweeper the one assigning rooms?

The staircase leading up to the second floor groaned with every step Shaunak took. Each creak beneath his slippers echoed through the empty corridor, as if the building itself disapproved of his presence. The hallway was narrow, dimly lit by a flickering tube light that buzzed with a low, irritating hum.

He found Room 203 at the very end—its door chipped, handle rusted, the number hanging on a crooked nail like a tired soldier.

He pushed the key into the lock. It took a jiggle, a little force, and a moment of doubt before the door finally clicked open.

The room inside greeted him with a musty smell—moist walls, unwashed sheets, and a lingering hint of something burnt long ago. The tube light above flickered, struggling to stay alive, casting brief flashes of the decaying corners.

The bed stood like a neglected corpse, its bedsheet crumpled and stained with stories better left untold. Dust lay thick on the table. A rusty fan churned slowly above, as if it had seen too many nights and given up trying to be useful.

Behind him, the sweeper peeked in, leaning against the doorframe. "Want me to clean it?" he asked casually, almost like he already knew the answer.

Shaunak looked around, took a deep breath, then shook his head. "No, it's fine. I used to live in rooms like this during my college days," he said with a tired smile. "I just need to sleep."

The sweeper gave a lazy nod and turned around without another word. Shaunak closed the door behind him and locked it. Twice.

He dropped his bag to the side, kicked off his slippers, and stared at the bed. He sat down on it, only to immediately flinch—the mattress was damp, the sheet emitted a sour smell, and something crunched beneath the fabric. He didn't want to know what it was.

"Hell with this," he muttered.

He pulled off the entire bedsheet, crumpled it, and threw it to the floor. Then he snatched the lone pillow from the bed and examined it. Even that carried a faint smell, but he was too drained to care. He placed it over his face—not just to block out the light, but the world too—and lay back down on the bare mattress.

His legs curled. His arms fell limply to his sides. The chill of the damp fabric seeped into his skin, but his mind was too scattered to complain. His body begged for rest, his eyes weighed heavy.

Just sleep... forget everything... forget the flat, the bed, the figure... the silence...

He tried to sink into unconsciousness, but the noises of the room kept poking at him. The fan above made a rhythmic *tick... tick... tick*, as though counting down to something unknown. Somewhere outside, a dog howled. Footsteps echoed in the corridor, then stopped, then continued again. Or maybe he imagined it.

Shaunak tightened the pillow over his ears and muttered, "Just let me sleep..."

The night wore a strange silence. Shaunak, after the earlier odd experience in his room, had finally managed to settle into his bed. The dim light from the street lamp seeped through the curtains, painting a soft amber glow on the ceiling. He lay still, trying to quiet the chaos in his mind, hoping that sleep would erase the discomfort that had settled in his chest.

Suddenly—**BOOM!**

A deafening sound pierced through the stillness of the night. Then, again—**BOOM!**

Shaunak sat upright in his bed, his heart skipping a beat. The sound was sharp, metallic, almost like a blast. "Must be a transformer," he muttered to himself, his voice rough with sleep and uncertainty. The area had seen a few of those before. Nothing new.

But something felt off again.

He got up, looked outside his window briefly—quiet lanes, distant dogs barking, nothing unusual. He turned back and forced himself under the covers, wanting nothing more than a few hours of peaceful sleep.

Minutes passed.

Then came the **knock**.

A light, hesitant knock on the front door.

He ignored it.

"Maybe someone drunk... wrong door," he thought.

But the knocking didn't stop.

It grew louder. Stronger. Angrier.

DHAK DHAK DHAK DHAK!

Shaunak threw off his blanket in frustration and stormed to the door, rubbing his half-sleepy eyes. His patience, already hanging by a thread, snapped.

He unlatched the bolt, flung open the door and shouted, **"Who the fuck is it? Why the hell are you knocking like that at this hour?"**

Before the words had even settled into the air, a hand shot forward and grabbed him by the collar, yanking him with force. Shaunak's neck jerked and his back hit the doorframe. Instinct kicked in—anger flooded his system.

Without thinking, he grabbed the man's collar in return and slapped him across the face, hard.

The sound echoed down the empty lane.

Everything stopped for a moment.

And in that stillness, Shaunak saw clearly for the first time—the man standing in front of him wasn't a drunkard. He wasn't a thief. He was wearing a crisp police uniform. The stars on his shoulders shone faintly under the streetlight. His cap had fallen from the slap, revealing his stone-cold glare.

Shaunak's breath caught in his throat.

Before he could say a word, a flurry of footsteps surrounded him. Within seconds, **10 to 20 officers** appeared like shadows from the dark, surrounding him from all directions. Some in uniforms, some in civil dress—but all of them had their eyes fixed on him like he was a criminal.

One of them growled, **"You slapped a senior officer... and you think you'll walk away from this?"**

Another whispered near his ear, **"You really thought you'll get away with *that* crime?"**

Shaunak was stunned. *"What crime? What are they talking about?"* His mind spun, confusion and fear crashing into each other. He looked around desperately, searching for someone to explain what was happening. But all he saw were judging eyes, murmuring lips, and furious faces.

"Must be one of those rich brats," someone said. "Probably some minister's son who thinks he owns the world," another added.

Shaunak tried to speak. **"Wait... what crime? I haven't done anything! I was just—"**

But before he could finish, two officers grabbed his arms. Another twisted his wrist behind his back. The handcuffs clicked.

The night that had started with silence and shadows had now turned into a nightmare.

And Shaunak...

...was in the middle of a storm he couldn't even name.

Shaunak's wrists were still gripped tightly by the police officers. Every muscle in his body ached from the sudden assault—the punches, the slaps, the jabs of their wooden batons. His mind was spinning. Confusion clung to him like sweat, thick and suffocating. He tried to protest, to understand what was happening, but every word was met with violence.

Suddenly, through the corridor that led to the flat next to his, a sound pierced through all the noise—a girl screaming.

"Please! Please save me!!"

Her voice cracked with desperation. It wasn't just a cry—it was terror itself.

Shaunak's head jerked toward the direction of the voice. Even amidst the blows, his instincts snapped into alert. Something was **very, very wrong.**

The door to the adjacent flat was wide open, and from where he stood, barely able to move, Shaunak caught a glimpse inside.

His breath hitched.

There, sprawled across the bed, was a girl. Her body limp. Her clothes torn and blood-soaked. The white bedsheet beneath her had turned into a dark red canvas. Thick trails of blood snaked down to the floor, forming puddles that shimmered under the pale light.

Shaunak's heart sank. His eyes widened in horror. *"What... what is this..."*

He turned to the officers, desperation in his voice now, not anger.

"Sir! Please! Call an ambulance! She's alive—I just heard her scream! Please help her!"

But instead of compassion, all he received was the back of a palm—

SMACK!

A heavy blow sent him staggering back into the wall. One officer grabbed him by the collar again and snarled through gritted teeth,

"Now you're going to teach us what to do... after putting three bullets in her chest?"

Shaunak froze.

Everything around him seemed to blur for a second. The noise faded. Time slowed down.

"What the fuck did he just say?" his mind screamed.

Bullets?

Three bullets?

HIM??

"Wha—what are you saying? I didn't even step out of my room! I didn't do anything!" he shouted, his voice cracking under the weight of disbelief. "I just... I just heard a sound... I saw her body now. I don't even know her!"

But the officers weren't listening. In their eyes, he was already guilty. And the more he pleaded, the angrier they got.

Each denial was seen as an act. Each tear as manipulation.

To them, Shaunak wasn't a confused young man caught in a nightmare—he was a murderer trying to fake innocence.

He tried to explain again, stammering, "I was in my room... cooking... I don't own a gun... I've never even—"

Another strike. This time, with a baton across his ribs. He fell to the ground, gasping for air, blood trickling from his lip. His head was spinning. His vision blurred.

As the chaos raged around him, Shaunak's thoughts began spiralling—

Is this a setup?

Why him?

Who was that girl?

Why was he hearing her scream... if she was already lying there, dead?

Something didn't make sense.

And in the back of his mind, just faintly, the memory of that **shadow from his room** flickered again.

This wasn't just about blood. Or bullets.

This was something **darker.**

The cold night air was merciless, but what Shaunak felt was something far worse than just the chill—it was humiliation, confusion, and fear, all twisted together like a storm inside his chest.

Bloodied and bruised, Shaunak stood outside the rundown hotel, hands cuffed, lips swollen, shirt torn. The policemen dragged him across the muddy parking lot and threw him against a street pole like he was a bag of garbage. His breath hitched, his ribs ached with every inhale, but what broke him more than the pain... was the **stares.**

A crowd had started to gather.

Hotel residents, mostly couples, were forced out of their rooms—some in shorts, some wrapped in bedsheets, some hiding behind each other, confused and terrified. Their eyes scanned Shaunak like he was some animal caught escaping a slaughterhouse.

Whispers filled the air.

"That's the guy."

"He shot the girl."

"Monster."

"Rich people's spoiled kid, probably."

Shaunak's head hung low, but his heart screamed.

He hadn't even submitted any government ID at the hotel reception. He'd come here just to disconnect for a night, escape the noise of the world. He'd booked the shady hotel anonymously because he didn't want to be found—wanted a night of silence to write, to think, to maybe sleep away some pain. But now... that very choice had turned into a weapon against him.

"You didn't submit your ID."

"You didn't let the cleaner into your room."

"You stayed locked in like you were hiding something."

The accusations fell like lashes, each one cutting deeper than the last.

But how could he explain himself?

How could he tell them that he didn't let the sweeper in because he thought he saw a **shadow** near the bathroom mirror? That his heart had been thumping since the moment he entered the hotel? That he felt watched, followed, and maybe even haunted?

Who the hell would believe a story about ghosts, hallucinations, and paranoia in the middle of a **murder investigation?**

As the officers surrounded him, one of them landed another hard slap across his cheek.

"Speak up now! What were you doing in that room?"

Shaunak coughed, tasted blood.

"I told you..." he gasped, "...I didn't do anything. I told you to take her to the hospital. She was alive. I heard her scream! You all... you all waited. You beat me instead."

Just then, a younger officer ran toward them, panic etched on his face. He pulled the senior officer aside and whispered something. But Shaunak heard it anyway.

"Sir... she's gone. The girl. She's dead."

The words hit the gathering like a thunderbolt. A collective gasp swept through the crowd. The night, already heavy with tension, now felt like it might collapse under its own weight.

Shaunak's head lifted slowly.

He looked at the officer dead in the eyes and said, trembling but clear,

"I told you... to take her to the hospital. She was still alive when I saw her. YOU let her die."

But his voice was lost in the growing sea of judgment.

The crowd started whispering again, louder this time.

"He's a murderer."

"He's faking innocence now."

"Disgusting. Look at him."

Fingers pointed at him.

Eyes burned through him.

The couples held each other tighter, their fear painted across their faces.

Shaunak looked around, his vision dizzy, dirt on his face, hopelessness in his bones. The lights of the police jeep flashed behind him, the sirens drowned in the rising noise of people calling for justice.

And yet, deep within him, a strange, quiet voice whispered:

"You didn't do this... but something else did. And it chose you to witness it."

Was this punishment? A trap? A curse? Or a cruel twist of fate?

Shaunak sat on the cold floor of the lock-up cell, his back resting against the damp wall. His hands trembled—not from the pain, not even from the bruises, but from the weight of something deeper.

He closed his eyes tightly, pressing his head against the concrete, wishing... begging...

"Let this be a dream. Please. Let me wake up in my room, with the fan spinning above, the smell of Maggi still in the air... Let all this be over."

But the metallic clink of a baton outside the cell, the distant echo of police radios, the sting of dried blood on his lips—everything reminded him that this was no dream.

It was his *reality* now.

Every passing hour was a burden. He was barely questioned anymore. The policemen had started to look at him with puzzled expressions, as if the story was shifting, but the bruises on his body reminded him of how quickly they had assumed the worst.

Then, after almost an hour of silent stillness, chaos broke through the station.

A young man, barely in his late twenties, stormed in, tears in his eyes, holding a pistol in both trembling hands. He was crying, screaming, pleading to be arrested.

"I did it!" he shouted. **"It was me! I shot her... she was going to leave me... I lost control! This guy—this boy—they're beating—he had nothing to do with it! I don't even know him!"**

The entire station paused in shock. Officers ran to disarm the man. The pistol was secured, and he was pinned to the ground—but not before the truth fell from his lips like a thunderclap of redemption.

Shaunak, still behind bars, heard everything.

For a moment... just a brief moment... he couldn't breathe.

He gripped the iron bars, knuckles white, eyes wide. *It's real... someone else... it really wasn't me...*

But strangely, even in that moment of truth, the officers didn't rush to open his cell. They exchanged murmurs, scribbled notes, their eyes still flicking toward him with suspicion.

One officer muttered, "Maybe they knew each other." Another, "Maybe he helped cover it up."

Even with the confession, even with a murderer kneeling on the ground... **doubt still clung to Shaunak's name like a shadow.**

It took two more days—two long, silent days of questioning, checking security footage, comparing fingerprints, cross-verifying stories—before the police finally accepted that Shaunak had nothing to do with the crime.

On the third morning, the cell door creaked open.

A senior officer, the same one who had led the beatings, stepped in. His face was tired. Maybe guilty. But still distant.

"You can go," he said, avoiding Shaunak's eyes. **"We confirmed you weren't involved."**

Shaunak stood still, eyes sunken, skin pale.

The officer hesitated, then added,

"Sorry. We made a mistake. You... you should probably see a doctor. For your wounds... and maybe... for your

mind. Sometimes these things leave more than scars."

Shaunak didn't reply.

He walked out of the police station as if floating. The sky outside was the same pale grey, the world moving on like it always did. The hotel was sealed, the crowd gone, the city unaware of what he had just endured.

But inside him, something had shifted.

He was free... but not really.

CHAPTER XXXII

Stories Without Endings

Shaunak sat by the window, his eyes following the drops of rain tracing uncertain paths down the glass pane. The world outside was moving—cars splashing through puddles, people rushing with umbrellas—but inside, he was frozen in a moment that seemed to stretch endlessly. His mind wasn't in the room anymore. It had wandered somewhere deep... somewhere between childhood dreams and the harsh truths of growing up. He remembered the first time he heard a love story. Maybe it was in a fairytale told by his mother or an old Bollywood song playing in the background during dinner. There was always something magical about the idea—two people written in the stars, destined to meet, no matter how far apart they began. Back then, he believed in soulmates. Not just the romantic kind, but the kind of bond that felt inevitable, like gravity. The kind that made poems weep and skies blush. He believed that somewhere out there, there was someone who was meant just for him. Someone who would understand the silences between his words, who would hold his hand not just in pictures, but in pain. Someone who would not walk away. But life... life isn't a storybook, is it? Years passed, and every time he thought he had found "the one," life gave him a lesson instead. Some stayed for a while, painting his world with colours he never knew existed, only to leave without saying goodbye. Some never even noticed him, and some loved the idea of him more than the person he truly was. And now, sitting in the dimly lit room, alone with his thoughts and the sound of distant thunder, Shaunak wondered — What about all those stories I grew up believing in? What about soulmates? Were they just illusions sold by movies and novels? Or did they truly exist somewhere out there? Was he too late? Had he already missed the one meant for him? Or worse... had she walked right past him, smiling, never knowing they were meant to collide? He sighed and closed his eyes, listening to the rhythm of the rain. Maybe, just maybe, she was also out there, somewhere, looking at the sky and asking the same questions. Maybe two people lost in thought could one day find each other in the crowd. Or maybe, some people are meant to live stories without happy endings... and write them for others instead.

Author's Note

From a young age, we're told to look for our "better half." We grow up with the idea that someone, somewhere, will arrive to complete us—as if we were born lacking. But that makes me wonder... if we are looking for our better half, does that mean we are the worst part?

No.

We are not fragments waiting to be glued together.

We are not missing pieces of someone else's puzzle.

Love is beautiful, yes. But it's not meant to complete us—it's meant to meet us where we already are.

Whole.

Flawed.

Becoming.

This book is for those who have loved deeply, lost quietly, and still dare to believe in the poetry of human connection. It's for the ones who mistook pain for passion and silence for peace. For those who held on too long and those who let go too early. For the hearts that bleed quietly and bloom again anyway.

Rose Thorn is not just about heartbreak—

It's about the realization that even a thorn once belonged to a rose,

and even pain once came wrapped in beauty.

Thank you for holding these pages with your hands and your heart.

I hope, somewhere between the lines, you find pieces of yourself too.

— Gaurav Anand

About The Author

Gaurav Anand is a writer who paints emotions with words and finds poetry in pain, healing, and everything in between. Rooted in the soulful lands of Bihar, India, his stories carry the quiet strength, warmth, and unfiltered honesty of where he comes from—blending the simplicity of small-town life with the depth of heartfelt experiences.

After touching readers with his soulful work Pink Petals of Life, Gaurav returns with Rose Thorn—a haunting yet honest exploration of love, heartbreak, and the bittersweet beauty of letting go.

Born with the heart of a dreamer and the soul of a storyteller, Gaurav writes not to escape the world, but to understand it. His stories are not just narratives—they're conversations with the reader's deepest truths.

When he's not lost in his thoughts or drafting verses under rainy skies, he's either building software or building universes through his words.

Rose Thorn is more than a book—it's a piece of him.